Because of Gus McBride, he'd had nothing.

No father, no grandparents on either side. No one to chase away the monsters in his closet, no dad to teach him to fish. No knowledge of where he came from or where he was going.

His mother had tried to step up and fill the role of both parents, and she'd done a damn good job. But she'd needed a husband, and he'd needed a father. They'd had neither. Because Gus McBride had been halfway across the country, protecting his *real* family.

And Taylor would bet that his *legitimate* children weren't scared at night growing up. They didn't worry about paying the bills or having enough money. Growing up, they'd had it all. Taylor wouldn't have been surprised if they'd thought their daddy was a saint.

He wasn't. Unfortunately, they'd never know that.

Unless he told them.

Dear Reader,

The days are hot and the reading is hotter here at Silhouette Intimate Moments. Linda Turner is back with the next of THOSE MARRYING McBRIDES! in *Always a McBride*. Taylor Bishop has only just found out about his familial connection—and he has no idea it's going to lead him straight to love.

In *Shooting Starr*, Kathleen Creighton ratchets up both the suspense and the romance in a story of torn loyalties you'll long remember. Carla Cassidy returns to CHEROKEE CORNERS in *Last Seen...*, a novel about two people whose circumstances ought to prevent them from falling in love but don't. *On Dean's Watch* is the latest from reader favorite Linda Winstead Jones, and it will keep you turning the pages as her federal marshal hero falls hard for the woman he's supposed to be keeping an undercover watch over. *Roses After Midnight*, by Linda Randall Wisdom, is a suspenseful look at the hunt for a serial rapist—and the blossoming of an unexpected romance. Finally, take a look at Debra Cowan's *Burning Love* and watch passion flare to life between a female arson investigator and the handsome cop who may be her prime suspect.

Enjoy them all—and come back next month for more of the best and most exciting romance reading around.

Yours,

Leslie J. Wainger
Executive Editor

Please address questions and book requests to:
Silhouette Reader Service
U.S.: 3010 Walden Ave., P.O. Box 1325, Buffalo, NY 14269
Canadian: P.O. Box 609, Fort Erie, Ont. L2A 5X3

Always a McBride

LINDA TURNER

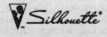

INTIMATE MOMENTS™

Published by Silhouette Books

America's Publisher of Contemporary Romance

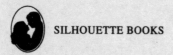

SILHOUETTE BOOKS

ISBN 0-373-27301-0

ALWAYS A McBRIDE

Copyright © 2003 by Linda Turner

All rights reserved. Except for use in any review, the reproduction
or utilization of this work in whole or in part in any form by any
electronic, mechanical or other means, now known or hereafter
invented, including xerography, photocopying and recording, or in
any information storage or retrieval system, is forbidden without
the written permission of the editorial office, Silhouette Books,
233 Broadway, New York, NY 10279 U.S.A.

All characters in this book have no existence outside the imagination of
the author and have no relation whatsoever to anyone bearing the same
name or names. They are not even distantly inspired by any individual
known or unknown to the author, and all incidents are pure invention.

This edition published by arrangement with Harlequin Books S.A.

® and TM are trademarks of Harlequin Books S.A., used under license.
Trademarks indicated with ® are registered in the United States Patent
and Trademark Office, the Canadian Trade Marks Office and in other
countries.

Visit Silhouette at www.eHarlequin.com

Printed in U.S.A.

Books by Linda Turner

Silhouette Intimate Moments

The Echo of Thunder #238
Crosscurrents #263
An Unsuspecting Heart #298
Flirting with Danger #316
Moonlight and Lace #354
The Love of Dugan Magee #448
Gable's Lady #523
Cooper #553
Flynn #572
Kat #590
Who's the Boss? #649
The Loner #673
*Maddy Lawrence's
    Big Adventure* #709
The Lady in Red #763
†*I'm Having Your Baby?!* #799
†*A Marriage-Minded Man?* #829
†*The Proposal* #847
†*Christmas Lone-Star Style* #895
**The Lady's Man* #931
**A Ranching Man* #992
**The Best Man* #1010
**Never Been Kissed* #1051
The Enemy's Daughter #1064
*The Man Who Would
    Be King* #1124
**Always a McBride* #1231

*The Wild West
†The Lone Star Social Club
**Those Marrying McBrides!

Silhouette Desire

A Glimpse of Heaven #220
Wild Texas Rose #653
Philly and the Playboy #701
The Seducer #802
Heaven Can't Wait #929

Silhouette Special Edition

Shadows in the Night #350

Silhouette Books

Silhouette Christmas Kisses 1996
"A Wild West Christmas"

Fortune's Children
The Wolf and the Dove

A Fortune's Children Christmas 2002
"The Christmas Child"

Crowned Hearts 2002
"Royally Pregnant"

A Colton Family Christmas 2002
"Take No Prisoners"

Under Western Skies 2002
"Marriage on the Menu"

The Coltons
The Virgin Mistress

LINDA TURNER

began reading romances in high school and began writing them one night when she had nothing else to read. She's been writing ever since. Single, and living in Texas, she travels every chance she gets, scouting locales for her books.

Prologue

He was a bastard.

Even before he'd been old enough to understand the meaning of the word, Taylor Bishop had known what he was. There was, after all, no avoiding the truth in the poverty-ridden neighborhoods of San Diego where he'd grown up. Dozens of kids were running around the street without fathers, and like recognized like.

Still, he hadn't understood the implications of the label until he was six and one of his school friends told him his mother must be a slut—otherwise his father would have married her. Outraged, his six-year-old pride stung, he'd defended his mother's virtue and his absent father's honor by punching his friend in the nose. All his bravery earned him was a split lip.

That was the day he'd begun to hate his father.

Thirty-five years had passed since then, and nothing had changed. He still hated his father…and he didn't even know his name.

That, however, was about to change.

Seated at his mother's kitchen table, her personal effects spread out around him in the small home she'd finally managed to buy after scrimping and saving for years, Taylor stared down at the sealed letter she'd left for him in her safety deposit box and knew without even opening what it said. After all this time, when it was too late for him to ask her any questions, she was finally going to tell him about his father.

"He's a good man. That's all you need to know."

Every time he'd asked his mother about the mysterious stranger who had sired him, the answer had always been the same. She'd promised to tell him the whole story one day, but she never had. Why? he wondered, scowling at the letter addressed to him in her neat handwriting. Had she thought that he would think less of her because he was obviously illegitimate? That he somehow blamed her for the fact that his father had been nonexistent in his life? Surely she had to know better.

For a moment, pain squeezed his heart at the thought that she might not have known how much he loved and admired her, but with a muttered curse, he quickly shook off his doubts. What the hell was he doing? Of course she'd known how he felt about her. As far as he was concerned, she'd been the best mother in the world. *She* was the one who'd been there for him as a child, the one who'd worked two jobs so that he could have the things he needed when he was growing up. Yes, money had been tight, but she'd done the best that she could, and he couldn't fault her for that. She'd been a single mother with no one to help her. When she lost her job at one of the local hotels because she refused to work nights and leave him home alone, she'd had to go on welfare for a while just so they could eat. Still, she'd held her head high and made sure he did, too. And as soon as she'd been able to find another job, she went off government assistance because, she'd claimed, there were poor people out there who needed it more than they did.

How could anyone not love a mother like that? He'd adored her. She taught him to be proud of who he was, to work honestly for what he wanted, to believe in himself and the future. Those things would get him through life, she'd claimed, not his father's name.

So why was she telling him now? he wondered with a frown. When she'd died unexpectedly last week of an apparent heart attack, the last thing he'd been worried about was his father's name. *She* was the one he loved, the one he cared about, and he would have gladly given up any chance of ever knowing anything about his father if he could have just had his mother back for five minutes.

That, however, was impossible. All he had left of her were her things…and a letter that had the power to change his life. His square-cut face carved in grim lines, he was half tempted to trash the thing, but it was the last communication from his mother. For no other reason than that, he had to read it. Reaching for it, he tore it open and began to read.

To my dear son,

You'll never know how much I love you. You've been the greatest joy of my life, a blessing I thanked God for every day. I know how difficult it was for you, growing up without your father, and I'm sorry for that. But your father wasn't the unfeeling monster you think he was, dear. He was a good man who had no idea you even existed. His

name is Gus McBride, and when we met, he lived
in Liberty Hill, Colorado.

We met in Cheyenne, Wyoming, when I was
there one summer visiting my grandmother. I never
believed in love at first sight until I met him. He
was in town for a rodeo and we had one wonderful
night together. That was all, dear. Just one night.
I fell in love with him, but please don't blame him
because he didn't return my feelings. He was still
in love with the girlfriend he had broken up with
the month before. She was all he talked about, but
I foolishly thought I could make him fall in love
with me. I was wrong. When he left town the next
morning, he probably went back to her.

Two weeks later, I returned to my parents' house
in San Diego. A month later, I discovered I was
pregnant. You must understand, dear, that times
were different then. My pregnancy was scandalous
to my parents, and their main concern was that I
get married as soon as possible. They didn't care
that Gus didn't love me. All they wanted was his
name so they could force him to marry me. They
didn't understand that if he'd known I was pregnant, they wouldn't have had to say a word to
him—he would have insisted on marrying me. He
was that kind of man. And if he'd loved me, I
would have agreed. But he didn't, so I kept his
name to myself—which is why your grandparents
disowned me.

Please don't feel sorry for me…or hate them,
Taylor, dear. If I could have turned back the clock
and done things differently, I wouldn't have. The
night I had with your father was magical, and you
were his gift to me. I never regretted it. It's im-

portant that you know that. You and I had a wonderful life together. When you remember me, remember that.

Love,
Mother

Grief squeezing his heart, Taylor sent up a silent prayer, asking her to forgive him for not respecting her final wish. He couldn't. Because in spite of the love he and his mother had shared, when he thought of her, it was the hardness of her life he remembered. And Gus McBride of Liberty Hill, Colorado, was responsible for that, he thought grimly. Somehow, some way, he was going to make him pay for that.

Chapter 1

"Hi, sweetie. Did I catch you getting ready for a date? What's the name of that boy you're going with? Micah? Mick? I never can remember. When's he going to wise up and ask you to marry him? I told your mother three years ago that he was too slow for you, but she thought he was the greatest thing since sliced bread."

Grinning, Phoebe Chandler had to laugh at her grandmother's disgusted tone, obvious even over the phone. Myrtle had never been one to keep her opinions to herself—which was one of the things Phoebe loved about her. "His name is Marshall, Gran, and we quit dating six months ago. Didn't I tell you?"

"Oh, of course," she said. "Now I remember. He was more interested in what your daddy left you than you. That's another thing I didn't like about him. He had dollar signs in his eyes."

Phoebe couldn't argue with that. She hadn't cared much for that particular trait of Marshall's, either. Luckily, her eyesight was as good as her grandmother's. "I sent him packing when he tried to borrow money from me. So what's going on? Mom said you were going on a trip with some old high-school friends."

Myrtle laughed gaily. "And here I thought everyone but me and Sara McBride were dead. By the way, I wish she was here. She'd love seeing the old gang again."

"When will she be back from her honeymoon?"

"Oh, not for another couple of weeks, at least. Longer, if they decide to take that cruise up the west coast to Alaska."

"So when's the trip? You are going, aren't you?"

"You know me, sweetie," she chuckled. "My bags are always packed. There's just a teensy problem...."

"Your antique store," Phoebe guessed with a smile. "You need someone to run it while you're gone."

"Well, yes," she admitted, "but there's another problem. I haven't had any boarders the last month, so I decided to turn the house into a bed and breakfast. I placed an ad in some travel magazines and I've got some reservations for the next couple of weeks."

"You're kidding! Gran, that's great!"

She chuckled ruefully. "It would be if I didn't want to go on this trip. I can't be two places at once. I've been trying to figure out what to do, then I remembered you always take the month of June off. How would you like to come to Liberty Hill and run my B and B for me?"

Phoebe didn't even have to think twice. "I'd love it!"

"Are you sure?" her grandmother asked worriedly. "You probably had plans—"

"I was just going to paint the house. I can do that anytime."

"What about the business? I don't want to put you in a bind just so I can run off with friends, sweetie. I can come up with a reason to cancel the reservations, if necessary…or stay home, for that matter. The world's not going to end if I don't get to go on this trip."

"No, but you want to go, and why shouldn't you? You'll have a great time. Call your friend back and tell her you're going. I'll handle things while you're gone."

"But who'll take care of your business while you're playing innkeeper for me? You deal with a lot of cash, honey. Do you really want to trust that to someone else?"

"Jason's going to work with me again this summer," Phoebe replied. "Dad always said not to let the business get so big that I couldn't handle it myself, but Jason's a good kid. And he's family. He won't steal from me."

Jason Chandler, her second cousin, was a high-school senior who had worked not only for her in past summers, but for her grandmother, as well. Honest and hard-working, he was saving his money for college and planned to be a doctor. It would never cross his mind to take anything that didn't belong to him.

Across the phone line, Myrtle sighed in relief. "Oh, well, if it's Jason, you don't have anything to worry about. He'll make sure every penny is accounted for."

"So when do I need to be there?"

"June eighth," her grandmother said promptly. "This is going to be so much fun, sweetheart—for both of us! You're going to love the guests who'll be coming in in a couple of weeks. They're newlyweds from Florida. They'll both be eighty in July."

"Eighty!"

"I know," she chuckled. "I was surprised, too, when I talked to the bride on the phone. I would have sworn she was at least thirty years younger."

"I guess that's what love does to you," Phoebe said with a smile. "It certainly agrees with Sara McBride. Who knows, Gran?" she teased. "Maybe your turn's next. You might find yourself a man on your trip."

Her grandmother laughed gaily. "When the cow jumps over the moon, sweetheart. I've had the love of a good man—nothing beats it. Now it's your turn."

If only that were true, Phoebe thought wistfully. She loved being in love. It was the most wonderful feeling in the world...until you came back to earth with a jolt and realized that the man you thought was the love of your life really wasn't Prince Charming at all. He was just a rat who knew how to say all the right things. She'd had too many run-ins with too many rats to believe in happily ever after anymore.

"Thanks, Gran, but I think I'll pass. All the good men are taken and I'm not interested in the dregs that are left."

"After Marshall turned out to be such a jerk, I can't blame you for thinking that, sweetheart, but don't give up. The world is full of good men. You just haven't met one yet. But your turn's coming. There's someone special for you out there and he's going to walk into your life when you least expect it."

Phoebe sincerely doubted that, but she knew better than to argue with her grandmother. Myrtle was an eternal optimist...and usually right. "I'll keep my eyes open," she said with a grin, "but how am I going to meet anyone when you've got all these newlyweds coming in to stay at the house? It's not as if we're going to get any walk-in trade. Liberty Hill's not even on the map.''

It was, of course, but she loved teasing Myrtle about how remote the place was. Liberty Hill was hardly more than a wide spot in the road and a thousand miles from nowhere, yet Myrtle still managed to find her share of guests and boarders, not to mention customers for her very successful antique store right next door to her house. Phoebe didn't know how she did it.

''That's all right,'' her grandmother chuckled, refusing to rise to the bait, ''go ahead and tease me. Liberty Hill might be little, but that just makes it easier for Mr. Right to find you, honey. So when can I expect you? You're going to be engaged by the end of the year, so there's no time to waste. Your mother will have a conniption if you even think about marrying someone you've known less than six months.''

''Gran!''

''I'm just being practical, dear,'' Myrtle chuckled. ''You want this marriage to work—''

''There is no marriage!''

''But there will be,'' her grandmother said calmly. ''You have to plan for these things, dear.''

Torn between amusement and frustration, Phoebe had to laugh. ''You're impossible. Do you know that? I'll be there on the eighth. Is that soon enough for you and Mr. Right, whoever he is?''

She didn't have to ask if her grandmother was pleased—she could almost feel her smile through the phone. ''That's perfect! I'll have your bedroom ready for you.''

Hanging up, Phoebe had to admit she was as excited as Myrtle. And she immediately felt guilty for that. She'd worked at her father's vending-machine business since she was eighteen years old, but she'd never liked it. It was a job, the family business, nothing more. Her father had always loved collecting the money from his vending machines around town and counting it, but she'd only seen that as a boring chore that had to be done every day. She'd hated it—though she'd never told her father that—and dreamed of quitting one day when he no longer needed her. But that day had never come. Six months ago, when her father had died unexpectedly of a heart attack, he'd left the business to her.

Even now, she couldn't believe it. *No!* she'd almost cried at the reading of the will. She didn't want the company! She had other plans. For as long as she could remember, all she'd ever dreamed about was having an old house like her grandmother's, where she could sell antiques and have a bed and breakfast. She didn't care about having a large place, just something cute and Victorian in a small town like Liberty Hill, where life moved at a slower pace and old-fashioned values still flourished.

She'd been saving for just such a house for years and had just enough money set aside for a decent down payment when her father had died. Just that quickly, with the reading of his will, everything had changed. Within the blink of an eye, she became the owner of her father's business. If she lived to be a hundred, she didn't think she'd ever forget the emotions that had washed through her at that moment. Dread, guilt, obligation. She'd felt trapped—she still did!—and there was nothing she could do about it. Her father had entrusted her with the business he'd spent his life building. She couldn't sell it without feeling as though she was stabbing him in the back.

A loyal daughter, she hadn't said a word to anyone

about her true feelings, but with Myrtle, she hadn't had to. Her grandmother knew her too well. She'd pleaded with her not to waste her youth protecting and nurturing someone else's dream—she needed to follow her own heart and do what was right for her. What Myrtle didn't understand was that *was* what she was doing, but on her own terms. She might not have her own shop or bed and breakfast, but she went antiquing with her friends, had guests over frequently, and surrounded herself in her apartment with the shabby chic decor that was all the rage and she just loved. Granted, that wasn't the same thing as having her own bed and breakfast, but for now, at least, there was nothing else she could do.

Except step in and sub for Myrtle occasionally. Her eyes sparkling at the thought, she sent up a silent prayer of thanks for being blessed with a grandmother who understood her so well, then hurried into the kitchen. If she was going to be at Myrtle's on the eighth, she had to get busy and plan the menu for the guests her grandmother had already lined up.

"Oh, goodness, Tom and Betty are going to be here any second and I haven't even finished packing yet. I don't know where the time went! Where did I put my spare set of glasses? You know, dear—the ones with the silver frames? I need them in case I lose my others. Oh, and I can't forget an umbrella…it looks as if it's going to rain. And Betty reminded me to bring my house shoes. They don't take up a lot of room and I can shuffle around in them in the motor home. My blood pressure pills! Where—''

In a tizzy, her hair still in rollers, Myrtle scurried around the house as though she was twenty minutes late to her own wedding, snatching up things she had yet to pack, and Phoebe couldn't help but laugh at her. "Stop, already! I've never seen you like this before. Will you slow down? This trip is supposed to be fun."

Stopping in her tracks, Myrtle drew in a huff of a breath, a rueful grin tugging at her lips. "Sorry, dear. I guess I am a little frantic this morning. I thought we'd have more time to visit. I wanted to tell you about the rest of the guests I've got lined up. Don't worry. You're not going to be swamped with a houseful of guests before you even have time to unpack your bags. A week from Friday, I only booked two rooms—that'll give you a little time to get your feet wet before the crowd hits. After that, you're on your own. From then on, we're booked solid all the way to Labor Day."

Stunned, Phoebe couldn't believe it. "You're kidding! How did you manage that? You only decided to convert the boarding house into a B and B a couple of weeks ago."

"You know how it is," Myrtle said with a grin. "You call a friend, they call a few people, and before you know it, you're talking to the head of the Aspen Visitor and Tourist Bureau, who turns out to have a grandmother who lives over in Wilson County. When I told her I was turning my boarding house into a bed and breakfast, she gave my number out to ten different callers by lunchtime. After that, I couldn't keep up with the reservations."

Suddenly realizing what she'd just said, she frowned at Phoebe over the top of her bifocals. "Am I putting too much on you, sweetheart? I was just so excited, I didn't stop to think how much work this was going to be for you, especially when you haven't done anything like this before. Maybe I should call Tom and Betty—"

Already guessing where her grandmother's line of thought was going, Phoebe said, "If you're thinking about backing out, you can just think again, Myrtle Henderson. You've talked about nothing but this trip for weeks! Don't you dare disappoint the Walkers. They're counting on you."

"But I can't just go off and leave you with all this work. It's not fair. When I called and asked you to hold down the fort for me, I never imagined that I'd be swamped with reservations. I should have turned some of them down."

"Don't be ridiculous," Phoebe scolded. "The more, the merrier. It'll be fun."

"But how are you going to take care of a whole houseful of people without any help?"

"I'll just add a few more eggs to the skillet in the mornings and double the biscuit recipe. It's no big deal, Gran. You know I love cooking for a crowd. I'll be fine."

When Myrtle hesitated, still unconvinced, Phoebe knew she was going to talk herself out of the trip if she didn't do something to stop her. "You're the one I'm worried about," she said quickly. "Do you have your blood pressure pills? And your glasses? What about your clothes? Did you take a sweater? I know it's summer, but the nights can still get cold in the mountains, and there's no telling where you'll end up with Tom at the wheel."

Safely redirected, Myrtle laughed. "That's because he leaves the navigating to Betty and half the time, she reads the damn map upside down. It's a wonder they haven't ended up in a ditch some-where."

Phoebe could picture the Walkers crisscrossing the country, making wrong turns everywhere they went, and not caring. It sounded wonderful. "You're going to have a great time," she said with a grin, "but you'd better be prepared for anything. When Tom heads for L.A. and you end up in the wilds of Montana, you're not going to be able to run to town for a toothbrush."

"He's not that bad, dear." Her grandmother laughed, only to jump, startled, when a horn suddenly blasted outside. "Oh, my goodness, they're here!" Frantic, she glanced around. "I forgot to get my pillow—I'll sleep better with it. And the mosquito repellant. You'll need my keys to the storage shed just in case you need to get in there for anything. And the reservation list. Where did I put it?"

Flustered, she would have rushed into her office, but Phoebe quickly stepped into her path. "I'll take care of the reservation list—it's around here somewhere. The keys to the shed are on the hook by the back door, and I already put the mosquito repellant in your bag. Here's your pillow," she said, stuffing it into her grandmother's arms with a grin. "Let's go."

She didn't have to tell her twice. Her beautiful wrinkled face alight with anticipation, Myrtle hurried out to greet her friends, while Phoebe trailed behind with her bag. Before her grandmother could think of something else to worry about, hugs and kisses were exchanged, her things were stowed in the Walkers' new motor home, and Myrtle only had time to wave before Tom fired up the RV and pulled away from the curb. In the time it took to blink, the motor home had disappeared around the corner.

Another woman might have immediately felt lonely, but Phoebe didn't have time. She had guests coming for the weekend. Her thoughts already jumping ahead to the elaborate breakfast she would serve them, she hur-

ried into the house to check to see what staples Myrtle
had the pantry stocked with. She had taken only one
step into the kitchen when she stopped in surprise, a
slow smile spreading across her face. Given the chance,
she would have given her grandmother a bear hug if
she could have reached her. Because there, on the table,
was the old flour tin Myrtle kept her favorite recipes in,
including the one for buttermilk biscuits she'd won with
at the state fair. Armed with nothing more than that,
Phoebe knew she could make the bed and breakfast a
success. Now all she needed was a guest!

The thunderstorm descended on the Colorado Rockies like the wrath of God. One moment, Tayler Bishop
was cruising through the mountain pass west of Liberty
Hill, his thoughts on his father and everything he would
say to him when he got the chance, and the next, a
driving rain was pounding the windshield of his black
Mercedes. Swearing, he jerked his attention back to his
driving just as a fierce crosswind buffeted the car, but
it was too late. He started to skid. Fighting the wheel
and the wind, he didn't realize he'd left the road until
a pine tree appeared right in front of him. He didn't
even have time to hit the brakes before he slammed into
it.

Dazed, he couldn't have said how long he sat there
in the dark as the storm raged around him. He held the
steering wheel in a death grip, his knuckles white from
the strain, and stared blankly at the air bag that had kept
him from hitting the windshield. Overhead, lightning
flashed like an exploding bomb, lighting up the night
sky and outlining the pine tree that had stopped his car
from careening down the mountain. In the dark, it
looked as big as a barn.

He supposed he should have been thankful the damn thing hadn't killed him. Then he forced open his jammed door and stepped out in the rain to get a good look at what the tree had done to his car. That's when he started to swear. He was still swearing when a wrecker arrived fifteen minutes later in response to the call he'd made on his cell phone to his road service.

Dressed in a yellow rain slicker, the wrecker driver took one look at the situation and whistled softly. "You took quite a hit, buddy. Are you okay? Want me to call an ambulance?"

"No, I'm fine," Taylor growled, disgusted, as he swept his dripping hair back from his face. "I had my mind on something else and didn't notice the storm until it was too late."

"Don't beat yourself up over it," the other man advised. "You're not the first person to take these mountains for granted. At least you were lucky enough to walk away. Where were you headed?"

"Liberty Hill," he retorted. "The last highway sign said it was ten miles from here."

The wrecker driver nodded. "If you'd made it through this last set of S-curves, you could have coasted the rest of the way without ever hitting the gas pedal." Noting the California plates on Taylor's car, he arched a brow in surprise. "It must be family bringing you to these parts because it sure ain't business—there ain't much in this neck of the woods. So who you visiting? I've been working a wrecker in this area for the past twenty years. Maybe I know them."

Studying him through narrowed eyes, Taylor didn't doubt that he probably knew Gus or had at least heard of him—which was why he had no intention of mentioning McBride's name. He'd planned his revenge carefully and knew the importance of surprise. He'd keep his identity—and his reasons for coming to Liberty Hill—to himself, casually seek out McBride and earn his trust, then find a way to make him pay for abandoning his mother when she'd needed him most.

Even to himself, the plan sounded ruthless and diabolical, and he knew if his mother was looking down on him from heaven, she wouldn't be pleased. However, he hoped she'd understand. This was something he had to do, and nothing and no one was getting in his way.

His expression grim, he looked the other man right in the eye and lied. "My cousin only moved here a couple of months ago, so I doubt that you know him. His name's Christopher Deacon. He bought some land east of town and moved a trailer in."

He didn't know if someone had moved a new trailer in or not, but the wrecker driver apparently didn't know either. Frowning, he said, "I don't remember doing business with anyone named Deacon, but my memory's not what it used to be. Since you got family here, and it's so late, I can tow you to their place tonight. Then you can have your car taken to Aspen tomorrow. No one else in these parts has a Mercedes dealership."

"Thanks for the offer, but Chris isn't expecting me, so I'd rather not disturb him tonight. Just take me into town and drop the car off at a local garage. I'll take care of everything in the morning."

He spoke in a cool tone that warned the other man not to argue, and with a shrug, he gave in graciously. "Suit yourself. Just give me a few seconds to get her all hooked up, and we can go. You can wait in the truck, if you like. I imagine you'd like to get in out of the rain."

Taylor generally had little patience for those who

stated the obvious. When he was thoroughly soaked and his wet hair was dripping down his face, he had even less. Somehow, however, he managed to hang onto the manners his mother had taught him and curtly thanked the man before heading for the truck.

Unfortunately, his mood improved little as he watched the wrecker driver hook his car to the tow truck. Assessing the damage, he swore roundly. When he'd planned how he was going to track down his father and confront him, he'd thought he'd accounted for every possible contingency. He'd been wrong. It would be at least a week or longer before his car could be repaired—if the local garage could get the parts in that quickly!—which meant he'd have to get a rental. And he seriously doubted that there was anything available locally. He'd have to call Aspen or Denver and see about having one delivered, which would take time. He'd be lucky if could start looking for Gus by the middle of next week.

Thoroughly irritated, his mood only darkened as the tow-truck driver drove him into Liberty Hill and he got his first look at the town where his father lived. It was smaller than he'd thought, though he supposed some would call it quaint. Old-fashioned streetlights lined Main Street, illuminating homes that looked as if they belonged in an old Jimmy Stewart movie. Nearly every house had a porch, a flower garden, and a swing set in the yard. In the mood he was in, Taylor saw little to admire about it. He liked cities, not small towns that weren't going anywhere. The rain had eased for the moment, but Liberty Hill's wet streets were still deserted. And it was barely ten o'clock at night! If the powers that be could have, he was sure they'd have rolled up the sidewalks by now. The only business that was still open was an old-fashioned diner by the name of Ed's.

"Here you go," the tow-truck driver said as he un-hitched his wrecked Mercedes in front of the town's only garage and gave Taylor a receipt for his credit-card payment. "Curtis Dean owns the place—he'll be in in the morning at six. He's a good mechanic. You won't find anyone who does better body work." Suddenly frowning as he watched Taylor pull his suitcase from the trunk of his car, he said, "Are you sure you don't want me to take you to your cousin's? Where are you going to stay tonight?"

Taylor was asking himself the same thing. He'd seen a sign for the town library and hospital, and they'd passed a beauty salon and a lawyer's office on the way to the garage. The one thing he hadn't seen was anything that even resembled a Best Western. "That's a good question," he retorted. "Aren't there any hotels around here?"

"Nope. Myrtle Henderson has a boarding house, though. I heard she was turning it into a bed and break-fast. You might try there. It's a big old Victorian house down the street on the right. You can't miss it. It's right next to the only antique store in town."

Considering how off the beaten track Liberty Hill was, Taylor doubted the place was booked for the night. "Thanks," he said. "I'll give it a try."

Myrtle Henderson's place was right where the tow-truck driver had said it was…and as dark as the rest of the buildings in town. Irritated, Taylor stood at the front gate and swore softly. What was it with this town? Did everybody go to bed with the chickens?

Scowling, he would have gone somewhere else for

the night, but there was nowhere else. He was well and truly stuck, and if he couldn't wake Myrtle Henderson, he'd be sleeping on a bench in the park...if this damn town even had a park!

Fuming, he pushed open the gate and strode up the walk to the front porch. Next to the old-fashioned, oval-glassed door, the doorbell glowed softly in the night. He jabbed it stiffly, sending the faint, cheery tinkle of its bell echoing through the silent house. Twenty seconds passed, then a minute, and still, the house remained as dark and quiet as a tomb.

Scowling, he swore and had just lifted his hand to pound on the door when he saw a light suddenly flare on inside the front entry of the old house. A split second later, the porch light was flipped on, and through the lace curtain covering the glass oval of the door, he saw the vague figure of a woman approach. Finally! he thought with a sigh of relief as she shot the dead bolt free. Maybe he wouldn't have to sleep on that park bench, after all.

His only thought was to get a room. It wasn't until the woman started to pull the door open that he remembered he had to look like something that had just crawled out of a swamp. His clothes were wet and torn, his hair plastered to his head. Any woman with sense would send him packing the second she laid eyes on him, not invite him in and rent him a room.

Idiot! he raged silently. He should have gone over to the diner and cleaned up some before approaching her. It was, however, too late for that. He'd have to muddle through an explanation the best he could and hope she believed him.

"I'm sorry for disturbing you so late," he began as the door was finally pulled open completely. "I had an

accident in my car when I was coming into town, and
I need a place to stay...."

That was as far as he got. No longer concealed behind
the lace curtain of the door was the most beautiful
woman he'd ever seen in his life. Stunned, he felt his
jaw drop and could do nothing but stand there like a
fool with his mouth hanging open. When the tow-truck
driver had said Myrtle Henderson was turning her
boarding house into a bed and breakfast, he'd assumed
for some reason that she was an older woman. Nothing
could have been further from the truth.

In the stark light of the entry hall's old brass chandelier, this woman quite simply stole his breath. Maybe
it was the angle of the light or simply the stress of
walking away from an accident that could have killed
him, but he took one look at her and felt as though he'd
stepped into a faded photograph from another century.
Everything about her was soft—the cascade of blond
hair that fell in soft waves past her shoulders, the old-
fashioned gown and robe that covered her completely,
but still somehow appeared to be as gossamer as a
dream. Obviously, she was fresh from her bath—he
could clearly smell the scent of her soap, and her hair
was damp around the edges—but he couldn't take his
eyes off her face. No woman had a right to look so
beautiful without makeup.

The thought had hardly registered—and had time to
irritate him—when he suddenly realized he was staring.
Stiffening, he reminded himself that he was there for a
room, nothing else. "The tow-truck driver said you
were turning your boarding house into a bed and breakfast," he continued stiffly. "I—"

Behind him, lightning suddenly ripped through the

night sky, and right on its heels was a crack of thunder so loud it could have stopped the devil himself in his tracks. Before Taylor could say another word, the lights went out.

Chapter 2

Startled, Phoebe gasped. Darkness engulfed her like a shroud, blinding her, and for a moment, she could see nothing but the sharp flash of the lightning outside and the silhouette of the stranger at the door.

In the darkness, he was huge! Phoebe felt her heart jump into her throat and reminded herself that she wasn't one of those women who was easily scared. After all, there was no reason to be nervous. She was in Liberty Hill, Colorado, for heaven's sake! There were no ax murderers here, no rapists, no serious criminals at all. She couldn't imagine a safer place in America.

So she wasn't afraid...exactly. It was just that her imagination had always worked overtime on stormy nights, and tonight was no exception. With her heart pounding crazily and the stranger filling the doorway with his dark silhouette, she could almost believe that he was some dark, avenging angel who'd been sent by her father to demand an explanation of why she was at

Myrtle's when she should have been home, taking care of his business. That was just the kind of thing Jack Chandler would have done. He'd never had much patience for following dreams, especially if it meant walking away from an established business. Money was the bottom line, and if her father somehow knew that she was at his mother-in-law's, trying her hand at running what he would have considered an artsy-fartsy bed and breakfast that had no chance of ever making a dime, he'd be spinning in his grave.

For a moment, guilt pulled at her, but then her common sense quickly asserted itself. *"Idiot!"* she silently chided herself. There was no reason to feel guilty. She was an adult and could spend her vacation—and her life—any way she chose.

As for the fierce stranger at the door, she'd taken one look at him before the lights had gone off and seen by the cynical curve of his mouth that he was no angel. He was just a man who was in trouble and needed help while she was standing there like a ninny, letting her imagination run away with her!

"Actually, my grandmother is the one who owns the place," she said huskily. "But I'm taking care of things while she's on vacation. If you'll wait a moment, I'll get a candle. The old wiring in this house doesn't handles storms very well."

Leaving him at the door, she turned away and quickly, blindly, made her way through the dark house, avoiding chairs and tables whose location she knew as well as the lines on the back of her hand. She hadn't lied about the wiring—it was nearly as old as her grandmother—and even though it could be an inconvenience at times, she'd loved it as a child when a storm blew the old circuit breakers. Unruffled, Myrtle would pull

out the oil lamps and candles, set water on to boil on
the gas stove, and they'd have a tea party in the dark.
Mrytle would tell her stories of all their dead ancestors
and how they'd come to Colorado in covered wagons.
Her stories had always been fun and magical and full
of adventure, and to this day, Phoebe still loved storms.

Smiling at the memories that pulled at her as she
reached the pantry, she quickly located the stash of
emergency matches and candles Myrtle kept there and
hurriedly lit a candle. Outside, the storm still raged, but
she didn't have time to enjoy it, not when the stranger
still waited for her at the front door. Placing a small
glass chimney around the candle, she hurried back to
the front door.

For a moment, she thought her unexpected guest had
left. The door was standing wide open, and in the flick-
ering light of the candle, there was no sign of him.
Frowning, she moved to the open doorway and lifted
her candle high…just as he stepped in front of her. Startled, she almost dropped the candle. He moved like a
cat in the darkness! "Oh!" she gasped softly. "I
thought you'd gone."

"I was just checking the sky," he retorted. "Do you
ever get tornadoes when it storms like this?"

She shrugged. "Sometimes, but I was watching the
weather channel earlier. The front passed through about
an hour ago, so all we have to deal with now is
rain…and wind, of course. It'll probably howl all night
long."

As far as she was concerned, there was no better
sleeping weather, but her guest looked far from pleased
with the forecast. His frown deepening, he scowled,
then obviously decided there was no use whining about
the weather. "As I was saying before the lights went

out, I need a room. Preferably something private, where I won't be disturbed.''

His tone was cool, almost snooty, and that alone told Phoebe that he was a man who was used to getting what he wanted. As a paying guest, he had a right to expect peace and quiet, and she would be as accommodating as she could, but she didn't like his tone at all. What was his problem, anyway? she wondered, narrowing her blue eyes at him in irritation. Hadn't his mama taught him he'd go a lot further in life if he used please and thank you?

Lifting the candle, she held it up so that it illuminated his face and made no secret of the fact that she was openly studying him. He was, she silently acknowledged, a good-looking man. Lean and rangy, with an angular face and a hard jaw, there was something about him that was vaguely familiar, though Phoebe was sure she'd never met him before. She would never have forgotten those eyes. Piercing, brown and sharp with intelligence, they met her gaze head-on and seemed to see into her very soul.

For no explicable reason, she felt her heart kick, and she didn't like the feeling at all. Frowning, she asked, ''How long were you planning on staying? Just tonight or until your car's fixed?''

''Actually, longer than that,'' he replied stiffly. ''Probably a month, maybe longer. At this point, I can't really tell you more than that.''

Phoebe loved Liberty Hill, but she wasn't blind to the fact that there was little about it that would attract a tourist for longer than a day or two. Especially one who appeared to be as sophisticated as this man. His clothes might be damp and torn from his accident, but even so, it was obvious that they were well-cut and expensive. What was his story? What was he doing here?

Curious, she arched a brow at him. "If you don't mind my asking, what are you going to do here for an entire month? You can walk from one end of town to the other in about ten minutes."

For a moment, he hesitated as if he didn't want to tell her, before he finally said, almost defiantly. "I'm a writer. I'm working on a book."

Phoebe couldn't have been more surprised if he'd told her he was the head chef for the *Titanic.* She liked to think she was a fairly good judge of people, but she'd never have guessed that the man had a creative bone in his body. He just didn't look like a writer. Not that a writer had any particular look, she admitted. But she'd always thought of writers and artists as exotic introverts who could do things with words or paint or clay that she and most people could never even dream of. In no way, shape or form did that describe her unexpected guest. If she'd had to guess what he did for a living, she would have taken him for some kind of power broker. He had class-A personality written all over him.

Still, he could have been friendly. He wasn't. In fact, he seemed almost angry. Granted, he had a right to be out of sorts after he'd wrecked his car in the storm, but she had a feeling his anger went deeper than that. And that disturbed her. She liked people…liked talking to them, cooking for them, getting to know them. Getting to know this man wouldn't be easy. Everything about him said back off.

For no other reason than that, she should have sent him back out into the rain in search of a room somewhere else. People who booked a vacation at a bed and breakfast weren't just looking for a place to spend the night. They were looking for an escape, a place where they could go to get away from the stress of their everyday lives. She didn't know if the other guests Myrtle had lined up for the next few weeks would be able to do that with this man in the house.

But how could she send him away? It was a miserable night and he'd already had more than his share of trouble. And it wasn't as if he could find someplace else in town to stay. The nearest hotel was thirty miles away! How was he supposed to get there? Walk? He'd wrecked his car!

Her ex-boyfriend would have told her she was a soft touch and whatever the stranger's story was, it wasn't her problem. But that was one of the reasons Marshall was an ex. She couldn't be that unfeeling, especially when someone was in trouble. Giving into her inherent need to help, she opened the door wider and invited him inside. "Please, come in. I'm Phoebe Chandler," she added with an easy smile as he stepped over the threshold. "I'm sorry. I didn't catch your name."

"Taylor Bishop," he growled.

Holding out her hand, she flashed her dimples at him. "It's nice to meet you, Taylor. I hope you'll enjoy your stay here."

He closed his fingers around hers, but only gave her hand a perfunctory shake before releasing it. "I'm sure it'll be fine."

He couldn't have insulted her more if he'd tried. After everything her grandmother had done to turn the place into a bed and breakfast—and all the work she, herself, intended to do to make the Mountain View Inn the best in the state—she wanted his stay to be a heck of a lot more than just *fine!*

Annoyed, she smiled, but it wasn't easy. "I hope it's

better than that. So if there's anything you need—or don't like—just let me know. If I can't fix the problem, I'll find someone who can.''

"I'm not particular about things. All I want is to be left alone to work in peace.''

Well, that was blunt enough, Phoebe thought, irritated. If he thought she was going to bother him, he could think again. He could have all the peace and quiet he wanted. "Then you should be pleased with your room,'' she said. "C'mon. I'll show you.''

Turning, she led him carefully up the stairs and found herself wishing the lights would hurry up and come back on. She'd never realized before just how intimate and inviting candlelight was. Or how quiet Myrtle's Victorian house was, even in the midst of a storm. As they carefully made their way up the grand staircase, she could almost hear the pounding of her heart as his shadow followed hers. Did he realize they were the only two people in the house? Was he as aware of her presence as she was of his? What the heck was going on?

Telling herself not to get fanciful, she led him to a room at the back of the house. "It's small, but I think it will suit you nicely. You won't be able to hear the street noise from here and it has a nice view of the garden. You won't be disturbed while you work.''

The room was, in fact, quite comfortable and was decorated with red plaids and heavy furniture designed to appeal to a man. Taylor Bishop took one look at it in the light of the candle she held and reached for his wallet. "This is fine. You do take credit cards, don't you?''

His tone was cool...and all business. Irritated, Phoebe reminded herself that he was only a guest— unfortunately, her first—and she didn't have to like him.

He wasn't going to stay forever. If he didn't care about his creature comforts, that was his problem. It was her job to see that his stay—and every other guest's—was as comfortable as possible, and that's what she intended to do.

Her tone as businesslike as his, she added, "The bathroom is across the hall—there are extra towels in the linen closet if you need them. Breakfast is served between seven and ten in the dining room. If there's anything in particular you would like added to the menu, just tell me and I can have it for you the following morning."

Not giving him a chance to say anything, she rattled off a list of the inn's other amenities. "If there's anything else you need, just let me know and I'll try to get it for you. Enjoy your stay."

Giving him a curt nod, she didn't wait to see if he had any questions, but simply turned and headed for her room further down the hall. She knew it was rude, but she couldn't help it. She didn't understand why someone like Taylor Bishop stayed at a bed and breakfast. He obviously wasn't the type to enjoy it. Logically, she knew he hadn't had any other choice—there were no other public lodgings in town—but he still irritated her. Taylor couldn't have cared less that the sheets and towels were line-dried so they would have that fresh scent that was impossible to get in a drier, or that she herself had experimented with dozens of new breakfast recipes, searching for just the right dishes that would make breakfast each morning memorable. He just wanted to be left alone to work.

Fine, she fumed as she stepped inside her own room and shut the door with a little more force than was nec-

essary. Let him hole up in his room. The less she had
to deal with him, the better!

Finally alone, Tyler found a phone book in the bottom drawer of the desk in the corner and wasn't surprised to discover that although the directory covered
several counties, it wasn't even an inch thick. After
waiting his entire life to track down his father, it took
him less than fifteen seconds to find the McBrides in
the phone book. There were two: Joe and Zeke.

Frowning, he refused to be discouraged. His father
could have an unlisted number, or there was always the
possibility that he had moved. After all, it had been
forty-one years since his mother met Gus at the Cheyenne rodeo that fateful summer. Gus had claimed he
was a cowboy, but there was no way to know for sure
that he was telling the truth. He'd been a cowboy sweet-
talking a pretty girl. That made anything and everything
he'd said suspect.

Still, there were McBrides in Liberty Hill, Taylor
thought in satisfaction. Whether they were related to
Gus or not remained to be seen, but the odds were in
Taylor's favor that they were. After all, Liberty Hill was
hardly bigger than a postage stamp. Everyone was
bound to be related to everyone else. Now all he had
to do was get either Joe or Zeke to tell him where Gus
was. Then he was going to hunt his old man down and
tell him exactly what he thought of him.

Over the years, he'd lost track of the number of times
he'd contemplated that meeting, but as he undressed and
climbed into the big, old-fashioned poster bed that dominated the room, he found he couldn't concentrate on
the old, familiar image as he usually did. The quiet still-
ness of the house surrounded him, and through the open

window, a gentle breeze stirred the night air with a freshness that reminded him all too clearly that he wasn't in San Diego anymore. Just that easily, he found himself appreciating the line-dried sheets—and thinking of Phoebe Chandler.

He could still smell the scent of her shampoo.

Irritated that he'd even noticed, he swore softly in the darkness. What the devil was wrong with him? He was on a mission and it had nothing to do with an innkeeper's granddaughter. Granted, she had a natural beauty that had caught him off guard, but she wasn't his type. He liked his women sophisticated and worldly, and from what he'd seen of Phoebe Chandler, she was neither of those things. Not that it mattered. He didn't have time for women right now. The only thing he was interested in was finding his father...and making him pay.

Satisfied that he had his priorities straight, he deliberately put her from his thoughts and concentrated instead on what he was going to say to Joe and Zeke McBride when he approached them about Gus. He generally didn't like to plan things too much—he worked better when he went with his instincts. Tracking down Gus McBride, however, was too important to leave to chance.

So, just as he did when he was working on an important trial, he tried to work out every possible contingency. Normally, he could have worked well into the night on a case without ever growing sleepy, but it had been a long, emotional day and evening. He yawned...and felt himself losing ground. With a sigh, he gave up the fight and let himself drift toward sleep.

His last thought should have been about his father. Instead, a whisper of the night breezes drifted in through the open window, teasing him with a sweet, faint scent that reminded him inexplicably of *her*. Like it or not, she was his last thought before he fell asleep.

When Phoebe came downstairs the next morning, dawn was still nearly an hour away. It was her favorite time of the day. There were no telemarketers calling on the phone, no TVs or radios blaring, no trucks shifting gears as they made their way down Main Street. Quiet echoed like a sigh, and for a while, at least, Phoebe could almost believe she was the only one in town awake. She loved it.

Unfortunately, this time she had to herself couldn't last. Although her guest hadn't told her what time he would like breakfast, she had a feeling he was an early riser. She'd be lucky if she had another two hours to herself. She planned to enjoy it before she had to deal with Mr. Personality.

A grin tugged at her lips at the unexpected nickname her psyche had come up with for Taylor Bishop. She didn't mean to be mean. After all, she didn't even know him. Like everyone, he was bound to have some good qualities. And she had to admit, he was an incredibly good-looking man. Looks, however, weren't everything. She'd never met anyone who could push her buttons so easily. And he planned to stay the entire time her grandmother was gone!

If he'd been anything other than a writer, she might have been groaning at the thought. But she doubted that she would see much of him. If he wasn't off somewhere doing research, he would, in all likelihood, be holed up in his room writing. If she was lucky, the only time she'd have to deal with him was at breakfast. And once the other guests arrived, she'd spend most of her mornings in the kitchen.

The cooking, more than anything else, was what she was really looking forward to. Breakfast was her favorite meal of the day, and as she stepped to the pantry to pull out her baking supplies, she could already taste the Virginia ham, apple strudel, and hot, homemade croissants that were planned for part of the morning menu. Mr. Personality hadn't blinked twice when she'd showed him to his room. She'd like to see similar restraint when he sat down to breakfast. If he was expecting ordinary bacon and eggs, he was in for a surprise.

Grinning at the thought, she'd just stepped out of the pantry, her arms laden with ingredients, when she thought she heard a cry in the predawn quiet. Surprised, she stopped in her tracks, listening. Then she heard it again.

"Oh, my God!" she said softly, "that sounds like puppies!"

Hurriedly dumping her supplies on the kitchen table, she grabbed a flashlight from the drawer by the refrigerator, then quickly unlocked the back door and rushed outside just as what sounded like an entire litter of puppies started to whimper and howl from under the porch.

The hems of her nightgown and robe trailing behind her, she flew down the steps, only to laugh when she peered under the porch and found six lab-mix puppies staring up at her warily. "Oh, poor babies! Are you hungry? Where's your mama?"

For an answer she got wagging tails, puppy grins and a couple of brave woofs. Just that easily, they stole her heart. Murmuring soothingly, she held out her hand to them. "It's okay. I won't hurt you. I'm just going to take you inside and find you something to eat. C'mon, that's it. Oh, aren't you sweet!''

Hungry and lonely, they cautiously came out from under the porch, and within seconds, little tails were wagging in greeting. Laughing, she scooped them all up and carried them inside.

His head buried under a pillow, Taylor came awake to the sound of yapping puppies and a woman's delighted laughter floating on the morning air. Disoriented and still half asleep, he found himself fascinated by the sweetness of the sound. Had someone new moved in next door? he wondered sleepily. She had a laugh like an angel. Who was she? He hadn't seen anyone new....

She laughed again, but this time, the fog of sleep clouding Taylor's brain parted and images of last night came rushing back. The wreck, Liberty Hill, Phoebe Chandler. *She* was the one downstairs, the one laughing, the one who fascinated him.

He swore softly, unable to believe he was thinking of her again. He kept waking up during the night because of her—every time he'd closed his eyes, all he could see was Phoebe, standing in the light of the entry hall in her old-fashioned gown and robe, her hair flowing around her shoulders as she opened the door to him. And now here she was, back again, walking out of his dreams into his waking thoughts.

And it was damn irritating! he thought, scowling. He didn't have time to lie around thinking about the old-fashioned lady downstairs. He had work to do. Throwing off the covers, he grabbed his clothes and stepped across the hall to the bathroom. Once he had a shower, he'd get on the phone, order a rental car from Colorado Springs, then get to work finding his father.

Ten minutes later, when he headed downstairs, he was all business. He'd ordered the rental car and decided to start his search for his father by paying a visit to the two McBrides listed in the phone book. No addresses were listed but he didn't expect that to be a problem. He'd call both McBrides at nine, and if he couldn't track them down, he'd walk over to the sheriff's office and see if he knew the McBrides. Surely in a town the size of Liberty Hill, the sheriff had to know just about everyone.

His thoughts on what he would say to the McBrides when he finally found them, he had no intention of eating breakfast. The scent of baking apples and cinnamon was incredible, but he intended to skip the traditionally elaborate meal that came with the cost of his room. He just didn't have time.

Considering that, he should have headed for the front door the second he reached the bottom of the stairs. But in the kitchen, Phoebe laughed softly and murmured something he couldn't quite catch, and with no conscious decision on his part, he found himself following the sound of her voice.

She was dressed as she had been last night, in the soft, flowing gown and robe that had made his sleep so restless, and for a moment, he cynically wondered if the lady always cooked breakfast in her nightclothes or if she had just done so this morning for his benefit. Then he realized she didn't even know he was watching, and he felt like an idiot.

All her attention was focused on the puppies, who were climbing all over each other, tumbling into her lap, their little tails wagging happily as they tried to get to her. Squirming and wiggling, they licked her on the face, making her giggle, and for the first time since his mother had died, Taylor found himself fighting a smile.

No woman had a right to look so pretty in the morning. She'd piled her hair up off her neck with a clip, but other than that, she'd done little to make herself beautiful. Her face was free of makeup, and she hadn't even bothered with shoes. From where he stood, Taylor could see her bare toes peeking out from under her gown and robe. Her nails were painted with a delicate pink polish, matching the natural blush of her cheeks, and with no effort at all, he could see her sitting in the old-fashioned bathroom, her foot propped against the clawfoot tub as she painted her toenails by candlelight.

A cynical man, Taylor readily admitted that he liked women who were sophisticated and politically well connected. From what he'd seen of Phoebe Chandler, she was neither of those things. He shouldn't have found her the least bit appealing. But he couldn't take his eyes off her. As he watched, she picked up each puppy, kissed it on the nose, and placed it in the cardboard box she'd used to make them a bed. With a will of their own, his eyes lingered on the curve of her mouth. Would her lips taste as soft as they looked?

Caught off guard by the direction of his thoughts, he would have sworn that he didn't make a sound, but suddenly, Phoebe glanced up and found him standing in the doorway. Not the least bit self-conscious, she smiled. "Good morning. I'm sorry I'm not dressed yet. I had a few unexpected guests under the back porch this morning. I hope they didn't wake you."

"I'm an early riser," he said gruffly. Nodding at the puppies, he said, "Where's the mama?"

"I don't know," she said with a shrug as she gave the last puppy a kiss and placed it in the box before rising to her feet. "I'm afraid she's abandoned them. There was no sign of her, so I called Merry McBride. She'll be by later to pick them up."

Surprised, Taylor couldn't believe his luck. When he'd taken the room last night and learned this woman was handling the bed and breakfast for her grandmother, he'd never dreamed she would know a McBride. "Who's she? Does she own the local animal shelter or what?"

"Actually, she's the vet," she replied. "She'll take care of the puppies and find them good homes."

Taylor opened his mouth to grill her about what she knew about the McBrides, only to remember just in time that he was supposed to be a writer, not a lawyer. He could ask as many questions as he wanted—he just couldn't cross-examine her as if she was on the witness stand.

So with a casualness he was far from feeling, he frowned and said, "McBride...that name sounds familiar. Is her husband a rancher in the area?"

Phoebe laughed. "McBride is her maiden name. Her husband's Nick Kincaid, the sheriff. Her family ranches, though. In fact, there's been a McBride ranching in Liberty Hill for over a hundred years. You definitely need to talk to them for your book."

Stunned, Taylor couldn't believe she'd given him so much information so quickly. Were the McBrides she spoke of his father's family? His mother had said his father was a cowboy. How was he related to Merry, the vet? And how did Phoebe Chandler know so much about the family?

Curious, he pulled out a chair at the kitchen table and asked her just that. "How do you know the McBrides? Are you friends with them or what?"

She smiled. "I've known them all my life. My grandmother and Sara McBride are best friends."

"And Sara McBride is…"

"Merry's mother. She and Myrtle have known each other forever. They were in first grade together, went to college together, and were in each other's weddings. I can't think of any major event in my grandmother's life that Sara wasn't there for. They're like sisters."

"So what about Mr. McBride? What's his name?"

"Gus."

She said his father's name so casually and didn't have a clue what she'd given him, Taylor thought. He'd found the son of a bitch! And he hadn't even been in Liberty Hill an hour. Never in a million years had he dreamed finding his father would be this easy. Now he just needed his address.

He couldn't, however, come right out and demand it, not without raising Phoebe Chandler's eyebrows. So he swore silently, clamped a lid on the anger that always boiled in him whenever he thought of Gus McBride, and reminded himself that he had a role to play. "If Sara's your grandmother's age, Gus must be getting up there in age, too. Is he still ranching? Or don't ranchers retire? What's his story?"

Surprised, she blinked. "Gus? Oh, I'm sorry. Didn't I tell you? He died years ago."

Chapter 3

Stunned, Taylor stood as if turned to stone. Gus was dead? He couldn't be, not now that he was so close to finding the jackass. God couldn't be so cruel.

But even as he tried to convince himself that Phoebe had to be mistaken, he only had to look at her face to know that there was no question she was telling the truth. She knew the McBrides. She had no reason to lie.

And that's when it hit him. There would be no revenge; Gus wouldn't have to account for his misdeeds. The bastard had used his mother, then walked away from her, leaving her pregnant and alone, with nothing but years of hardship and poverty ahead of her. And what punishment had he received for that? A life of wealth and privilege on one of the largest ranches in the area, a wife and children who'd never known what a skunk he was, happiness.

Bitterness coiled like a snake in Taylor's stomach. It just wasn't fair, dammit! He didn't care for himself so much, but for his mother. She'd come from a well-to-do family who'd lived by high standards. When she'd gotten pregnant without the benefit of a wedding ring on her finger, they'd shunned her, thrown her out, shut the door in her face. She'd never seen her parents again, never had any contact with her family at all. All because of Gus McBride.

"What do you mean...he died years ago?" he asked harshly. "When? Five years ago? Ten? He must have been a young man!"

"Oh, he was," Phoebe assured him. "If I remember correctly, it seems like Joe had just graduated from high school, so Gus was probably in his mid forties—I was just a kid at the time, so I don't really remember the particulars, except that he had a heart attack. It was a shock to everyone. He just dropped dead out on the ranch one day.

"The whole family was devastated, especially poor Sara," she continued. "She was devoted to Gus—from what I remember, they had a wonderful relationship. No one thought she would ever marry again, but I guess time really does heal all wounds. She and Dr. Michaels had been friends for years when they suddenly realized they were in love. They're in Mexico right now on their honeymoon." Smiling fondly, she said, "They had a wonderful wedding. The whole town turned out for it."

Taylor almost told her he couldn't have cared less about Sara McBride or her wedding. She was the woman his father had left his mother for, and for no other reason than that, he wanted nothing to do with her. Phoebe Chandler would no doubt be horrified by that, but dammit, the truth of the matter was, his mother's life would have been a hell of a lot happier if it hadn't been for Sara. Considering that, who could blame him for disliking her, sight unseen?

He thought, however, that he was hiding his hostility well. He wasn't. Something of what he was feeling must have shown in his expression because Phoebe's smile suddenly faded, and her eyes searched his. "What is it?" she asked, frowning. "What's wrong?"

Wrong? he wanted to growl. What *wasn't* wrong? When he'd taken a leave of absence from the firm to track down his old man, everything had seemed so simple. Unfortunately, the joke was on him. Gus was dead, and that was that.

Angry, bitter, his plans all shot to hell, he had to get away, had to think. "Nothing," he lied. "I just realized that I left my notes at home, and I need them for the book."

"Oh, I'm sorry. Is there someone you can call to send them to you?"

"No," he replied shortly. "I'll just have to redo the research. Is there a library around here? I can probably get what I need from the local history books."

There was no research, of course, no work he had to do except figure out where he went from here. Phoebe, however, accepted his story without so much as a blink. "It's down the street on the right," she said. "Across from the post office. You can't miss it. It's in the only redbrick building on Main Street."

Gruffly thanking her for her help, he turned to leave, but he'd only taken two steps when she cried out, "Wait! What about breakfast? I can have it ready in ten minutes."

"Save it," he growled. "I'm not hungry."

He was gone before she could stop him, leaving her staring after him with her mouth hanging open. That was it? He wasn't hungry? After she'd gotten up before the crack of dawn to cook breakfast for him? He couldn't be serious!

But the front door slammed behind him, and just that quickly, she was alone. Glancing at the apple strudel, Virginia ham and croissants she'd already made for breakfast, Phoebe didn't know whether to laugh or cry. Why, out of all the people she could have had for her first guest, had Taylor Bishop landed on her doorstep? Did the man know there was a reason the inn was classified a bed and breakfast? Breakfast was included with the cost of the room! What was she going to do with all this food?

It was a beautiful summer morning, cool and clear, and under other circumstances, Taylor would have enjoyed a brisk walk. But as he strode quickly down the street toward the library, every step he took echoed the anger seething inside him. Damn Gus McBride! For as long as Taylor could remember, he'd hated the faceless, nameless man who hadn't been there for him as other fathers were for their sons. He'd only wanted the answer to one question—Why?—and now he wasn't even going to get that. Because Gus McBride was dead and had been for a long time.

And that, more than anything, was what infuriated him the most. For years, he'd resented a man who was already dead, and he hadn't even known it. He felt like a fool. Somehow, he should have known, dammit. But not even his mother had guessed that Gus McBride was dead. If she had, she would have been devastated, and for the life of him, Gus didn't know why. The man had never loved her or he wouldn't have walked away from her. As far as Taylor was concerned, the jackass hadn't respected her, either, or he wouldn't have had sex with her without protecting her.

He should have had to answer for that, if nothing else, Taylor thought grimly. It was no more than he deserved. But, no! In this, too, he'd somehow managed to escape the repercussions of his behavior. Taylor knew he was being unreasonable—Gus hadn't died deliberately so he wouldn't have to face his illegitimate son—but that's what it felt like. And it infuriated him that Gus had that much control over his emotions, that this man that he had resented for as long as he could remember could tie him in knots from the grave and there wasn't a damn thing he could do about it.

What the hell was he going to do now?

Fuming, unsure what his next move would be, he almost walked right past the library. There was, he thought grimly, no longer any reason to keep up the charade that he was a writer. He might as well go back to the Mountain View Inn, pack his bags, and head back to San Diego. There was nothing he could do here.

But instead of returning to the inn, he found himself walking up the front steps to the library, after all. This was, he thought bitterly, his one and only chance to find out everything he could about Gus McBride and try to understand what his mother had possibly seen in such a worthless man. Then he planned to go home and forget the man he should have grown up calling Dad ever existed.

His chiseled face set in grim lines, he stepped inside the library and wasn't surprised to find it practically deserted. After all, it wasn't even nine o'clock in the morning. An old woman sat at a desk in the genealogy area, obviously working on a family tree, and a thin man with bottle-thick glasses was comfortably ensconced in an old leather chair in the periodical section, reading the Denver paper. Other than the librarian, who was busy dusting the shelves, they had the place to themselves.

Which was just the way he wanted it, Taylor thought as he found the local history section and the newspaper archives. He wanted to be left in peace to satisfy his curiosity about Gus, then he was getting the hell out of Liberty Hill.

Deciding to start with the end of his father's life and work backwards, he pulled out the newspaper archives and began searching for his obituary. A computer would have made the job go much faster, but the Liberty Hill library was obviously caught in a time warp. There wasn't a computer anywhere in sight.

Not that that was a problem, he soon discovered. Even though Gus had died years ago, searching for his obituary wasn't nearly as difficult as it would have been in a city. Liberty Hill was a small community, and there were only a few deaths recorded in the local paper each week. Finding the obits from twenty years ago only took a matter of minutes.

GUS MCBRIDE DIES!

The all-cap headlines of the obituary seemed to jump right off the page and slap him in the face. Taylor stiffened, and just that easily, found himself reading about his father's life.

Gus McBride died October 3, 1983, at his ranch in Liberty Hill, at the age of 44. He is survived by his loving wife, Sara J. McBride, children: Joseph

McBride, Jane McBride, Zeke McBride, and Merry McBride, and numerous nephews and nieces.

A member of one of the founding families of Liberty Hill, Gus was president of the Colorado Cattlemen's Association from 1979 to 1983, a Boy Scout leader for the last fifteen years of his life, and a deacon in his church. A loving father and husband, he will be sorely missed.

Visitation will be Tuesday night, October 5, between 7:00 p.m. and 9:00 p.m., at Liberty Hill Funeral Chapel. Funeral services will be at 10:00 a.m., Wednesday, October 6, at the funeral home, with interment following at the McBride family cemetery at Twin Pines, the family ranch.

Later, Taylor couldn't have said how long he sat at one of the library's time-worn oak tables, staring at his father's faded obituary, before the words finally sank in. Phoebe had, without being aware of it, already informed him he had a sister. Now, it turned out, he had another sister and two brothers. When he'd planned the trip to Liberty Hill to search for his father, he'd known, of course, that there was a good possibility that he had a couple of half brothers or sisters walking around Colorado that he knew nothing about. He'd never dreamed there were four of them.

And he felt nothing. Nothing but resentment.

If his mother had been alive, she would have been less than pleased with him. In spite of the fact that she'd been disowned by her own parents, she'd valued family and had always regretted the fact that she couldn't give that to him. Although she'd never discussed the matter with him, he knew she would have wanted him to give his father's other children a chance if they showed an interest in developing a relationship with him.

It wasn't going to happen.

At the thought, he could almost hear his mother clicking her tongue at him in disapproval. But it took more than blood to make a family. The *legitimate* children of Gus McBride had been raised on the family ranch. *They* had grown up with all the rights and privileges of a McBride. They knew who their father was, their grandfather, where the family came from, where they, themselves would live and die. Hell, they even knew where they would be buried!

And what had been his birthright? Because of Gus McBride, he hadn't had a father, hadn't had grandparents—on either side! When he was little, there'd been no father to chase away the boogeyman in the closet when he had bad dreams, no dad to teach him to fish or hunt or the million and one other things a good father taught his children.

His mother had tried to step up and fill the roll of both parents, and he had to give her credit. She'd done a damn good job. But she couldn't do it all. She was a woman, and there were times when she had to deal with her own fears. She'd needed a man, a husband, to protect her, just as he'd needed a father. They'd had neither.

Because Gus McBride had been halfway across the country, protecting his *real* family.

And Taylor would bet money that Zeke, Merry, Joe and Jane weren't scared at night when they were growing up. They hadn't worried about the bills or having enough money for new clothes for school each year. They didn't hate the neighborhood they had to live in. They'd grown up in the Colorado Rockies, for heaven's sake, on a ranch that was started by some of the first settlers in the area. That alone was like growing up in a national park.

Did they know how lucky they were? Growing up, they'd had it all. Taylor wouldn't have been surprised if they'd thought their daddy was a saint. He wasn't. Unfortunately, they'd never know that.

Unless he told them.

Deep down inside the very core of him, a voice reminded him that he wasn't the kind of man—or lawyer—who hurt innocent people. Normally, he would have agreed, but the bitterness that rose in him every time he thought about Gus McBride drowned out his common decency. All he could think of was that it wasn't fair that his father had escaped the consequences of his actions by dying. The truth had to be told.

And he was just the person to tell it, he thought grimly. The only problem was, it wasn't just Gus's children who needed to be told the truth about him. He wanted Sara to know. She was the one Gus had left his mother for. She was the reason he'd grown up without a father. If it hadn't been for her, his mother would probably have contacted Gus as soon as she found out she was pregnant. She'd loved him. Because of Sara, she'd spent the rest of her life without him.

Nothing he could do now could change that or the heartache his mother had suffered. He still intended to tell Sara just what kind of man her deceased husband was, if for no other reason than it was time the truth came out. The only problem was…she was on her honeymoon and he didn't know when she was coming back. It didn't matter, he decided. He could wait.

"Oh, Phoebe, they're adorable!" Merry McBride Kincaid cooed as she cuddled one of the puppies that had showed up under Myrtle's back porch earlier that morning. "Are you sure you don't want to keep one? It seems like fate that they ended up here, almost as if they're supposed to belong to you. Maybe you should reconsider."

"Oh, no you don't!" Phoebe laughed. "Don't even think about trying to pawn one of them off on me. They're just as sweet as they can be, but a puppy's the last thing I need."

"But it would be such company for you," Merry said, her blue eyes twinkling. "C'mon, Phoebe, at least consider the idea. You know you want to. There's no better way to get unconditional love."

Phoebe didn't doubt that—and there was nothing she loved more than a puppy—but the timing was all wrong. Her future was up in the air, her plans too uncertain. If working at Myrtle's bed and breakfast turned out to be half as enjoyable as she knew it was going to be, then she had some major career decisions to make when she went back home. If she decided to follow her heart and open her own bed and breakfast, she'd have to find the appropriate location, sell her father's business, move, get the business up and running. And she couldn't do that with a puppy underfoot.

"Nice try," she said with a grin, "but it's not going to work. I've got too much going on right now. Maybe next year."

"Give me a call when you're ready," Merry said, understanding, as she returned the puppy she held to the box where his brothers and sisters were sleeping. "Someone's always bringing me a stray litter of puppies."

"You're the first person I'll call," Phoebe assured her as Merry hefted the box of puppies and started down the central hall to the front door. "Here, let me get the door for you."

Pulling the door open for her, she pushed open the screen door and stepped out onto the front porch, only to find herself face to face with Taylor as he came up the steps to the porch. "Oh!" she said, startled, frowning as her heart skipped a beat at the sight of him. Why did she always have this crazy reaction whenever she laid eyes on the man? She didn't even like him! "I thought you were at the library."

"I found everything I needed," he replied, and glanced past her to Merry, who'd just stepped through the front door with the box of puppies.

Phoebe saw him catch his breath and wasn't surprised. Everyone reacted to Merry that way when they met her for the first time. She was drop-dead gorgeous...and one of the nicest women Phoebe knew. Like all the McBrides, she would give the shirt off her back to someone in need.

"Merry, this is my first guest, Taylor Bishop," she said, breaking the silence that had fallen with Taylor's arrival. "He's a writer. He's doing a book on the ranching families that helped settle Colorado."

"Oh, really?" Smiling easily, she said, "Then you need to talk to my mother and brothers. And Janey, too," she added. "She did the family genealogy and traced the McBrides all the way back to Scotland."

Still dazed, Taylor hardly heard her. This was his half sister? This was unbelievable. She was beautiful. She was—

"Taylor? Are you all right?"

Glancing up from his thoughts, he found both Phoebe and Merry grinning at him. For the first time in a long time, a blush stung his cheeks. "I feel like I just put my foot in my mouth and I didn't say a word."

"I seem to have that effect on people," Merry chuckled. "It's nice to meet you, Taylor. Welcome to Liberty Hill."

"Thank you," he said gruffly, and only just then realized that the puppies she was holding had to be heavy. "Here, let me take those for you. Where did you want them?"

"In my truck," she said, nodding toward the white Explorer sitting at the curb. "Thank you."

"No problem," he assured her, and easily carried the puppies to the truck.

"He's nice," Merry said quietly to Phoebe, "when he lets down his guard. He should do it more often."

Phoebe didn't know if she would have described him as nice or not, but she had to agree with Merry. When he forgot to be so angry, he was devastatingly attractive. Who would have thought it?

Walking with Merry out to her truck as Taylor carefully deposited the puppies in the back seat, she was still marvelling at the change in her guest's attitude when he turned back to Merry and said solemnly, "Phoebe said your father is dead. I'm sorry to hear that. I was hoping to talk to as many of the old ranchers in the area as possible about the old days."

"Dad would have enjoyed that," she said with a smile. "I remember when I was a kid, he used to tell us stories about the ranch that his father told him."

"How old were you when he died?"

"Twelve," she replied. "It was a shock for all of us—he was only forty-four. My mother was in shock, of course, but I think it was hardest on my brother Joe. He was eighteen and about to go off to college when

Dad died. Mom wanted him to go on and go, but Joe knew she couldn't run the ranch by herself and raise the rest of us. So he did it for her.''

''What about college?'' Taylor asked. ''Did he ever go?''

''No,'' she said simply. ''Zeke went on to get his Ph.D, I went to veterinary school and Janey became an RN, but Joe never went. We owe him a lot. If he hadn't run the ranch and helped put all of us through school, there's no telling what any of us would be doing now.''

Taylor doubted that any of them would have ended up waiting tables—they all sounded too intelligent for that—but there was no question that their lives would have been different if it hadn't been for the fact that Joe had sacrificed his own education for theirs. And that gave him a lot to think about. He'd always thought that if his father had any other children, they'd probably been blessed with a golden childhood, free of the worries and lack of security he'd grown up with. Apparently, they'd gone through rough times, too, if Joe had to give up college to keep the family afloat.

For a moment, he almost felt sorry for the unknown Joe. But then a bitter voice in his head pointed out that while he, himself, had been living in roach-invested government housing as a child, his half brothers and sisters had been growing up on a ranch that was, no doubt, nearly as big as Rocky Mountain National Park. Poor Joe? He didn't think so.

''You would all have probably still found a way to go to college,'' he retorted. ''And your brother would still have turned out to be a rancher whether he went to college or not. It's obviously in his blood.''

''Actually, it's in all our blood,'' Merry replied with a smile. ''Janey and I might not be working the ranch

like the boys, but we love it as much as they do. I guess
that's why we all built our homes within a few miles
of the homestead. It'll always be home.''

Because she was a McBride, Taylor thought grimly.
A *legitimate* McBride. They all were. He wasn't and
never would be. There would be no home on the range
for him, no sense of family, no belonging that they took
for granted. Because their father—and his—had not
been an honorable man.

''You know, you really should come out and see the
ranch,'' Merry told him with a smile. ''We all get together once a week for dinner, just to keep in touch and
find out what's going on in each other's lives. We're
going to Joe's tonight. Why don't you come? You, too,
Phoebe,'' she added. ''We always have enough food for
an army, and I know everyone would love to see you.''

Surprised, Phoebe blinked. ''Oh, no, I couldn't. It's
a family get-together. I wouldn't want to intrude on that
or Taylor's work. I can see everyone another time.''

Elated—he'd never dreamed he'd be invited to the
ranch this quickly!—Taylor was determined not to lose
this chance. ''You wouldn't be intruding, Phoebe,'' he
assured her, ''at least, not on my work. Most of my
research involves talking to people, recording their con-
versations, and transcribing the tapes later. There's no
reason why you can't be there, visiting with your
friends. And I don't have a car. Remember? I called
Colorado Springs to see about getting a rental, but it
won't be delivered until tomorrow morning. So, in the
meantime, I'm afoot. If you've got other plans and can't
go, I understand, but I could really use a ride. And if
you're going to drive me out there, you might as well
stay to eat and visit.''

Put on the spot, she couldn't come up with a reason

to turn him down, especially when his plan made perfect sense. Reluctantly, she agreed. "If you're both sure..."

"It'll be fun," Merry assured her, hugging her. "Be at Joe's at seven. And don't worry about bringing anything. Like I said, there'll be plenty to eat." The puppies chose that moment to cry out from her truck and she grinned. "It sounds like the natives are getting restless. I've got to go. See you both tonight."

She was gone so fast, Phoebe didn't have time to reconsider what she'd agreed to until it was too late. Then it hit her. For all practical purposes, she had agreed to attend a dinner party with Taylor. Dear God, they had a date and she didn't even know how it had happened!

She should have backed out immediately. She loved the McBrides and didn't doubt that she'd enjoy visiting with all of them, but not with Taylor. She hadn't forgotten how her heart kicked at the sight of him. There was something about him that put her on edge, and for the life of her, she didn't know why. She didn't want to be so aware of him, but she couldn't seem to help herself. And that troubled her. She hardly knew the man, and what she did know about him she wasn't sure she liked. He was moody and surly, and too sophisticated for a woman like her. Knowing that, she should have kept her distance, been as cool and reserved as he, and looked forward to the day he checked out. Instead, she'd stupidly agreed to go to the McBrides' with him. She must have been out of her mind.

At ten minutes to six, Phoebe stood in front of her closet, frowning at the meager supply of clothes she'd brought with her and wondering what in the world she was going to wear on a date that she was determined wasn't going to be a date at all. She'd had all day to think about it, and she'd realized that the only reason Taylor had pushed her to accept Merry's invitation was so that he'd have a ride out to the ranch. That should have calmed the butterflies that had fluttered in her stomach all afternoon. She was just giving him a ride, and for convenience's sake, she'd stay to visit with her friends while he worked. In no way, shape or form, could that be considered a date.

So why did it feel like one?

Frowning at the thought, Phoebe told herself to grab something from the closet, anything. It didn't matter what she wore—she didn't have a date! She was just having dinner with some old friends and a guest who wasn't the least bit interested in her. And that was fine. She wasn't trying to attract his attention or look pretty for him. She could throw on anything decent, pull a brush through her hair, and she was good to go. No problem.

But knowing that and doing it were two different things. Every time she reached for something simple and comfortable, she found her hand drifting, instead, to something a little nicer, something soft and feminine that brought out the blue of her eyes. It was damned irritating.

Frustrated, she muttered, "You're running out of time, Phoebe. Pick something!"

Closing her eyes, she grabbed the first hanger her fingers touched and told herself she would wear it regardless of what it was. When she opened her eyes to discover that it was one of her favorite blouses—and one of the most feminine ones she owned—she hesitated. It was a soft, gauzy material, with frilly cap sleeves and a little bit of lace at the neck, and it looked good with anything, including jeans, which she'd intended to wear tonight to Joe's. It was, however, also a date blouse, something that she felt pretty and feminine in and men generally noticed. The question was, did she want Taylor to notice?

When she hesitated, she knew she was in trouble. She had to be losing her mind. He was cold and unfriendly and angry. Why would she want a man like that to notice her? Afraid to go there, she pulled the blouse off the hanger and hurriedly slipped it on. This was ridiculous. It was just a blouse. She wasn't going to beat herself up wondering if she'd made the right choice.

By the time she came downstairs ten minutes later, she was sure she was ready to face Taylor. She'd tied her hair back in a neat ponytail and applied a minimal amount of makeup. She didn't even wear lipstick—lip gloss was all she needed for dinner with friends. Then she found Taylor waiting for her in the parlor.

She took one look at him and felt her mouth go dry. After seeing him last night when he'd managed to look incredibly handsome even dripping wet from a thunderstorm, she'd thought he couldn't possibly find a way to look any better. She'd been wrong. He'd showered and shaved, and sometime over the course of the afternoon, he'd found the time to get his dark hair cut. It was his clothes, however, that created such a change in his appearance. Instead of the expensive business clothes he'd worn last night, he'd changed to khakis and a white polo shirt that, while still of high quality, were much more casual.

He almost looked approachable, she thought. Now if he would just relax and smile.

For a moment, she thought he was going to do just

that. The corner of his mouth twitched as his eyes met hers, and she found herself holding her breath. Then he obviously thought better of it. Lifting a brow at her, he merely said, "Ready?"

Disappointed—and more than a little annoyed with herself for being so—she should have said of course, she wasn't ready! He looked too good, smelled too good, and in the small confines of her car, neither of them would be able to move without the other being aware of it. It was time to call the whole thing off.

But when she opened her mouth, she was horrified to hear herself say, "Just let me lock up."

It won't be so bad, a voice in her head assured her. It's not that far to Twin Pines and all you have to do is concentrate on the ranch and your driving. You'll be there before you know it, and tomorrow, he'll have a rental car and won't need you to act as his chauffeur anymore. So just grin and bear it.

That was good advice. Or so she thought until she slid behind the wheel of her Volkswagen Bug a short while later and he joined her in the passenger seat. His shoulder brushed hers as he reached for his seatbelt and just that quickly, everything changed.

Her heart thumping, Phoebe told herself she imagined the sparks that seemed to jump between them. But her eyes locked with his and she couldn't, for the life of her, look away. Why hadn't she noticed before how big he was? She'd known he was tall, of course, but his shoulders were much broader than she'd first thought, and he had a presence about him that somehow made her feel safe and protected.

Stunned—and more than a little alarmed—she told herself that this was crazy. She hardly knew the man!

How could he possibly make her feel safe when she didn't even like him?

Afraid even to try to figure out the answer to that one, she reminded herself that she wasn't looking for a man. Not at this point in her life, when she wasn't sure where she would be this time next year. And when she was ready to get back into a relationship, she assured herself, she would never be attracted to a man like Taylor. He might be incredibly good-looking, but there was a reserve to him, a coolness, that had No Trespassing stamped all over it. He wouldn't be an easy man to get to know…or to love.

So why was her heart pounding like a locomotive on a downhill run? She felt as though she'd never seen him before, and suddenly she had this crazy need to touch him. And she didn't know why. It was something about the way he sat, the way he stretched out his long legs as far as he could in the small car, the way he moved with an animal grace that was so sensuous. She couldn't take her eyes off him.

Alarmed, she almost changed her mind about taking him to the McBrides right then and there. But they were already in the car, and what excuse could she possibly give him? She was attracted to him? She didn't think so!

The scent of his cologne teasing her senses, she quickly distracted herself from his closeness by saying the first thing that came into her head. "What do you do when you're not writing? Are you the kind of person who's bored easily? I hope not, since you're staying at least a month. There's not much to do around here. Of course, there are the mountains. You can go hiking and camping if you like. And Aspen's not that far."

"I'm not here to sightsee," he growled. "I don't have time to be bored. All I want to do is work."

From the moment she'd met him, Phoebe had suspected that anyone as intense as he was had to be a workaholic. Obviously, she was right. Whatever Taylor Bishop chose to do, she didn't doubt that he would be successful. But she pitied the woman who gave him her heart. In all likelihood, he'd be so busy working that he wouldn't notice.

And that was just one more reason not to get involved with the man.

Still, she couldn't resist reminding him, "You know what they say about all work…"

Taylor wasn't really surprised by her attitude. He'd seen her kind before. She dressed like a hippy and had probably been raised by flower children of the sixties who encouraged her to float through life smelling daisies. That didn't pay the rent, he thought grimly. And she wasn't going to get very far working in a bed and breakfast, either—if you could call that work. She would never understand the value of real hard work or his need to prove himself.

Knowing that, he should have seen her as a means to an end, nothing more, and not given her a second thought. But she was a difficult woman to ignore. When he should have been focusing all his attention on the upcoming meeting with the McBrides, she was all he could think of. And it had nothing to do with the fact that her scent was alluring or that she looked touchably soft in a blouse that was about as substantial as a whisper. It was just Phoebe…her smile, her total lack of artifice, her feminity. Dammit, why did she have to be so pretty?

Chapter 4

Scowling, he was still pondering that question fifteen minutes later when they arrived at the entrance to Twin Pines, the McBride ranch. Tension crawled up his spine, tightening the muscles of his back one by one. He'd expected some kind of grand, impressive entrance, but other than two pines trees that stood side by side to the left of the gate, there was nothing out of the ordinary about it. There was a cattle guard flanked by two old fieldstone columns and a long drive that cut through a pasture to disappear into the trees on the horizon.

"That's Merry's office and house over there," Phoebe said, nodding to several rock-and-log buildings that he hadn't noticed fifty yards to the right of the entrance. "Joe's place is a couple of miles down the road, and the others are scattered further back. It's a big place."

"Where's the homestead?"

"About a mile from Joe's. Sara and Janey lived there

together for years, but then when they both got married, they had some decisions to make about the house. Janey and Reilly wanted their own place, just like all newly-weds, but they were also aware of the fact that Sara and Dan weren't getting any younger. In the end, they decided it would be better for everyone if they stayed at the homestead.''

''So they're all just one big happy family,'' he retorted.

If Phoebe noted his sarcastic tone, she gave no indication of it. ''Actually, they are,'' she replied. ''That doesn't mean tempers don't get short sometimes, but they all seem to find a way to get along. And all the kids are thrilled that Sara has Dan in her life. As a wedding present, they're remodeling the east wing for them so they'll have their own separate space. They're going to be so surprised when they get back from their honeymoon.''

They were going to be surprised, all right, Taylor thought grimly. Especially Sara. But then again, maybe now that she had remarried, she wouldn't care that her first husband was not the man she'd thought he was. Either way, it was time she and her children were told the truth. If they didn't like it, that wasn't his problem.

''Most families don't get along that well,'' he said as he spied the two-story house and outbuildings in the distance. ''I'm surprised that they're all able to live on the ranch peacefully.''

''They're a great family,'' she assured him. ''You've already met Merry. The others are just as nice. Sara and Gus did a good job raising them.''

While you were growing up without a father in California, a voice in his head reminded him. Yeah, they're a great family.

Phoebe, of course, didn't know that, so he couldn't blame her for thinking the McBrides walked on water. She and the rest of Liberty Hill, however, would know the truth soon enough. It was just a matter of time.

They drew up in front of Joe's place then, and Taylor was surprised to discover that the house was just an ordinary two-story home that couldn't have been over twenty-two-hundred square feet. He'd been expecting something a little more elaborate than an ordinary ranch house. After all, the McBrides owned thousands of acres and were one of the original founding families of the area. He'd thought all his brothers and sisters would be living in high-dollar houses and driving new pickups. Apparently, he'd been wrong.

"Looks like everybody's here," Phoebe said, nodding toward the vehicles in the driveway, all of which were at least a couple of years old. "I hope Janey made banana pudding. I thought my grandmother's was good, but Janey's got hers beat by a mile. C'mon. You're going to love it."

Food was the last thing he was interested in—every nerve in his body was on alert—but Taylor knew neither Phoebe nor the McBrides would ever guess that he was so uptight about the evening to come. He was a damn good lawyer, and he knew how to hide his emotions when he found himself in an adverse situation. Granted, he might not be in a courthouse, but he was definitely walking into a trial, and he knew next to nothing about his opponents. He wouldn't be able to drop his guard for so much as a second.

Escorting her to Joe McBride's front door, he stood behind Phoebe as she knocked, his heart slamming against his ribs with an emotion he couldn't put a name to. Would Joe or Zeke McBride look like his father? Would they favor *him?*

Stiffening at the thought, he swore silently at himself for not thinking about that sooner. He should never have met all his siblings when they were together in one group—if he favored them, one of them was bound to notice. Then what was he going to say? It was too soon to tell them who he was—Sara wasn't here, and he wasn't ready. But he might not have any choice. On edge, ready for anything, he tensed as the door was abruptly pulled open. It was showtime.

All of his life, whenever he'd stood before a mirror, he'd wondered if there was anyone in the world he looked like. It was a lonely feeling. His mother had always said that he was nearly the spitting image of his father, but he'd had no pictures of Gus McBride—or his mother's family, for that matter. He didn't know who he looked like—which was why it was so disconcerting when he found himself face to face with Joe McBride. At first glance, they didn't appear to look anything alike, but he saw himself in the eyes of this man who was his brother.

Whatever Joe McBride was, he was nobody's fool. That much, at least, was instantly obvious. Taller than Taylor by an inch or so, he had the hard, weathered look of someone who spent his days working in the sun. His square-cut face was tanned and chiseled, his shrewd brown eyes as sharp as a barbed wire fence. In a single glance, he looked him over, then turned his attention to Phoebe. Only then did he smile, and the transformation in his face was amazing. With nothing more than a smile, his entire demeanor changed.

"Well, if it isn't Miss Chandler, queen of the vending

machines," he teased. "Long time no see. You're looking good."

"So are you," Phoebe said with a grin. "Angel must be between pictures. I heard you're a bear when she's gone."

"Myrtle's been talking about me again," he retorted, not the least apologetic. "Okay, so I get a little grumpy when my wife is off kissing some other man. I'm not jealous."

"Of course you're not," Phoebe agreed with twinkling eyes. "Why should you be? You're the one she comes home to."

"You're damn straight." Glancing past her to Taylor, he said, "You must be the writer who's staying at Myrtle's. Merry told me about you. It's nice to meet you. I'm Joe McBride."

"Taylor Bishop," Taylor replied, stiffly shaking the hand he held out to him. "I hope I'm not intruding."

"Not at all," Joe assured him. "The more the merrier. Though you must be wondering what kind of family we are since my wife goes around kissing other men. She's an actress," he explained, and there was no denying the pride in his eyes. "Angel Wiley. You might have heard of her."

Taylor couldn't have been more surprised if he'd been hit over the head with a two-by-four. "You're married to Angel Wiley?!"

"Did somebody mention my name?" Stepping to her husband's side, Angel Wiley gave Taylor a sweet smile that had been seen on movie screens around the world. "You must be Taylor. Hi, I'm Angel. Joe's keeping you talking on the doorstep, isn't he? Please, come in and meet the rest of the family."

Taylor normally took pride in the fact that he wasn't

a man who was easily impressed. He didn't care what
someone did for a living—he was more interested in the
kind of person they were. The McBrides were nothing
like he'd expected. Within seconds, he was surrounded
by them. They greeted him with friendly smiles and
handshakes, then drew him into the gathering as if
they'd known him for years.

At first, he thought they had to be crazy. He was a
stranger—all they knew about him were the lies he had
told them. Didn't they realize what a risk they were
taking by inviting someone they didn't know into their
home? But as Merry introduced him to her husband,
Nick Kincaid, the sheriff, and he met Zeke and his wife
Elizabeth, who both had their doctorates, and Janey, a
nurse, and her husband, Reilly Jones, a heart surgeon,
he realized that these were educated people who were
all successful in their careers. And even though Joe had
never made it to college, he'd made Twin Pines one of
the most successful ranches in the state. He and the
others hadn't gotten where they were in the world by
being stupid. They sized him up with a quick look and
accepted him for who he said he was.

He wasn't normally a dishonest man, and though he'd
thought he could pull off this charade with ease because
he was only seeking justice for being denied a father
all these years, he discovered that he wasn't comfortable
with the lie. Not when he was a guest in his half
brother's home and taking advantage of his hospitality.
For the first time in his life, he was surrounded by family, and all he wanted to do was tell them who he was.

Guilt pulled at him, angering him. Dammit, this
wasn't supposed to happen! He wasn't supposed to like
them! That wasn't why he was here. He just wanted
them to know what kind of man their father had been.

And he couldn't tell them until Sara returned from her honeymoon and he could confront her with the truth. In the meantime, he planned to keep his silence and remember what he was there for.

They didn't make it easy for him. They were so damn likable! And then Janey caught him off guard by saying the one thing he'd been dreading. Seated across the table from him, she studied him with intelligent brown eyes, then frowned in confusion. "You look awfully familiar. I know you said you were from San Diego, but are you sure you don't have relatives living around here somewhere? You just look so familiar."

"Are you holding out on us?" Zeke teased him. "Is that why you decided to focus your book on Liberty Hill? Tell the truth. You're related to Abner Hawkins, aren't you? You've sort of got the look of him."

"He does not!" Merry retorted with a grin, then confided, "Trust me, Taylor, nobody thinks you're related to Abner. Zeke is just pulling your leg."

Not the least repentant, Zeke just grinned. "When Abner hears you've been talking about him, he's going to be hurt, sis. You know he's had a crush on you for years."

Merry just rolled her eyes, and Taylor couldn't help but grin with the others. "Why do I have the feeling that I've been insulted? Just what does this Abner character look like?"

"Don't ask," Nick advised, chuckling.

"Trust me," Janey added, struggling to hold back a smile, "you don't look anything like Abner. But you do look familiar."

The need to tell the truth pulled at him again, this time stronger than before, but the words wouldn't come and the moment was lost. Shrugging his shoulders, he said, "I guess I just have one of those faces that everyone seems to know. I don't know how you could know me. I'm sure we've never met before."

When she continued to study him with a frown of puzzlement, he told himself he was doing the right thing even if it didn't feel like it. When the time was right, the McBrides would know who he was, and that was only fair. In the meantime, he was keeping his identity to himself.

Ruefully accepting his explanation, Janey laughed at herself. "I guess my imagination is playing tricks on me. So, are you hungry? We've got enough food to feed an army. C'mon, everyone, let's eat."

She didn't have to tell them twice. Everyone headed for the dining room, where the table and buffet were loaded down with casseroles, grilled chicken, ribs and what looked like every kind of dessert known to man. Grabbing plates from the buffet, they quickly served themselves and found seats at the table. As Joe said grace, Taylor sighed quietly in relief. The subject of who he was and who he might be related to was, at least for the moment, dropped. That didn't, however, mean he could drop his guard. His half brothers and sisters were an intelligent group. If he didn't want to give himself away before he was ready, he'd have to watch every word he said.

Seated across from Taylor, Phoebe realized almost immediately that she should have found somewhere else to sit at the table. Every time she looked up from her plate, he was right in her line of sight. And something wasn't right. Unobtrusively watching him, she couldn't help but notice that although he seemed to enjoy the McBrides' company, his rare smile never quite reached his eyes. He was tense—she could see it in the stiff set of his shoulders—and for the life of her, she didn't know why. She'd always liked the McBrides—they were a great family—and when they invited you into their home, they treated you like family. That should have put Taylor at ease. So why wasn't he? What was going on?

A frown knitting her brows, she was tempted to ask him, but then Joe asked, "Have you talked to the Thompsons yet, Taylor? Or the Clarks? They've been ranching here as long or longer than we have. If you'd like, I can introduce you to them. Marlin Clark is pushing ninety and can tell you stories about this area that go back before the Civil War. He'd make a great addition to your book."

"That sounds great," Taylor said easily. "I can use all the help I can get. Why don't I give you a call in a couple of days and we'll set something up? At your convenience, of course," he added. "I don't want to interfere with your work. The ranch has to keep you pretty busy."

"I should have some time next week. I'll call Marlin tomorrow and set something up."

"You need to see the ranch, too," Zeke added. "Elizabeth and I are heading up into the back country for a couple of days to check on the wolves. Why don't you come with us? You can't really see a ranch until you see it from horseback."

Surprised, Taylor lifted a brow. "Did you say wolves?"

Zeke's wife, Elizabeth, grinned, her green eyes sparkling with amusement. "I'm a wolf biologist. A couple of years ago, I was in charge of a government project that reintroduced wolves into the Liberty Hill National Forest."

"She wasn't very popular around here for a while," Zeke added grimly. "She almost got herself killed."

"I knew when I started the project that there would be a lot of opposition," she said simply. "People didn't understand." Her eyes momentarily clouded with something that looked an awful lot like sadness, but before Taylor could be sure, she blinked it away. "Anyway, Zeke and I ride up into the back country every year just to check on the wolves and see how they're doing. We'd love for you to come."

"It sounds fascinating," he admitted. "Just tell me where and when you're going, and I'll be there."

Pleased, Elizabeth turned to Phoebe with a smile. "What about you, Phoebe? You've never seen Napoleon's pups, have you? They're beautiful animals. And there's nothing like seeing them in the wild. You should come, too. I know you'd love it."

Phoebe didn't doubt that. She'd heard about the wolves for years and had always been fascinated with the story of how Elizabeth had released them back into the wild despite the sometimes violent opposition of the locals. And from what she remembered of the story, Elizabeth *had* come very close to being killed. Still, she had done what she'd set out to do, and Phoebe couldn't help but admire her for that. She'd never seen a wolf anywhere but at the zoo. How could she possibly pass up a chance to see some in the wild?

Be careful, a voice in her head warned. This little trip has a price tag. Taylor's going along. Are you prepared to be paired with him again? Keep this up and the McBrides are going to start thinking of you as a couple. Is that what you want?

No, of course not, she automatically assured herself. But the evening hadn't turned out to be so bad. And she wanted to see the wolves! This was likely to be her only opportunity. Not even hesitating, she said, "I'd love to."

"Good," Zeke said. "You haven't been up in the back country with us since you were a kid. This'll be fun."

Phoebe didn't doubt that. She always enjoyed the McBrides' company. And having other people around would, she hoped, distract her so she wouldn't be so aware of Taylor.

You've been surrounded by other people all evening, the irritating voice in her head reminded her. *You're still aware of every move the man makes. If you want to get him out of your head, let him go into the mountains with Zeke and Elizabeth, and you stay home.*

She should have. That certainly would have been the wiser thing to do. But she'd always wanted to see the wolves, and she wasn't going to deny herself this opportunity just because Taylor had been invited, too. So what if she found herself attracted to him? It was just a fleeting physical attraction and certainly something she could control. After all, she didn't even like the man!

The conversation turned to what they would each need to bring for the weekend campout, then shifted back to Taylor's book and the research he was still doing. Ranching was in Joe's blood, the red dirt of the land as much a part of him as the lines in the palm of his hand, and there was nothing he liked more than talking about the ranch. As soon as the meal was over, he invited Taylor to take a look at the new bull he had just bought, and the men all headed for the barn.

As soon as they were gone, Merry immediately turned teasing eyes on Phoebe. "It's about time we got some time to ourselves to talk. So what's Taylor's story, Phoeb? Is he married? He's not wearing a ring—"

"That doesn't mean he's not married," Angel said dryly. "Jerks who fool around on their wives never wear rings."

"He doesn't seem the type," Elizabeth argued before Phoebe could say a word. "Has he asked you out yet?"

"If he hasn't, then you need to get busy, girl," Merry told Phoebe. "Have you looked at that man? He looks like he just stepped out of *Jane Eyre*."

"It's his eyes," Janey said. "They're so dark and brooding."

A grin pulling at the corner of her mouth, she added, "It's a good thing Myrtle's not here or she'd be match-making like crazy. She's been wanting you to settle down and give her great-grandbabies for years."

Alarmed, Phoebe said, "Don't you dare call her! There's no relationship here!"

"Maybe not yet, but give it time. The man's hand-some, intelligent, and appears to be available. What's not to like?"

"If you play your cards right, you could be engaged by Christmas."

The McBride women grinned at her with broad grins, granting her no mercy. Frustrated, Phoebe couldn't help but laugh. "I should have known you all would do this to me. He's just a paying guest, ladies. In a month, he'll be gone. And so will I! So don't start planning the en-gagement party. It's not going to happen!"

"Never say never," Merry warned, her blue eyes twinkling. "You're asking for trouble."

"He's not my type," Phoebe assured her, confi-dently. "It's not going to happen."

Phoebe knew they were just having fun teasing her,

but later, as she and Taylor said their goodbyes and climbed into her car, the awareness that she told herself she wanted nothing to do with was back, stronger than ever. Horrified, she tried to ignore it, but as they approached Myrtle's, she felt like a teenager on her first date and the evening was about to end. Would he kiss her?

Mortified by the direction of her thoughts, she sent up a silent prayer of thanks that it was so dark inside the car. Otherwise, he would have surely seen the blush firing her cheeks.

Sure he must be able to hear the pounding of her heart, she blurted out, "The McBrides are great, aren't they? When I visited my grandmother when I was a kid, I loved going out to the ranch. Sara had a photo album on the coffee table and it was filled with all these old pictures of their ancestors when they first came to Liberty Hill in a wagon. I loved it. While Myrtle and Sara visited, Janey and Merry would tell me stories about their great-grandparents and the long-lost uncle who was a Pony Express rider who was killed by the Indians in Oklahoma. His wife moved to the ranch after he died and started the county's first school...."

Desperate for something to distract her from his closeness—why did she have to pick now to notice how long his legs were next to hers?—she rattled on like an idiot about the McBrides. If he noticed, he didn't say anything, for which she was heartily grateful, but she was still more nervous than she'd ever been in her life. She couldn't seem to stop talking. Then, before she realized it, she was pulling into Myrtle's driveway.

Her heart slamming against her ribs, she told herself to get a grip, but her palms were sweating, for heaven's sake! She'd never been so skittish around a man in her

life, and there was nothing she could do but try to end
the evening as quickly as possible.

It should have been easy. All she had to do was un-
lock the front door, wish him good night, and escape to
her room, where she could die of embarrassment in private. But as she hurried up the sidewalk to the front
door, he was right there with her, step for step. And
when her fingers were suddenly trembling slightly and
she couldn't hold the keys steady enough to fit the key
into the dead bolt on Myrtle's front door, one of his
hands closed over hers, steadying it as he guided it into
the lock. Just that easily, he stopped her heart beating
in her chest.

"Thank you," she said huskily. "I don't know
what's wrong with me tonight. I guess I'm tired. Did
you get what you needed from the McBrides? Joe and
Janey are the two that can probably help you the
most...."

Taylor had never heard a woman talk so much in his
life. Normally, he would have been irritated, but he'd
have been blind not to notice that she was jittery about
something, though he didn't have a clue what. Obviously, she'd known the McBrides all her life and enjoyed their company, so it was doubtful that anyone had
said anything to upset her. So what was going on? He
wanted to thank her for all her help—without her con-
nections to the McBrides, it could have taken him
weeks to track down his brothers and sisters and find a
way to meet them—but he couldn't get a word in edge-
wise. If she'd just give him two seconds to say what he
had to say...

Giving in to impulse, he did the only thing he could
think of to shut her up. He leaned down and kissed her.

The second his lips brushed hers, he knew he'd made

a mistake. From the moment he'd first met her, there'd been something about her that had teased his senses. He couldn't get her out of his head, and kissing her, he realized, only made the situation much, much worse. Dear heavens, her lips were soft! He'd kissed his share of women, but never one this soft, this sweetly arousing. The subtle, delicate scent of her surrounded him, enticing him until all he could think of was her...the good humor that invariably sparkled in her eyes, the tenderness of her touch as she'd cradled a puppy close that morning for a good-morning kiss on the nose, the grace and sensuality of her figure as she moved about the kitchen, cooking a gourmet breakfast fit for a king.

More than once, he'd told himself she couldn't be for real. But there was no question that the woman who hesitantly kissed him back was real right down to the soles of her delicate feet. With nothing more than a kiss, she made him want more. Before he could stop himself, his arms folded her close.

That's the way to get the lady out of your head, a voice in his head taunted sarcastically. *Kiss the stuffing out of her, then go upstairs to your room alone and try to go to sleep. Yeah, right. That'll work.*

He liked to think he wasn't a stupid man, but at that moment, he'd never felt more idiotic in his life. What *was* he doing? He'd come to Liberty Hill for one reason and one reason only—to make his father pay for what he had done to his mother. That goal hadn't changed just because Gus McBride was dead. His children and widow had to know what kind of man he was, and he wasn't going to let anyone get in the way of his plans, especially a woman who didn't seem to care about anything but what she was going to make for breakfast tomorrow. He liked smart, ambitious women, and that description didn't quite fit Phoebe. Oh, he didn't doubt that she was intelligent—she'd held her own with the very educated McBrides at dinner, moving from one topic of conversation to another without so much as a blink of an eye—but he'd never seen anyone so laid-back when it came to business. How did she expect to succeed in life when she seemed to have no other ambition than to run her grandmother's bed and breakfast? Liberty Hill was hardly a tourist hot spot, and to add insult to injury, it was over fifty miles from the nearest interstate. She'd be lucky if she kept it booked one month out of three!

She had to know that, he reasoned. She was too smart not to. But her lack of overnight guests didn't seem to bother her—from what he'd seen, little did. While that might be refreshing for a while, he was sure that with time, her laid-back manner would drive him right up the wall.

And here he was kissing her as if there was no to-morrow.

Abruptly coming to his senses, he set her from him, but it wasn't easy. He ached for her, damn it! Then she looked up at him in dazed confusion, her big blue eyes clouded with a passion she obviously didn't understand any more than he did, and need tightened in his gut like a fist.

Taking a step back from her was one of the hardest things he'd ever done. Fighting the urge to reach for her, he said roughly, "It's late, and I've still got some work to do. Thanks for taking me to the McBrides."

He turned and strode up the stairs without looking back, but it wasn't until Phoebe heard his bedroom door shut firmly that she came back to earth with a jolt. Shaken, she dropped down onto an antique bench in the entry hall and stared up the stairs as though she'd never seen them before. What had she done? she wondered wildly. She didn't go around kissing men she barely knew…especially not the way she'd just kissed Taylor! If he hadn't been the one to come to his senses, she would have been in serious trouble.

Because she'd loved kissing him.

The thought terrified her—she had to be losing her mind!—but she wasn't a woman who lied to herself. She was attracted to him, and for the life of her, she didn't know why. She was a romantic with a soft heart, and Taylor was a hard, cynical man who had openly admitted that he didn't care about anything but work. Getting involved with him could never be anything but a mistake.

Not, she quickly assured herself, that she was involved with him. He was a paying guest, nothing more, and the one kiss they'd shared hardly classified as a relationship.

Logically, she knew that and accepted it. The problem was that the kiss he'd given her was anything but ordinary. Her toes were still tingling, for heaven's sake!

Troubled, more unsure than she'd ever been in her life, she told herself to go upstairs and go to bed and the situation would look better in the morning. But she was asking the impossible. As she made her way up to her room, she couldn't help but be aware of his presence in the house. Even though he'd shut his door and she couldn't hear a sound coming from his room, she knew every step he'd taken, every chair he'd sat in, since he'd first walked in her grandmother's front door. And when she changed into her nightgown and crawled into bed, all too easily she could picture him lying in the four poster down the hall, staring at the ceiling, just as she was. It was, she knew, going to be a long night.

Taylor didn't sleep. He told himself it was because he'd finally met all of his half brothers and sisters after wondering all his life if they existed or not, and his mind was too active to allow him to sleep. But deep in his gut, he knew there was only one person responsible for his sleeplessness, and it was the woman down the hall. What the hell was he going to do about her?

The answer evaded him all night, frustrating the hell out of him. By the time the sound of Phoebe's alarm floated softly down the hall to him the next morning before dawn, he knew he had to put some space between himself and the lady, and damn soon, before he did something stupid—like kiss her again.

So he quietly dressed, then waited in his room for the arrival of the rental car, which was being delivered by nine that morning. He had some reading to keep him busy, some case work he'd brought with him to work on in the privacy of his own room. Concentrating, however, turned out to be a heck of a lot harder than he'd anticipated. Downstairs, Phoebe started breakfast, and soon the enticing scent of fresh-baked muffins drifted up the stairs. Without even closing his eyes, he could picture her moving quietly about the old-fashioned kitchen. She would be humming softly to herself, and she'd look as fresh as the summer morning. And after the way he'd kissed her last night, she could be dressed in a suit of armor and he'd still have a hard time not reaching for her.

Swearing softly, he realized he wasn't going to be able to wait for the delivery of the rental car before he got out of there. Not when she was so damn tempting.

His face etched in grim lines, he grabbed his cell phone and quickly punched in the number of the rental car agency in Colorado Springs and requested that the car be delivered to Ed's Diner instead of the bed and breakfast. A few minutes later, he quietly made his way downstairs and let himself out the front door.

In the kitchen, Phoebe had unconsciously been listening for his step on the stairs for an hour or longer, wondering all the while what she was going to say to him when they came face-to-face. She needn't have worried. Just as she pulled the muffins from the oven, she heard the front door shut. Surprised, she frowned. She'd known Taylor's rental car was being delivered that morning and that he would, no doubt, be out most of the day doing research on his book. After all, that's what he was there for. But what if his plans had changed after last night? With the delivery of his rental car, he would no longer be afoot. He didn't have to stay in Liberty Hill. He could go wherever his research took him.

She shouldn't have cared. She would be losing a guest, but that was the nature of the hospitality industry. People changed their plans all the time. There would be other guests, and with time, she'd forget all about him. It was probably for the best.

Yeah, right, a voice drawled in her head. *So why do you suddenly feel as if you're going to cry?*

She told herself she wasn't. She was fine. But even as she assured herself she didn't care what Taylor Bishop did, she checked to make sure nothing on the stove was in danger of burning, then hurried upstairs to his room.

It wasn't locked, and with a twist of her wrist, she pushed it open and took in the contents of the room in a single glance. The room was neat as a pin—he'd even made the bed—and for a moment, it looked empty. Then she spied his suitcase in the corner. When her heart started beating crazily in her chest, she didn't know if she was relieved or not that he was still there.

Chapter 5

Ed's Diner was packed with the lunch crowd, and there wasn't a spare seat in the place. Seated at the counter, the keys to his rental car in his pocket, Taylor finished the hamburger and fries he'd ordered, and could find no complaint with the food. In fact, for diner fare, it was damn good. After he'd left Phoebe's earlier that morning, he'd stopped there for breakfast, and it had been equally good. It couldn't, however, compare to what Phoebe whipped up in her grandmother's kitchen.

Just that easily, she slipped back into his thoughts, and he swore softly. After the rental car had been dropped off at the diner and he'd paid for his breakfast, he'd driven for hours, trying to get her out of his head. She hadn't made it easy for him. Hours after he'd kissed her, he'd still been able to feel the softness of her in his arms and taste her kiss. And that had only frustrated him more. He couldn't remember the last woman who had dominated his thoughts so easily.

Disgusted with himself, he considered finding another place to stay. Under the circumstances, it was the logical thing to do. Myrtle Henderson's house might be a huge, sprawling Victorian, but he and Phoebe were living there alone together and it had begun to feel damn small. He couldn't take a breath without breathing in her scent. Everywhere he turned in the house, he was aware of her. He'd never experienced anything like it in his life. He could even smell her on the damn sheets! It had to stop!

He'd go to Colorado Springs, he decided. He'd feel more like himself in a city. And now that he had the rental car, he didn't have to stay in Liberty Hill. He could commute back and forth, and use the driving time to concentrate on his reason for being there in the first place—the McBrides. Whenever Phoebe was anywhere within touching distance, he tended to forget that.

He didn't know how she'd gotten under his skin so easily. It wasn't as if she was flirting with him or seeking him out. In fact, he got the distinct impression that she wasn't any happier about this attraction between them than he was. So what the hell was the matter with him? He shouldn't have given her a second thought. Instead, she was all he could think of.

That would change as soon as he got a room in Colorado Springs, he assured himself confidently. He'd be able to sleep nights without her being right down the hall, distracting him just by breathing. Maybe then he could focus on the McBrides and how he was going to expose Gus to them for the bastard he was.

She's your ticket to the McBrides, an irritating voice in his head reminded him. *They wouldn't have been nearly as quick to accept you if it hadn't been for*

Phoebe's introduction. And don't forget, every invitation that they have extended to you has included Phoebe. How many more times do you think they're going to ask you to their house if you cancel your stay at their friend's bed and breakfast?

The answer to that was quick and irritating. None.

He had no choice but to accept the inevitable. Like it or not, he wasn't going to get very far with the McBrides without Phoebe. From what he had seen of his brothers and sisters, they were a loyal bunch and protective of friends and family. He was an outsider and someone they barely knew. If his leaving cost Phoebe money or in any way inconvenienced her, he doubted that the McBrides would extend another invitation to him, let alone let him get close enough to Sara to tell her the truth about her deceased husband and the man she no doubt thought had been faithful to her his entire life. The family would continue to think Gus was some kind of saint, and they'd never know the truth...all because Phoebe could, just by walking through his air space, make him forget his common sense.

It wasn't going to happen, he thought grimly. He'd resented his father for as long as he could remember, and he'd promised himself on his mother's grave that Gus McBride was going to pay for not being there for her. Gus might be out of his reach, but he would still see that his mother was avenged by telling the McBrides the truth about Gus. He didn't doubt that they would be hurt when they realized just how they'd been duped all these years, but their hurt couldn't compare to the lifetime of loneliness and poverty his mother had suffered because she'd made the mistake of giving her heart to

Gus. Let them all walk in her shoes, and then they'd talk about hurt.

"I was going to ask if I could join you," a familiar male voice drawled in amusement, "but now I'm not so sure. You look like you could take somebody's head off if they looked at you wrong, and I'm kind of fond of mine."

Jerking back to his surroundings, Taylor looked up with a scowl to find Joe McBride standing by the empty chair next to him, grinning down at him as if they'd known each other all their lives. Later, he knew that was going to bother him—how could the McBrides be so damn friendly when they didn't know a thing about him?—but all he said was, "Don't worry, your head's safe. It's somebody else's I'd like to take off. Pull up a chair. What are you doing in town at this time of day?"

"Buying some barbed wire," Joe replied as he pulled out the chair across the table from Taylor and sank into it. "Some idiot drove through the fence down the road from Merry's office, and I've spent all morning rounding up cattle. It's time for a break. I've been thinking about Ed's chicken-fried steak all morning."

The waitress appeared at their table then and didn't bother to hand him a menu. "The usual, Joe?" At his nod, she glanced and Taylor and smiled. "Sure I can't tempt you with a piece of chocolate pie? Ed's famous for it."

"You won't regret it," Joe told him with a grin. "I don't care what kind of fancy desserts you've eaten in California, you've never had anything like Ed's chocolate pie. If you don't believe me, ask Angel. She's got all her friends in Hollywood hooked on it."

Taylor didn't care two cents about dessert, but he

wasn't about to pass up an opportunity to get to know Joe better and grill him about their father. Later, when Joe found out who he really was and why he was there, he would, no doubt, hate his guts for using him, but Taylor told himself he didn't care. His mother's feelings were the only ones he was concerned with, and even though he could no longer do anything to help her, he was holding the McBrides accountable for the years of loneliness and hardship his mother had suffered because of Gus.

"Okay," he said, giving in. "It looks like I'm outnumbered. I'll have the pie."

"Good choice," she replied, giving him a wink. "I'll be right back with your order."

When she took his empty plate with her, Joe commented, "I guess I don't have to ask how the food is at Myrtle's. From the time she was old enough to stand at the stove, Phoebe was always damn good in the kitchen. She should have gone to cooking school after she graduated from high school—she can do more with a handful of ingredients than anyone I know."

"So why didn't she?"

"Because for as long as I can remember, her father groomed her to take over his business. She was an only child, and there was no one else to leave it to. She could have sold it when he died, of course, but she was grieving and I think she felt guilty. And that's a damn shame. Life's too short to do something you hate."

Surprised, Taylor said, "I thought she worked for her grandmother. I didn't realize she had a real job."

"You'd better not let her hear you say that," he said with a laugh.

He didn't have to tell Taylor twice. Phoebe might

look like a flower child from the 60s, but from what he'd seen, she took her responsibilities seriously at her grandmother's place and worked hard to make sure it was a success. He didn't doubt that she worked just as hard or harder to make sure her father's business was successful.

"What kind of business is it?"

"Vending machines," he replied with a grimace. "The money's good, but it sounds boring as hell. She has to collect the money every day, then count it and deposit it in the bank because she can't trust anyone else with that much cash."

"So she's tied to the business all the time?"

Joe nodded grimly. "Pretty much. I think she has a cousin or someone who comes in for her when she's sick or on vacation, but according to Myrtle, she handles it completely on her own most of the time. Personally, I don't know how she stands it. If you knew Phoebe, you'd know that's just not her. I'm not saying she can't do it—she obviously can—but she'll never enjoy it. She likes people—taking care of them, making them feel comfortable, cooking for them. I just can't see her counting change at her kitchen table every night like a miser hoarding his money."

Taylor couldn't either. As a lawyer, he worked with hard-nosed businessmen all the time, and their main goal in life was to do whatever they had to to make more money. They were cutthroat and ruthless and they would work sixty hours a week or more if they had to to increase their coffers. If Phoebe had to run with that pack to keep her business going, she'd get eaten alive.

"From what I've seen, she doesn't seem to care two cents about money," Taylor said. "The first time I saw her, I would have sworn she'd stepped out of some kind of time machine or something. It was during the middle of the storm on Tuesday night, and the lights were out. She opened the door to her grandmother's house holding a candle and I thought I'd stepped back into another century. It was weird, but she looked right at home. Has she always been like that?"

Joe grinned. "Always. That's why she loved spending the summers with Myrtle when she was a kid. The house was always filled with antiques, so she'd pretend she lived in the 1800s. Every night, she and Myrtle would cook dinner on the old wood stove on the back porch, then eat dinner by the light of an oil lamp. She loved it."

Taylor couldn't blame her for that. It sounded like she'd had a magical childhood. "No wonder she volunteered to help her grandmother out. The two of them must be very close."

"They are," Joe replied. "Myrtle's great—she always has been. She taught Phoebe how to can peaches, and every summer, the two of them get together with my mother and sisters and make the best peach preserves you ever tasted. If she ever decides to sell her dad's business, she can operate a bed and breakfast with one hand behind her back. Hell, she even knows how to make soap!"

His eyes alight at the memory, Joe laughed. "Poor Phoebe. She got the recipe out of an old book of Myrtle's and tried making it in the backyard. Talk about a mess! You could smell it all over town, and trust me, it didn't smell anything like Irish Spring! We teased her about it for years!"

"She must have improved her recipe," Taylor replied

with a crooked smile. "There's some soap in the bathroom across the hall from my room that smells like rainwater."

"That's sounds like something she'd come up with. She always was a romantic." Eyeing him quizzically, Joe frowned slightly. "But you're not, are you? So what *are* you still doing at Myrtle's? I know you had car trouble and temporarily needed a place to stay, but the Best Western in Colorado Springs seems more your speed. I was born and raised here and wouldn't want to live anywhere else, but a man like you must be bored stiff. There's not much to do around here during the day, let alone at night. The mayor rolls in the sidewalks at seven."

Taylor froze at his words. *A man like you.* What kind of man did he think he was? Had he guessed that he wasn't who he claimed to be? He couldn't have, Taylor assured himself. He'd done nothing to give himself away. Joe was just curious, not suspicious.

Still, he felt like the word *liar* was tattooed on his forehead. His tone was casual, however, when he said, "Actually, I like the change of pace. It's quiet, and the research I need to do is here."

"I'm glad you brought that up," Joe said promptly. "What are you doing today?"

Avoiding Phoebe, Taylor thought, but he wasn't stupid enough to admit that. Instead, he lied, "Doing research at the library. Why?"

"I'm thought you might like to ride with me out to Leonard Cooper's ranch east of town. He's a crusty old goat, but I think you'll like him. He's a local history buff, and his great-great-grandfather was one of the original settlers of the area. He can probably give you a lot of information for your book while I check out a bull he's got for sale.''

When Joe had volunteered last night to introduce him to the other ranchers in the area, Taylor hadn't really thought the offer was anything more than lip service. After all, the McBrides didn't know him—in spite of their kindness last night when he was their guest, people didn't go out of their way for strangers. Or at least the people he knew didn't.

So maybe you're hanging around the wrong people. You wanted to meet your family. This is who they are.

He didn't want to believe the voice in his head—he'd hated his brothers and sisters too long without even knowing for sure that they existed—but there was no doubting Joe's sincerity. His plan was working better than he'd ever imagined, he thought, stunned. In less than two days, he'd not only met his brothers and sisters, he'd got them to drop their guard and invite him into their lives. All he had to do now was wait for Sara to return, and then he was going to hit them all with the truth about Gus.

At the very least, he should have felt satisfaction. Instead, he found he didn't like himself very much at the moment.

''So, you want to go or not? I'm going, anyway, but I thought you might want to ride along. If you're busy, it's no big deal. Leonard's not going anywhere. You can meet him another time.''

''No!'' he said quickly. ''I can work at the library anytime. Let's go.''

Leonard Cooper *was* a character. And if Taylor had really been writing a book, he would have definitely included the old man in it. He was a wealth of information—not only about his own family, but about the McBrides. The two families had been neighbors for well over a century, and Leonard was only too happy to tell him all about Gus and his parents, the grandparents Taylor knew nothing about.

"They were great people," he told Taylor in his gravelly voice. "Isabel—that was Gus's grandmother—was the prettiest girl in the whole county…and a damn good shot. According to my grandmother, every man in the county was half in love with her, including my grandfather. But she never had eyes for anyone but old Ben McBride. He and Isabel built the homestead themselves, then filled it with sons. Granny said they were quite a pair, especially at country dances."

"I can remember my grandfather talking about those dances," Joe added with a grin. "They must have been something else. Half the county would come, everyone would bring enough food for their own family, and the dance would last for three days."

Leonard's faded green eyes twinkled with memories behind the lenses of his bifocals. "Travelling wasn't as easy back then as it is now. So when people took the trouble to get together, they didn't want it to end. All that changed, of course, with the Model T—they still had country dances, but they didn't last three days any more."

"I'll bet you and Dad went to a few of those dances, didn't you?" Joe said with a grin. "I heard you were as wild as a march hare."

Grinning, Leonard Cooper didn't deny it. "Your dad did his share of sowing some wild oats. But then he met your mother, and he settled right down. A good woman will do that to a man. I wasn't so lucky. It took me another five years before I found my Betsy.''

Taylor stiffened at his words, anger flashing in his eyes before he quickly controlled it. His mother had been a good woman, too. Gus could have been happy with her, *should* have been happy with her. Timing, he thought grimly. Happiness was all about timing. Sara met his father first, and she must have made a hell of an impression. In spite of the fact that Gus had turned to his mother on a wild weekend in Wyoming, she'd never really stood a chance. Because of Sara.

Bitterly, Taylor decided he'd heard enough. He thanked Leonard for all the information he had given him, and soon after that, he and Joe headed back to Liberty Hill with the bull Joe had bought in the stock trailer hooked to the back of his truck.

They'd talked easily on the way to Cooper's ranch, but Taylor had little to say now. Not surprisingly, Joe noticed. "You're awfully quiet. What'd you think of Leonard?"

"He's a tough old coot," Taylor retorted. "I liked him."

"When Dad died, he got a bunch of the neighbors together to help us with the spring roundup that year. I don't know what we would have done without him."

"You were still grieving."

It wasn't a question, but a statement. Joe nodded. "He was a good father. We lost him too soon."

Too soon? he echoed silently, scowling. Joe had had his father for eighteen years. And because of that, he, Taylor, had had nothing. His father had never seen him, had never even known he existed. And nothing was ever going to change that.

His stomach knotted with resentment, Taylor wanted to hate Joe for that, for all the Christmases and birthdays and just ordinary days on the ranch he and the rest of the legitimate McBride children had had with *his* father. But he couldn't. Joe was his brother, whether he knew it or not, and a good man. He liked him, dammit! He liked them all, and that was something he hadn't planned on. Now what was he supposed to do?

Long after Joe dropped him at the library, where he'd left his car, Taylor was still asking himself that same question. He didn't mind admitting that he was a damn good lawyer, and when it came to the law, he always played to win. He could be cutthroat when he had to be, and he didn't apologize for that. That was his job. His clients paid him a hell of a lot of money to go after the opposition and win a satisfactory judgment for them, and that's what he did.

When his mother had died and he'd discovered who his father was, his plan had been simple enough. Find Gus McBride and make him pay for being the deadbeat father that he was. In San Diego, Taylor had been confident he could do that with one hand tied behind his back. And he wouldn't feel an ounce of remorse, he'd assured himself.

But that was before he'd known Gus was dead. Damn the man for once again managing to escape accountability. How was he supposed to make a dead man pay for what he'd done? His brothers and sisters were good people who hadn't asked for a father who betrayed them or a half brother they still didn't know existed. When they found out the truth, they were going to be hurt, and like most people, they'd no doubt look for someone to blame. It didn't take an Einstein to figure out who that would be. They'd loved Gus and would find a way to excuse his behavior. Taylor knew they wouldn't do the same for him.

And neither would Phoebe.

She slipped into his thoughts uninvited, and there wasn't a damn thing he could do about it. After Joe left him at the library, he spent what was left of the afternoon finding what he could about the McBrides in local history books and avoiding going back to Myrtle's. For a while, he managed not to think about how good Phoebe felt in his arms, but the memory had been right there on the edge of his consciousness all day, waiting for a chance to dominate his thoughts.

What the hell was he going to do about her? When she found out who he was and his real reason for being in Liberty Hill, she was going to feel that he'd used her to get to the McBrides. She'd hate him for that, and he couldn't say he blamed her. He had.

He tried to justify his actions—he was only doing what he had to, what was right—but the guilt tightening like a fist in his gut told him there was nothing right about what he was doing. If he intended to go through with his revenge on the McBrides, he had no right to involve her in that. He didn't need her anymore to gain access to the family or the ranch. Joe was right—bed and breakfasts weren't his speed. He needed to get a room at the Best Western in Colorado Springs.

But when he left the library and headed back to Myrtle's, he knew he wasn't going anywhere. Not yet. Right or wrong, he'd come too far to change his plans now. He regretted that he'd had to use Phoebe, but at the time, he'd had no other choice. Moving to Colorado Springs wouldn't change that at this late date. As for that kiss they'd shared, it wouldn't happen again. It couldn't, he warned himself grimly. He couldn't let the lady get to him any more than she already had.

Determined to keep his distance, he intended to go upstairs the minute he stepped through Myrtle's front door, but Phoebe was in the front parlor and there was no avoiding her. She looked up, his eyes met hers, and an emotion he couldn't put a name to tugged at him, stopping him in his tracks. It had been nearly twenty-four hours since he'd kissed her. Suddenly, it only seemed like seconds.

"If you haven't had supper, there's a meatloaf and scalloped potatoes on the stove," she said quietly. "Feel free to help yourself."

Why did he suddenly feel as if he owed her an explanation of where he'd been all day? He hardly knew the woman. He'd kissed her one time, for heaven's sake! They weren't involved or anything. It just a kiss. One kiss. One unforgettable kiss.

Swearing silently, he growled, "Thanks, but I'm not hungry." He should have gone upstairs to his room then—it would have been the smart thing to do—but his feet refused to budge. Instead, he lingered, his gaze falling to the material bunched in her lap. Only just then noticing the needle and thread in her hand, he frowned. "What are you doing?"

"I'm just patching this old quilt," she replied, spreading out the quilt slightly so he could see its old-fashioned design. From across the room, a blind man couldn't have missed the tears in it. "My grandmother bought it at an auction and was going to make it into pillows for the bridal suite, but I think I can repair it. It's a wedding-ring quilt," she added.

He didn't have to know much about quilt patterns to know that at one time, brides-to-be made wedding-ring quilts to take with them into their marriages. While he could appreciate the handwork that must have gone into making one, it wasn't something he normally would have given more than a second glance. But when Phoebe held it with gentle hands, smoothing it over her lap as if she herself had made it, he couldn't look away. With no trouble whatsoever, he could see the two of them making love under that same quilt.

Like any man, he had his share of sexual fantasies, but not like this. The image was so real, he could almost feel her, taste her, as surely as if she were in his arms. He tried to push the sensual image from his mind, but he was fighting a losing battle. Suddenly hot, aching for her, all he wanted to do was reach for her.

"Taylor? Are you all right?"

Caught up in the fantasy, it was a long moment before he heard her. When he finally realized that he must be staring at her like a starving man who'd suddenly laid eyes on a hot meal for the first time in a month, he felt like a complete idiot. "I'm fine," he growled. "I just remembered a phone call I have to make. Excuse me."

He strode up the stairs before she could do anything but blink in surprise, leaving Phoebe staring after him with a pounding heart. For a moment, she'd thought she'd seen something in his eyes…something that made her heart skip and her knees go weak…something that reminded her of yesterday and the kiss they'd shared. Had he felt it, too? That need that wouldn't go away? Is that why he'd rushed upstairs like the devil himself was after him? Or was her imagination running away with her?

Confused, she was tempted to go knock on his bedroom door and demand some answers. But did she really want to know if he was as attracted to her as she was to him? After all, most of the time, she didn't even know if she liked him or not!

Disturbed, she decided this wasn't the time to pursue the subject. It had been a long day, she was tired, and she'd been thinking about him for hours, wondering where he was, if he was as shaken as she was by a kiss she couldn't forget. He obviously didn't want to talk, and that might be for the best. The last time she'd felt this way, she'd ignored her common sense and rushed headlong into a relationship with a man who'd only wanted to use her. She wasn't doing that again. Taylor didn't seem the type of man to use a woman, but then again, she hadn't thought Marshall was, either. When it came to men, she always followed her heart, and invariably, she ended up getting hurt. Not this time. This time, she was going to use her head. And her head was telling her to step back and remember what she did know about Taylor. He was an angry, class-A personality from San Diego who was only staying at Myrtle's because there wasn't another motel for miles. When he finished his research and returned to California, he wasn't taking her heart with him.

Satisfied that she finally had her head on straight, she put away her sewing, made sure the house was locked up tight for the night, and went upstairs to bed. Falling asleep should have been easy. In order to get Taylor out of her head, she'd spent the day cleaning the house, and she was exhausted. She took a hot bath, slipped into her favorite nightgown, and crawled into bed.

Later, she couldn't have said how long she lay there,

staring at the dark ceiling over her head—it seemed like forever. And when she finally did fall asleep, Taylor was there in her dreams, waiting for her. He smiled in greeting, held out his hand to her, and just that easily, she stepped into his arms.

When her alarm went off the next morning, she remembered little of the details of her dreams...except that she kept reaching for Taylor. Shaken by a need that she wanted no part of but that refused to be ignored, she felt panic rising in her and could do nothing to stop it. Later in the day, she and Taylor were going to be riding up into the high country of the McBride ranch with Zeke and Elizabeth. They'd be together all weekend, riding together, possibly sharing a tent....

Images teased her, hot, intimate, sensuous. Her heart slamming against her ribs, she stiffened. No! She couldn't do it. Not when she'd dreamed of him all night. Not when all she wanted was for him to kiss her again. He'd take one look at her, her face would give her away, and she'd die of mortification. If he ever guessed, she'd want to kill herself.

She'd just make her apologies and he would go without her, she decided as she hurriedly dressed in jeans and a simple white cotton blouse, then went downstairs to start breakfast. The McBrides would understand—after all, the only reason they'd probably included her in the invitation to begin with was because she was Myrtle's granddaughter and Taylor was staying at Myrtle's. They hadn't wanted to exclude her since she obviously heard them invite Taylor along on the trip, and she appreciated that. She really did want to see the wolves she'd heard so much about, but she still couldn't go. Not with Taylor.

The decision made, she knew she was doing the right thing. Still, she couldn't stop her heart from skipping a beat when she heard his steps on the stairs. Her hands suddenly not quite steady, she quickly pulled fresh cinnamon rolls from the oven.

"Good morning," she told Taylor as he stepped into the dining room just as she set the rolls on the sideboard. "The coffee's hot, there's homemade jam and fresh fruit on the table, and I was just about to cook some eggs. How would you like yours? Poached? Fried? Scrambled? Or I could make you an omelette—"

"The cinnamon rolls are enough," he replied. "What time are we supposed to be at the McBrides'?"

Put on the spot, she hesitated, then finally said, "Ten-thirty, but I'm not going to be able to go, after all. I don't know what I was thinking of when I told Zeke I could go. I've got two couples coming in next weekend, and I've got a lot of work to do before they get here. I've got grocery shopping to do, not to mention two bedrooms to clean, sheets to wash. I'd love to see the wolves, but even if I could find a way to go, you don't need me to tag along. You have work to do, and I don't want to get in the way of that."

Taylor should have been relieved. He'd thought of nothing but her and that damn wedding-ring quilt all night, and by dawn, he'd decided that he had no business going anywhere with her, least of all into the back country, where they would be cut off from the rest of the world for the entire weekend. Granted, Zeke and Elizabeth would be there, so it wasn't as if he would be completely alone with her, but an entire army of people could have been with them and he knew it wouldn't have made a difference. There was just something about Phoebe that he couldn't ignore. The way she moved, the way she kissed...

Irritated with himself for letting his thoughts drift there, he opened his mouth to tell her that he would give the McBrides her regrets, only to hear himself say perversely, "You can't back out at the last minute. Zeke and Elizabeth are expecting you."

"They'll understand."

"Maybe they will, but I don't. I thought you wanted to see the wolves."

"I do."

"Then why are you looking for an excuse to back out?"

"I'm not!"

"Good. Because if anyone should be going, it's you. The McBrides are your friends—and you're the one who wanted to see the wolves."

Even as the words rolled off his tongue, Taylor wondered what the hell he was doing. He needed some space, some time to get his head on straight and put this crazy desire he had for her in perspective. So what was he doing? Pushing her to go! He was losing his mind—there was no other explanation. And it was all her fault!

So why are you pushing her to go? a voice in his head demanded. *You wanted some space—she's giving it to you. Accept it and be grateful for it!*

He should have. He meant to. But in the time it took to blink, he heard himself say, "You were the one who told me I needed to play more. The same applies to you. And don't worry about all the work you've got to do. I'll help you."

　　　　　　　　　　　　　Always a McBride

Hesitating, Phoebe couldn't believe she was hearing correctly. "You're going to help me with the laundry?"

"If you need me to. Unless you've got a problem with that, of course."

"You're a guest," she reminded him. "Guests don't do the laundry."

"And innkeepers don't drive guests all over the countryside, introducing them to their friends and neighbors," he pointed out. "But that didn't stop you from helping me. This is your opportunity to see the wolves. I don't think you should miss that."

She should have thanked him for the offer and politely turned him down. Her eyes only had to meet his for her to know that that would have been the smart thing for her to do. But he touched a yearning in her she couldn't resist, and it had nothing to do with the wolves. She was playing with fire, but she couldn't resist. Giving in, she sighed, "All right. But you're not helping me with the laundry when we get back!"

Chapter 6

They were only going to be gone for the weekend, but Zeke and Elizabeth brought enough food and supplies for an army. They were still packing the horses outside the barn behind the homestead when Taylor and Phoebe arrived and added their own bags to the mix. ''You never know what you're going to need,'' Zeke said with a twinkle in his eye as he looked pointedly at his wife. ''Some people insist on eating like they're just going into town to a steak house. We've got T-bones and pork chops and wine—''

Grinning, Elizabeth retorted, ''Don't forget the feather bed. It seems to me I heard someone say he wasn't a kid anymore and couldn't be expected to sleep on the ground. I think he even brought his pillow.''

''You must have been talking to Joe again,'' he tossed back, flashing his dimples at her. ''You know how he is, sweetheart. He's getting old—''

Stepping out of the barn at that moment, Joe warned

teasingly, "Watch who you're calling old, little brother. You're the one who needed help getting off your horse the last time we went riding. If I remember correctly, you weren't moving too good for about a week after that. Elizabeth said you went through a whole tube of Ben-Gay in one day."

"I own stock in the company," he retorted. "I do what I can to help my fellow shareholders."

Rolling his eyes, Joe snorted. "Yeah, right." Turning to Phoebe and Taylor, he grinned. "Angel and the kids went to visit her dad for a few days, so I thought I'd go check out the wolves with the four of you...just in case you need my help getting Zeke off his horse."

Phoebe grinned. "This might be the time for me to admit that it's been a while since I've been riding. *I* may be the one you have to help off a horse."

Far from worried, Joe chuckled. "You've been getting on and off horses by yourself since Janey and I taught you to ride when you were five years old. The day you can't do that, it's time for all of us to get rocking chairs."

"Actually, you might want to get a ladder, instead," Taylor said ruefully. "I've never been on a horse in my life."

"Then it's about time you were," Joe replied, undaunted. "C'mon, let's get you saddled up. I've got a chestnut in the barn that's just perfect for you."

The chestnut looked as big as a house, but with Joe's assistance and instruction, Taylor soon found himself observing his surroundings from the back of a horse. It was, he had to admit, a different perspective. He hadn't lied when he'd said he'd never ridden, and though he wouldn't have said he was nervous, he would have been a fool not to have been at least cautious.

He needn't have worried. The minute Joe had him walk his mount around the corral, he felt as comfortable as if he'd been riding all his life.

Pleased, Joe said, "Not bad for a city slicker. I'd say you're a natural."

Without knowing it, Joe had struck a nerve. If he was a natural, then it had to be in the genes, Taylor thought grimly. Anger, old and familiar, tightened like a fist in his gut, but it wasn't his brothers and sisters he was angry with. It was Gus. *He* was the one who'd been irresponsible, the one who had left a woman pregnant when he returned to the one he claimed to really love. And he'd never looked back, never, apparently, thought there was any need to.

"You're going to be a sore natural by the end of the day," Zeke warned with a grin. "But then, again, you won't be the only one. Let's go."

With their gear loaded onto the pack horse, the five of them fell into line and soon left the homestead behind. To the west, the mountains beckoned. Taking the lead, Zeke set an easy pace and headed through the trees toward the first ridge.

When Zeke had invited him to join them on their trip to the back country, Taylor had seen it as a chance to learn more about his family. He hadn't stopped to consider that he would also have an opportunity to explore the ranch where his father—and ancestors—had lived and died.

He'd known the ranch was big, of course—he'd already checked out the deed at the country courthouse—but it was impossible to visualize its vastness until he was actually in the middle of it. Almost in the time it took to blink, civilization was left behind. He knew the homestead was less than ten miles away, but as they climbed higher into the mountains, it seemed as if there wasn't another living soul for a thousand miles or more. And just that easily, he knew how the first McBrides must have felt when they moved to Colorado after the Civil War.

It was a humbling feeling.

Just weeks ago, he would have deeply resented the fact that his brothers and sisters had grown up with an incredible wilderness right in their backyard. He, on the other hand, had lived in a series of bare-bones apartments that hadn't even had a community playground for the kids, let alone mountains and streams and a vista of trees that stretched for as far as the eye could see. But how could he be angry and resentful in such an incredible setting?

"It's pretty awesome, isn't it?" Phoebe said as she dropped back to ride beside him for a few moments. "The first time I went camping with the McBrides, I was ten years old and I thought we'd stepped back into the Old West. Can you imagine going over these mountains in a covered wagon? Especially in the winter? I don't know how people did it."

"They had to be pretty tough," he agreed, and felt a pride in his McBride ancestors that surprised the hell out of him. He knew next to nothing about these people, not their names, where they came from, what they stood for. He might share the same DNA with them, but the McBrides weren't his family and never would be. Regardless of how tough they were, how hardy or tenacious, or what kind of empire they'd managed to carve out of the wilds of Colorado, they and their descendents meant nothing to him. So where the hell did this feeling of pride come from?

Confused and more than a little annoyed, he discovered a part of him that wanted to come up with an excuse to go back to town. The rest of the crowd wouldn't have to change their plans—Phoebe could give him a key to Myrtle's and continue with the others up into the mountains. Some time by himself might be what he needed to get his head on straight.

But even as he acknowledged the wisdom of that, he couldn't deny the connection he felt to the land, and that surprised him. He'd never considered himself a rural man—he liked cities and all the amenities that they had to offer—but there was something about the ruggedness of the mountains, the whisper of the wind through the pines, the cry of a hawk in the distance, that seemed to call to a hollow spot in his soul. He told himself he was crazy—his imagination was playing tricks on him—but he couldn't bring himself to turn around and ride back down the mountain.

When they finally reached the canyon where they planned to spend the night, the afternoon was half gone and a storm was gathering high up in the mountains. Zeke took one look at the darkening sky and said, "I don't like the look of those clouds. We'd better set up the tents before it starts pouring."

He didn't get any arguments from the others. "Let's set up under those big pines over by the creek," Joe said. "The ground's not as rocky there, and the trees'll protect us some if it rains."

They all quickly dismounted and began the task of setting up camp. First, the horses had to be taken care of. They were stripped of the gear they carried and their saddles, then fed and watered. Only then did Joe and Zeke begin constructing the tents.

Already setting up the camp kitchen, Elizabeth said, "Phoebe, why don't you and Taylor collect some firewood? I'll use the Coleman stove to cook dinner, but we'll need some wood for a fire later. It'll get cold once the sun goes down."

"We'd better hurry before it rains and the wood gets wet," Taylor said, casting a wary eye at the darkening sky. "It looks like it's going to pour any minute."

Phoebe had to agree. Just in the last few minutes, the wind had picked up, and in the distance, the rumble of thunder could clearly be heard. "We'll be back as quickly as we can," she assured Elizabeth, and hurried away from camp with Taylor at her side.

Later, she couldn't have said how far they wandered from the campsite. Their eyes trained on the ground in front of them, they picked up one piece of fallen wood after another, but much of it was decomposing and wouldn't burn well. So they moved deeper into the canyon and never noticed that the clouds gathering overhead were becoming darker and darker.

Then, from out of nowhere, lightning split the sky with an angry crack of thunder. Startled, they both jumped, and only just then noticed that camp was nowhere in sight. "Damn!" Swearing, Taylor dropped the few pieces of wood he was carrying and grabbed her hand. "C'mon!"

Running, he pulled her with him toward a spot in the canyon wall fifty yards away where a rock jutted out, creating a shallow cave. Breathless, her heart pounding, Phoebe matched him step for step, but they were both running a race they couldn't win. Twenty feet from the cave, it started to rain. And what began as a few sprinkles quickly turned into a downpour.

Gasping, her hair falling into her eyes, blinding her, Phoebe slipped on a slick rock, but before she could fall, Taylor snatched her up into his arms as if she weighed no more than a baby. With three long strides, he reached the cave.

Taylor released her almost immediately, but he couldn't step back—there was no room. The cave was little more than an alcove big enough for two. If either one of them moved the least little bit, they would find themselves standing in the rain.

Phoebe had never been afraid of storms, but then again, she'd never been trapped in one before. Overhead, lightning ripped across the dark sky with a crack of thunder that seemed to make the very ground tremble beneath their feet. The wind picked up, tearing at the trees, and the rain turned into a downpour.

Her heart racing and her eyes trained on the wild display being put on by Nature, Phoebe didn't realize she'd instinctively crowded closer to Taylor until she found herself pressed against him. Startled, she would have stepped back, but then suddenly, from the corner of her eye, she caught sight of something moving through the trees in the rain. Her eyes narrowing, she peered through the misty rain, only to gasp when her gaze locked with the steely dark gaze of a wolf.

Beside her, Taylor went perfectly still, and she knew that he, too, saw the wolf. It stood near the edge of a thick stand of pines, blending into the shadows, its fur wet from the rain as it gazed unblinkingly at the shallow cave where she and Taylor had sought protection from the rain. Watching it, Phoebe felt tears sting her eyes. It was the most beautiful animal she'd ever seen in her

life. It showed no fear, no concern that humans had
invaded its territory, but studied them as carefully as
they studied it. Then, without warning, it silently
slipped off into the trees like a gray ghost, disappearing
as quietly as it had appeared. And just that easily, she
understood why Zeke and Elizabeth had fought so hard
to reintroduce the wolves back into this area of the Colorado Rockies.

How long they stood there, staring at the spot where
the wolf had disappeared, she couldn't have said. The
magic of the moment was still in her eyes when she
made the mistake of looking up at the same time Taylor
looked down. Something passed between them, something shared, something hushed and intimate that set her
heart pounding.

"That was pretty incredible, wasn't it?"

His low, rough growl reached out and stroked her like
a caress, stealing her breath, and it was a long moment
before she could find her voice. "I've heard about the
wolves for years, but I never expected to feel like this
when I saw one," she said huskily, and prayed he didn't
ask for an explanation of what she meant by *this*. Because *this* was the wonder of seeing the wolf…with
him, of sharing it…with him. Did he have a clue what
his nearness did to her? Could he hear the pounding of
her heart? Did he know how much she wanted him to
touch her? Hold her? Kiss her?

She prayed her expression wouldn't give her away,
but there must have been something in her face, a look
in her eyes, that caught his attention. His gaze narrowed
on hers, and, for a moment, she couldn't seem to catch
her breath. Then he reached for her and stepping into
his arms seemed to be the most natural thing in the
world.

Lightning flashed overhead, but the world could have stopped rotating on its axis and she never would have noticed. Her heart pounding, every bone in her body melting, she didn't want him to ever let her go. Later, she knew that would bother her, but for now, she didn't want to think, didn't want to do anything but kiss him again and again and again. Crowding closer, she sighed his name, aching for more.

He was losing his mind.

Taylor told himself he had to stop this—now, while he still had some measure of his common sense left. But how was he supposed to think straight when the feel and scent and taste of her went straight to his head? He couldn't remember the last woman who had felt so damn good in his arms. She kissed him back with a hunger that matched his own and all he wanted to do was pick her up and carry her off to some dry spot in the woods where he could spend the rest of the day and night making love to her.

Images played in his mind, teasing him, heating his blood, and before he could stop to consider the wisdom of his actions, he gave in to the need and swept her up in his arms. Startled, she gasped softly…and sweetly wound her arms around his neck. That easily, he was lost. Groaning at the feel of her against him, he unthinkingly stepped out from under the protection of the rocky ledge that protected them from the weather.

Cold rain pounded down on their heads and shoulders, bringing them back to their surroundings with a jolt. Startled, they broke apart with a gasp…and looked up at the sky as if they'd never seen rain before. Almost immediately, they were both soaked; the mood was broken.

"Well, damn!" Taylor swore. Normally, he would have been furious with himself for losing his head and forgetting where he was, but when he looked down at Phoebe, water was streaming from her hair, her blouse was plastered to her breasts, and she looked like a drowned rat. Any other woman he knew would have been, at the very least, less than happy with him for carrying her out into the middle of a storm, but as his gaze met hers, her lips twitched and her blue eyes sparkled with amusement. And suddenly they were both laughing.

"Sorry about that," he said with a rueful grin as he quickly stepped back into the shallow cave and set her on her feet. "I lost my head there for a second."

Surprised that he'd admitted it—losing control wasn't something she suspected he acknowledged often— Phoebe was amazed that a kiss and a little rain could turn him into such a likable man. Who would have thought it?

"Me, too," she said with a smile. "I forgot all about the others. They'll be wondering where we are."

It was the wrong thing to say. His smile faded. "We need to get back." Casting an eye at the still-dripping sky, he said, "It looks like it's just about passed over us. It's clearing to the west."

The sky was, indeed, clearing—the words were hardly out of his mouth when the sun broke free of the clouds low on the horizon. Disappointed and hurt—was he *that* anxious to get back to the others?—she forced a smile that never reached her eyes. "Then I guess we'd better go. I'm sure Zeke's figured out by now that we're not going to find any dry wood. I hope he brought down sleeping bags. It's going to be cold tonight."

The temperature had already started to drop because

of the rain—and she was quickly becoming chilled. She tried to tell herself that it was because of her wet clothes, but she knew it had more to do with Taylor's cool insistence on returning to camp. How could he kiss her as though he didn't want ever to let her go, then turn around and walk away as if nothing had happened between them? Was he really that cold?

Hurt, confused, she would have liked nothing more than to head back to town then and there, but that was impossible, of course. It would take hours just to reach the homestead, and it would be dark long before then. So she headed for camp instead, uncaring that the trees were still dripping. Behind her, she could feel Taylor right on her heels, taking every step she did. Fighting sudden, foolish tears, she never looked back.

"Hey, there you are!" Zeke greeted them as they walked into camp twenty minutes later. "We were beginning to wonder if you were in trouble."

"Hey!" Joe exclaimed. "What do you mean *we?* I knew they were fine. Didn't I tell you they were both smart enough to find a place to get out of the rain?"

"If I remember correctly," Elizabeth replied with a grin, "you were giving them five more minutes, then you were going to go looking for them.

"I kept telling them both you wouldn't show up until it stopped raining," she continued, smiling at Phoebe, "but would they listen to me? Of course not."

Her clothes still damp, sure that the kiss they shared must somehow be stamped all over her face, Phoebe forced a smile. "We found a small cave where we could get out of the storm. That's when we saw the wolf."

"What! Which one?"

"A big gray one," Taylor said. "I think it was a male, but it was hard to tell in the rain."

"It was magnificent," Phoebe added. "He just appeared out of nowhere, and the next thing we knew, he was gone. He never made a sound."

Pleased, Elizabeth smiled. "Thank God! That must have been Napoleon's grandson, Duke. I haven't seen him in a while. I was afraid something had happened to him."

"I told you he was fine," Zeke told her, slipping an arm around her shoulders to give her a hug. "He looks just like Napoleon. He can take care of himself." Suddenly noticing that neither one of them had collected any wood, he said, "What happened to the firewood?"

"We dropped it when it started to rain," Phoebe admitted. "Sorry."

"Don't worry about it," Zeke assured her. "We brought plenty of charcoal along, just in case. You never know what the weather's going to do up here, even in the summer, so we've learned to be prepared. Don't worry. We won't freeze tonight."

"Or go hungry," Elizabeth added. "We threw a tarp over the kitchen stuff once we realized it was going to rain, so we won't have to eat wet sandwiches tonight, thank God. I don't know about the rest of you, but I'm starving!"

Thankful to have something to do to get her mind off Taylor, Phoebe said, "What can I do to help you get dinner ready?"

"Make a salad while the guys set up the table," Elizabeth replied promptly. "We're having fettuccine Alfredo, and I brought the sauce from home. All we have to do is boil the water for the noodles, heat the sauce, and we can eat."

She didn't have to tell any of them twice. It had been a long day, and it had been hours since lunch. The men quickly had a makeshift table set up, folding chairs arranged around it, and a charcoal fire started to ward off the already falling temperatures. A lantern was lit, the food brought to the table and it was time to eat.

They were in the middle of nowhere, and as comfortable as they'd been that night they'd had dinner at Joe's. Phoebe would have sworn she'd never be able to relax—let alone eat—seated across from Taylor. But they were surrounded by the night, the mountains, the sweetly fragrant scent of damp pine in the air, and the rest of the world seemed very far away. Phoebe found herself laughing at the good-natured ribbing between Zeke and Joe and fascinated by the stories Elizabeth told about her precious wolves. If her heart seemed to stop in her breast every time her eyes chanced to lock with Taylor's, the others soon distracted her with another joke or story. Glad she hadn't backed out of the trip that morning, after all, she thoroughly enjoyed herself.

Watching Phoebe laugh at something Zeke said, Taylor couldn't take his eyes off her. She sat comfortably relaxed in a folding camp chair, her legs stretched out in front of her, her cheeks pink from the sun she'd gotten earlier in the day during the ride up into the mountains. The rain had brought out the curl in her hair and washed the makeup from her face, but she was still beautiful. How the hell did she fascinate him so? he wondered in confusion. She wasn't his type. They didn't have a damn thing in common...except this incredible chemistry that flared to life every time their eyes met. Touching her, kissing her, only made the need she stirred in him worse.

Irritated, he told himself he never should have come on this trip. Any way he'd looked at it, he'd known it was wrong of him. He was too attracted to Phoebe— spending a weekend with her under rugged conditions was only going to make it worse. Then there were the McBrides themselves. He liked them, dammit. That still amazed him. He hadn't planned this, didn't want it. Liking them only made it more difficult for him to carry out the revenge he'd planned. But how the hell could he *not* like them? Right from the beginning, they'd trusted him to be the man he'd said he was. Just as Phoebe had. Once, that wouldn't have bothered him. Now, however, his revenge had become a double-edged sword. Did he really want to go through with his plan to expose Gus to his legitimate children and their mother? What purpose would it serve? His own mother was dead. It wouldn't change the sadness and hardship of her life. And it wouldn't give him the father he'd never had.

"You're awfully quiet," Joe told him with a grin. "You're not falling asleep on us, are you?"

Forcing a smile, Taylor said, "Actually, I was wondering how the hell I'm going to get out of this chair when it's time to go to bed. I feel like I'm about a hundred years old."

"Wait till tomorrow," Zeke teased. "You'll be lucky if you can move."

"Don't worry," Elizabeth said, chuckling, "we brought plenty of horse liniment. Everybody gets their own bottle."

Phoebe rose to her feet with a grimace, her grin rueful. "I think I'm going to need two."

"That's what happens when you spend so much time in the city," Joe retorted, his brown eyes twinkling with amusement. "Here. I brought you a present."

When he tossed her a hot-water bottle, she burst out laughing. "My hero!"

"Hey, what about mine?" Taylor protested. "I'm from the city, too!"

For an answer, Joe tossed him another hot-water bottle.

Taylor scowled at the luminous dial on his watch and swore softly in the darkness. Midnight. It had been two hours since they'd all turned in for the night, and he'd spent every second of that time staring at the peaked roof of his small tent. He tried to convince himself it was because he was still sore, despite the liniment and hot-water bottle, but he knew his stiff muscles had nothing to do with his insomnia. It was Phoebe, dammit! She slept less than ten yards away, and from where he lay, he swore he could hear every breath she took.

Idiot! he silently chided himself. What the hell's the matter with you? Since when did you let a woman tie you in knots? Especially one who doesn't appear to be losing any sleep over you. You don't hear her tossing and turning, do you? Forget this afternoon and what happened in that damn cave and go to sleep!

He tried, but he was fighting a losing battle. Every time he closed his eyes, she was all he could see. Her smile, her laughter when Joe had tossed her the hot-water bottle he'd brought for her, the soft, heated passion he'd seen in her eyes when he'd kissed her—and he wanted her all over again.

Swearing, he jerked down the zipper to his sleeping bag and threw it off. In the dark, he reached for his clothes and pulled them on, wishing he'd had the sense to bring his laptop. He could have at least gone over the weekly report his secretary had e-mailed him on some of the bigger cases his partners were handling while he was gone. Instead, all he had to read was an old paperback Western he'd found in the bookcase in his room at Phoebe's grandmother's. He didn't usually have much time for fiction—especially Westerns—but anything that would take his mind off Phoebe tonight would do. Grabbing it from his overnight bag, he slipped quietly out of his tent.

The last of the rain had cleared hours ago, leaving behind a night sky full of stars and a crescent moon. Joe had banked the campfire before everyone had turned in for the night, but the coals still had a glow that would spark into flames again with nothing more than a few small twigs. He saw thankfully that the damp wood that had been neatly stacked nearby was nearly dry. Hoping it would burn easily, he started to reach for a couple of branches, only to look up sharply when he caught sight of movement out of the corner of his eye.

In the shadows of the night, he just caught a glimpse of a woman in the clearing fifty yards away, but he knew it was *her*. Phoebe. Even in the dark, with scant moonlight to illuminate the curve of her cheek, the glow of her wavy blond hair, he knew her as well as he knew the shape of his own hand.

His common sense ordered him to turn around and go back to his tent…immediately! Everyone else was asleep—he had no business being alone with her. Not when he'd lain awake for the last two hours thinking of nothing but her.

He prided himself on doing the right thing. He was a logical man—he liked to think that the only time he'd ever let his emotions control his life was when it had come to his father. He certainly hadn't ever let a woman overcome his common sense. But instead of doing the smart thing and walking away, he headed straight for her.

In the shadow of the surrounding mountains, Phoebe spread a blanket out on the ground in the middle of a clearing that was within a short walk of the camp, then settled down to stargaze. It had been a long day—she should have been exhausted. But when everyone had gone to bed and she'd crawled into her sleeping bag, her mind had refused to shut down enough for her to fall asleep. In desperation, she'd escaped outside, hoping she'd find some peace in the quiet of the night.

The open field...and a view of the stars...drew her away from camp, to a clearing nearby that was bathed in the soft glow of the moon. Spreading out her sleeping bag, she sank down onto the ground and lifted her eyes to the sky full of stars. A soft breeze caressed her face, and for the first time in what seemed like hours, she smiled. This was just what she needed.

Later, she couldn't have said when she first realized she wasn't alone. The night was as quiet as ever, the breeze that played with her hair little more than a sigh. She would have sworn nothing moved, but suddenly, she could feel the touch of eyes on her. She tried to tell herself that her imagination was playing tricks on her, but the goosebumps running up and down her arms were all too real. Had Elizabeth's wolf followed them back to camp? she wondered suddenly. Did wolves eat people? Horrified at the thought, she jumped to her feet and whirled, half expecting to find herself face to face if not with Duke, then with a bear or some other wild animal. Instead, Taylor stood at the edge of the clearing, his silhouette just barely visible in the moonlight.

Relieved, her knees melted. ''Thank God!'' she said with a shaky laugh as she sank down to the sleeping bag. ''I thought you were a wolf!''

Unable to take his eyes off her in the soft glow of the moonlight, Taylor said, ''What are you doing out here by yourself?''

''Stargazing,'' she said simply. ''I couldn't sleep. I guess you couldn't, either. What's the matter? The ground's too hard for you?''

''Something like that,'' he said dryly. ''I'm not much of an outdoorsman.''

''You do look as if you'd be more comfortable in a boardroom than a tent,'' she replied with a smile. ''So why'd you accept Zeke's invitation to ride up here? He wouldn't have been offended if you'd turned him down.''

''Research,'' he said, wincing at the lie that came easily to his tongue. ''It's easier to write about something you've experienced first-hand.''

Guilt knotting in his gut, he half expected her to ask why he chose to write about something that obviously wasn't his thing, but she was more trusting than that. ''Well, you've certainly had that so far, and the weekend has barely started. First a storm in the mountain, then Duke. I know the whole purpose of the trip was to check on Elizabeth's wolves, but I never really thought that we'd see one. It was so eerie the way he just appeared out of the mist that way, wasn't it?''

She had that look on her face, that same soft, pretty one that had been his undoing right after Duke had disappeared into the rain. He'd taken one look at her and lost his head. And he was doing it again. He had to get out of there!

"Yeah," he said gruffly. "Speaking of which, you were stargazing and I interrupted you. I'll let you get back to it—"

He turned back toward camp, but he'd only taken a step when she stopped him. "No! Wait!"

Chapter 7

"Phoebe, this isn't smart."

"I know," she said huskily. "Stay anyway. I want you to stargaze with me."

He shouldn't. They both knew what would happen if he made the mistake of joining her on her sleeping bag, but she didn't care. Couldn't he feel how special the night was? The others may have been fifty yards away, but surrounded by the mountains and trees, with the moon and a sky full of stars above them, it felt like they were the only two people in the world. And there was nothing she wanted more than to spend the night with him.

Even in the dark, in the glow of the moonlight, she knew he had to see that in her eyes, but she didn't look away, didn't hide the need that had been building in her ever since he'd kissed her. And that shocked her. She'd never been so bold in her life! Especially with a man who was so wrong for her. But from the moment they'd met, they had been dancing a slow, seductive dance around each other, making their way toward this moment in time. It was fate, karma, inevitable. Couldn't he feel it?

When he hesitated, she felt her heart sink. If he walked away, there was nothing she could do about it, but she refused to believe that he didn't want her. She'd been on the receiving end of his kisses. She'd seen the passion in his eyes when he looked at her. But she wouldn't ask him to stay again. She couldn't. She did have some pride, and she'd gone as far as she could.

His eyes locked with hers in the darkness, Taylor told himself that staying could be nothing but a mistake. It was late, he wasn't thinking clearly, and if he went anywhere near her, he wouldn't able to keep his hands to himself. If he had a lick of sense, he'd run, not walk, back to his tent.

He knew that, accepted it and took a step. But it wasn't away from her.

He'd lost his mind—it was the only explanation. But if this was madness, he couldn't regret it. Not now. Not when her hair caught the soft glow of the moonlight and she looked at him with a hesitancy that matched his own. She was as unsure as he, he realized, and just as confused by this need that sparked between them without rhyme or reason. And that only made him want her more.

Later, he never remembered closing the distance between them, but in the blink of an eye, he found himself standing at the edge of the sleeping bag she sat on. Holding out her hand to him, she smiled, and he felt a sigh of contentment ripple quietly through her. And once again, he felt the need to run…because it seemed as though he'd been waiting his whole life to hear a woman do that when his hand closed around hers.

Before he could even think about running, however, she tugged gently at his hand, pulling him down to her. "Lie down with me," she said huskily. "It's the only way to really see the stars."

He could no more have resisted her than Elizabeth's wolves could resist the call of the wild. Without a word, he sank down to his knees beside her and drew her down with him to the sleeping bag. A heartbeat later, he was flat on his back, staring up at the star-studded sky, lying shoulder to shoulder with her, their heads just inches apart as she pointed out to him the constellations in the vast sea of stars above them.

"There's the Big Dipper," she said huskily. "See it? It's beautiful! And so close! It looks as if you could just reach out and touch it."

Shifting slightly to follow the direction of her pointing finger, Taylor's head came to rest against the cloud of her hair, and his senses scrambled. He couldn't have seen the Big Dipper if it had been ten feet in front of his face. Between one heartbeat and the next, the elusive scent of ginger and peach and something that was uniquely her filled his lungs, teasing him, intoxicating him, heating his blood.

His heart pounding, he rasped, "Where's Orion?"

"There," she said softly, and turned to point to the constellation that was low in the night sky to the west of where they lay. In the time it took to blink, they lay face-to-face on the sleeping bag, so close they could see the anticipation reflected in each other's eyes.

Lying perfectly still, her breath catching in her lungs,

Phoebe wanted him so badly, she ached. How long had she wanted him? Days? Weeks? Years before she'd even met him? She didn't know how or why, but it seemed as though the knowledge of him had somehow always been there. She only had to look into his eyes to know that he was the one she had dreamed of all her life.

She could fall in love with him.

The knowledge whispered through the deep, dark corners of her soul and should have scared the hell out of her. He didn't live in her world—when he left and returned to California, she didn't want him to take her heart with him. But when he was this close, she couldn't think, couldn't guard her heart. She wanted him too badly. He reached for her, and the future seemed a long way away. There was only now…and Taylor. With a sigh that was his name, she melted into his arms.

"We shouldn't do this," he murmured, echoing her thoughts, then covered her mouth with his.

Stardust. His kiss tasted like stardust and magic and every dream she'd ever dreamed. The camp—and the others—were fifty yards away and asleep in their tents. They might as well have been on the other side of the moon. He gently wooed her, seducing her in a way no man ever had, and made her feel as if she was the only woman on earth.

Her head spinning and her heart pounding, she clung to him and kissed him wildly. "Don't stop. Please…"

"I'm not going anywhere without you," he rasped. "Let me make love to you."

She couldn't refuse him, not when she wanted him as badly as he wanted her. He kissed her again and again, long, drugging kisses that stole her breath and heated her blood and made her ache. Their clothes melted away and their hands were free to touch, to stroke, to linger.

He was driving her crazy. Bare skin rubbed against bare skin, and nothing had ever felt so good. She wanted the night to go on forever, but he knew just where to touch her to make her gasp, just where to kiss her to drive her over the edge. And she loved it.

"Taylor!"

It was the sound of his name on her lips that destroyed what was left of his unraveling control. She was so sweet, so giving! She held nothing back, kissing him, moving with him with a passion that drove him crazy. Need burned in his belly. On fire for her, he lost himself in her and only wanted more. A groan ripping from his throat, he rolled her under him and took the loving deeper.

High up in the heavens, the stars glowed softly, silently, in the night, but Taylor never noticed. Every breath, every touch, every thought was focused on Phoebe and the pleasure he took in her. Making love had never been like this before. When she came apart in his arms, he was the one who came undone.

Dawn was just a promise on the eastern horizon when they quietly made their way back to camp. Even then, Taylor didn't want to let Phoebe go, and that shook him to the core. He wasn't a man to linger after he'd made love to a woman. He'd never wanted to let anyone get that close to his emotions. But there was something about Phoebe....

He told himself it was just sex, but he'd never been very good at lying to himself. In the predawn light, she was beautiful. Her hair was a mass of tossed curls, her mouth sweetly swollen from his kisses. When she hesitated outside her tent, her blue eyes lifting to his, he wanted to reach for her so badly, he could taste it. But if he touched her now, he knew he would never let her go.

So he kept his hands to himself and cursed the dawn. "The others will be up soon," he said quietly.

No! Phoebe wanted to cry. She wasn't ready for the night to end—or to walk away from the intimacy they'd shared. She needed him to hold her a little longer, to assure her that this wasn't the only night that they were going to have together. But no promises had been given, no words of affection or caring whispered in the night. Was need all he'd felt?

Afraid of the answer…and examining her own feelings too closely…she said huskily, "I guess I'd better go in, then. Good night."

She ached to kiss him one last time, but she couldn't. So she turned and ducked into her tent, and never let him see the tears that suddenly welled in her eyes. Even though his own tent was only steps away, she'd never felt so lonely in her life.

And that horrified her. What was wrong with her? She'd known when she made love with him that she was taking a risk. After all, when two people were that intimate, there was no way to remain emotionally distant. But she'd thought she could handle her feelings, thought she could enjoy the experience and still walk away with her heart intact. She'd been wrong.

Stunned, she sank down onto her sleeping bag and called herself seven kinds of a fool. She had to be losing her mind. Taylor wasn't the kind of man she could let herself care for. Aside from the fact that he was a writer, she knew next to nothing about him...except that he was everything she wasn't. Driven, reserved, a loner. When the time came for him to leave, he would do so without a backward glance.

The thought left her shaken, and that's when she realized she couldn't touch him again. She didn't care how good a kisser he was or how he could melt her bones just by taking her into his arms, she couldn't afford to go anywhere near him again. He was just too dangerous to her peace of mind. Not that she'd be able to avoid him completely, she assured herself. After all, he was a guest. She'd be friendly, but no friendlier than she would be with any other guest. Then when he left, he wouldn't take her heart with him.

She should have been relieved that she'd come up with a plan. But when she lay down on her sleeping bag to wait for the others to wake up, she might as well have saved herself the effort. Taylor was all she could think of.

"Hey, are you okay?" Elizabeth asked with a worried frown as they saddled their horses and prepared to ride further into the canyon to look for the rest of her wolves. "You didn't say two words during breakfast. Is something wrong?"

All too aware of the fact that Taylor was well within hearing distance and had been watching her all morning with those dark, probing eyes of his, Phoebe forced a smile. "Will I sound like a city slicker if I admit that I'm a little stiff this morning? It's been a while since I've ridden this much."

Relieved, Elizabeth chuckled. "Ah, so that's it. A

little saddle sore, are we? Thank God! I thought I was the only one.''

''But you and Zeke come up here all the time and go camping, don't you?'' Phoebe said with a frown, surprised.

''We did—before we had the kids,'' Elizabeth admitted ruefully. ''It's not so easy once you've got a four-year-old and a toddler. We'll have to wait until they're a little older before they can make the trip.''

Seeing her wistful smile, Phoebe said, ''You miss it, don't you? Being alone together up here?''

Elizabeth didn't deny it. ''It was wonderful. Sometimes we stayed for weeks at a time.''

Phoebe could well understand why. Last night, lying in Taylor's arms and making love under the stars had been the most romantic evening of her life. If they'd been newlyweds, she would have wanted to stay there forever.

Memories from last night tugged at her heart, and for a moment, she could almost feel the tenderness of his touch, taste the hunger of his kiss. Without even looking, she knew where he was at all times. She'd developed a sixth sense where he was concerned, and when she glanced over to where the men were saddling their own horses, she wasn't surprised to find Taylor watching her. They'd been aware of each other's every move all morning, and it was driving her crazy. Even though she'd resigned herself to the fact that she had to keep her distance, her body still ached for him. Given the least amount of encouragement, she would have walked into his arms.

He, however, was as reserved as she and not the kind to make any kind of overture to her in front of the

others. She should have been thankful. Wasn't that what
she wanted? Some time and space to get her head on
straight? He wasn't pushing her for anything more than
they'd already shared or she was prepared to give. Why
did that make her so unhappy? What was wrong with
her?

Confused, in desperate need of some time to herself
to think, she would have liked nothing more than to
head back home right then and there, but Elizabeth still
needed to check on the rest of the wolves. So when
Zeke gave the signal, she climbed onto her horse, then
fell in line with the others. She was thankful that the
terrain grew rougher as they climbed higher into the
mountains, and she couldn't afford to be distracted by
thoughts of Taylor. All her concentration was focused
on following Zeke and making sure her horse didn't
take a misstep and send them both tumbling down the
side of the mountain.

It was Zeke who first spotted the wolf standing silently in a thick stand of pines, watching them with
intelligent gray eyes that missed little. Without a word,
Zeke pulled up. "Up in the trees to the right," he murmured to Elizabeth when she brought her mount to a
stop alongside his. "It looks like Queenie."

"No, it's Duchess," she said softly. "We didn't see
her last time. I was afraid something had happened to
her." Looking past the watchful female, she suddenly
grinned broadly. "Look! She's got pups!"

The young gray wolf did, indeed, have two pups with
her, but they were far more cautious than she. Blending
into the shadows and half hidden under the underbrush,
they lay on their bellies near their mother and didn't so

much as blink as they watched the riders a hundred yards down the mountain from them.

"That's Queenie and Napoleon's granddaughter," she explained to Phoebe and Taylor. "Isn't she beautiful?"

"Where's her mate?" Taylor asked quietly. "Wolves mate for life, don't they?"

Smiling, she nodded. "He's somewhere nearby. He'll show himself when he's ready."

The words were hardly out of her mouth when a large alpha male silently appeared in the trees off to their right. "That looks like the same one we saw yesterday," Phoebe said in a hushed voice that didn't carry past their ears. "He had that same white collar of fur around his neck."

"I'm surprised they showed themselves," Taylor said quietly. "This area's so remote. They can't see many humans."

"They accepted Elizabeth a long time ago," Zeke replied. "They know they have nothing to fear from her."

"They don't let me get any closer than this, though," Elizabeth quickly added. "They always seem to know when I'm here and come to check me out. Once they're assured everything's okay, they leave. See," she said, nodding toward the female wolf. "There goes Duchess now. The others will follow."

True to her words, the pups slipped further into the underbrush, disappearing from view. The alpha male stood like a gray statue, its sharp, intelligent eyes quietly studying them, assessing them. Shrouded in silence, no one moved. Just when they began to wonder if the wolf saw them as some kind of threat, he turned and soundlessly slipped into the trees. As quickly as he had appeared, he was gone.

In the silence of their leavetaking, it was a long time before anyone spoke. Then Taylor said gruffly, "I can see why you've spent so many years studying them. They're magnificent."

Phoebe had to agree. In all the years that she'd heard about Elizabeth's wolves, she'd never dreamed that seeing them in the wild could strike such awe in her. "Now I understand why you and Zeke set up the wildlife preserve. They need a place where they are protected."

Blinking back the tears that glistened in her eyes, Elizabeth gave them both a watery smile. "It's where they belong. It took a while to convince the neighboring ranchers of that, but time has a way of working things out."

"Time and a lot of hard work," Joe added dryly. "People can act like real idiots when they don't understand something."

"If they'd just gotten the facts before they rushed to judgment, there wouldn't have been a problem," Zeke added grimly. "But I guess that's human nature. What's important is that they finally came around and the wolves are safe."

The trip a success, there was no need to venture further into the mountains—they'd seen what they'd come to see and the ride back to camp would take several hours. It was already well past midday. By mutual agreement, they turned around and headed back down the mountain to the canyon where they'd made camp the night before.

Dinner that night was a celebration. The wolves were all safe and accounted for and all was right with the world. In anticipation of that, the McBrides had brought champagne and all the makings of a feast. Laughing and talking, everyone working together, they had the meal together in a remarkably quick time, then gathered around the campfire to eat.

It was a wonderful summer evening, cool and clear, and the food was fantastic. Normally, Phoebe would have thoroughly enjoyed herself, but she couldn't stop thinking about last night...and Taylor. Sometime between the long hours of the night, when he'd made love to her again and again, and today's ride up into the mountains, something had changed between them, something she couldn't put her finger on. She just knew that he was already regretting last night.

Oh, he hadn't said anything. He hadn't even tried to avoid her. He'd joined in the conversation with the others, offered suggestions as Zeke grilled the steaks, and didn't seem the least bit uncomfortable in her company. But there was something in his eyes, a reserve, a distance when he looked at her that made her want to cry.

Don't! she wanted to tell him. She'd given herself to him freely, without strings, and it had been one of the most wonderful nights of her life. No one had ever made her feel the way he had. The last thing she wanted was for him to regret it.

She didn't, however, have any control over what he thought or felt. He was like a fish out of water in Liberty Hill and driven by something she would probably never understand. His stay there was only a temporary one, and when the time came for him to leave, he would, no doubt, do so without giving a second thought to her or the time they'd spent making love under the stars. The sooner she accepted that, the better.

Still, it hurt, and that shook her to the core. She hadn't realized last night, when she'd given herself to him without a thought to the future, that she'd also given him the ability to hurt her. Tears stung her eyes, but she quickly blinked them back. No, she told herself fiercely. She wouldn't cry! If he didn't have the good sense to appreciate her, then the loss was his.

Shaking off the hurt that squeezed her heart, she forced herself to join into the easygoing conversation around the campfire after the meal. She smiled at an outrageous story Zeke told and even managed to eat a piece of the chocolate cake that Elizabeth had brought along to celebrate the thriving of the wolves. Phoebe didn't doubt that it was delicious, but she'd lost her appetite and she could have been eating sawdust and wouldn't have tasted it. She made sure that no one, especially Taylor, had a clue how she was feeling. When her eyes met his across the campfire, she smiled as if she didn't have a care in the world and finished her cake with a flourish.

She wasn't smiling, however, when she retreated to her tent later. But then again, she didn't need to. There was no one there to see.

Taylor reached for her during the night…and cursed himself for his actions. He never should have made love to her. He'd known at the time that it would turn out to be nothing but a mistake, but he hadn't been able to stop himself. Idiot! He hadn't come all the way to Colorado to let his thoughts get tangled up with a woman. Sara McBride would be returning from her honeymoon soon, and he had yet to decide how he was going to confront her about Gus. *That's* what he should have been concentrating on, not Phoebe!

Just the thought of his father should have been enough to distract him from thinking of her, but the old familiar anger and resentment that usually knotted in his gut at the mere mention of Gus's name was surprisingly absent. Scowling, he cursed softly in the darkness. What the devil was wrong with him?!

The question nagged at him all that night and the next morning as they broke up camp and headed back down the mountain. If he was too quiet, the others were as well, and he couldn't say he blamed them. It was time to go back to the real world.

And the further they made their way down the mountain, the grimmer Taylor became. When he'd first arrived in Liberty Hill, there hadn't been a doubt in his mind about what he'd come there to do. Now he wasn't sure of anything, and he didn't like the feeling at all.

He wasn't an impulsive person who was ruled by his emotions, he assured himself. Whether he was considering strategy for a trial or for his life, he carefully considered his options, weighed the pros and cons, then made a decision based on logic. And he very seldom made mistakes.

So why was he having second thoughts now?

Lost in his thoughts, he didn't notice that Zeke, who was in the lead, had taken a detour from the main path until he and the others brought their horses to a halt and began to dismount. Surprised that Zeke had called a break when the homestead was in clear view in the valley below, he started to ask if there was a problem when he suddenly saw the old, weathered headstones of a mountain cemetery.

When he'd first learned that Gus was dead, he hadn't given a thought to where he might be buried. After all, the old man hadn't even known he existed when he was living, so he certainly hadn't given a rat's ass where Gus spent eternity. Then he saw his half brothers head for a gray granite headstone that was the newest in the rows of markers that were spread out under the pines on the side of the mountain.

So this was his father's grave. He didn't have to read the nearby headstones to know that all the McBrides were here…grandparents, great-grandparents, aunts and uncles and cousins who had settled this land high in the mountains and carved a homestead out of the wilderness that would be there for generations to come.

Dismounting, he stood back under the trees, silently watching the McBrides clean the pine needles from the graves. Their love and respect for not only Gus, but their grandparents and the rest of the family that had come before them was evident in every move they made. Never had he been more conscious of what he had missed out on his entire life.

Once, that would have stirred nothing but bitterness in him, but as his eyes wandered over the headstones, noting the names, the dates, the history of the McBrides, an emotion he couldn't put a name to reached out and grabbed his heart. And for the first time in his life, he knew what it was like to feel a connection to family.

Stunned, he stood as if turned to stone and wondered how the hell this had happened. He didn't want to feel anything for Gus or the grandparents he'd never had the opportunity to know. But he could see himself in Zeke and Joe—the way they stood, the curve of a brow, the set of their jaw—and too late, he realized that by meeting them, getting to know them, he'd opened a door to feelings he'd never anticipated. They were family...*his* family.

Call off the revenge.

The thought whispered through his head, urging him to do what he knew, deep in his heart, was the right thing. But then he remembered his mother and the loneliness and hardship of her life, the sacrifices she had made. She'd never complained, but she hadn't had to. Even as a child, Taylor had known that she did without so that he could have the things he needed. She'd seldom bought herself any new clothes, and the only new car she'd owned in her life was the one he'd bought her after he'd graduated from law school. Before that, she'd only been able to afford used cars that seemed always to break down.

And that was only one person's fault—Gus McBride. He couldn't forgive him for that, not without betraying his mother.

"We always stop here on our way back home," Zeke said as he walked over to join him. "It brings Dad closer. He died too young."

"What about your dad?" Joe asked. "I know you said your mom was dead, but you never mentioned your father."

He couldn't have asked for a better opportunity to tell them who he was, but Sara wasn't there. If he was determined to do this, then he was going to do it the way he'd planned. "He's dead, too. I never had the chance to know him."

His tone was flat and cold and didn't encourage further questions. Taking the hint, Elizabeth politely changed the subject. "Is anyone besides me getting hungry? It seems like it's been hours since we've eaten. How does taco salad sound? I've got all the makings back at the house. I can have it ready in less than a half hour once we get home.''

She didn't have to say it twice. Stomachs grumbled at the mere mention of food, and suddenly they all realized they were starving. Within minutes, they were all mounted and headed for Zeke and Elizabeth's house.

Two hours later, it was time to go back to the real world. They'd had dinner, Phoebe had helped Elizabeth with the dishes, and outside, it was growing dark. Phoebe knew it was time to leave, but sadness pulled at her at the thought. She knew she was crazy—she should have been eager to be alone with Taylor again—but she knew what would happen when they returned to Myrtle's. He would retreat to his room, using the excuse that he had to work, and she would be alone with her memories of the weekend, of the loving they'd shared, of his withdrawal, of the feelings she was starting to have for him that she didn't know how to handle. And she wasn't ready to deal with any of it, least of all her feelings. Unfortunately, they couldn't stay at the McBrides forever.

So she forced a smile and hugged Zeke, Elizabeth, and Joe good-bye. ''Thank you for the weekend. It was wonderful! I still can't believe we saw the wolves.''

''We'll have to do it again sometime,'' Elizabeth said. ''Next time you're in town, don't be such a stranger. And you're welcome any time, Taylor,'' she added, turning to him with a smile. ''I hope you had as good a time as we did.''

''I won't ever forget it,'' he said solemnly. ''It was incredible.''

Her heart skipping a beat at his words, Phoebe wanted to believe that he wasn't just talking about seeing the wolves in the wild, but the night they'd shared together, too. His eyes, however, still didn't meet hers. And when they climbed into her car a few minutes later and headed back to Liberty Hill, silence fell between them like a rock. He didn't say a word the entire way back to Myrtle's.

They needed to talk. Phoebe didn't know about him, but she couldn't pretend that the night they'd spent in each other's arms had never happened. But every time she glanced over at him to say something, his jaw was set in granite and he was staring straight ahead. She told herself to wait until they got to the house, but the opportunity was lost the second they stepped inside. ''I've got some writing to do,'' he muttered. And without another word, he disappeared upstairs.

''Well,'' she sighed aloud as the firm shutting of his bedroom door echoed through the house, ''so much for discussing things.''

Tears stung her eyes, horrifying her, and she quickly blinked them back. She would not cry, she told herself fiercely. She'd known when they'd made love that there were no promises between them, no words of caring, no commitment. She couldn't complain now just because she was starting to care and he wasn't.

Still, it hurt.

''So, find something else to think of,'' she muttered. ''Like what you're going to do with the rest of your life.''

That was an issue she had put off dealing with, but

she wouldn't, she knew, be able to do that much longer. Myrtle would be back from her trip in a matter of weeks, and she would have to return home. Just thinking about it made her cringe. She'd never liked the business her father had loved so much, but since his death, she'd thought she'd come to terms with the fact that she was responsible for keeping it going. Granted, there was nothing exciting about it, but it was lucrative. Instead of complaining about it, she should have been grateful that her father had thought enough of her to leave her a business that would support her the rest of her life.

And she *was* grateful. She just hadn't realized how much the tediousness of it stifled her soul until she took over running Myrtle's bed and breakfast for her. She loved the house, loved cooking and cleaning for guests, loved the peace and quiet of life in Liberty Hill. How was she going to find the strength to leave it all behind and go back to the lonely existence of a business and life she hated?

Pain squeezing her heart, she reminded herself that she didn't have to do it today. She still had a couple of more weeks before Myrtle came home, and she wasn't going to ruin that time by worrying about the future. One way or the other, it would take care of itself. In the meantime, she had guests to think of. They would be arriving Friday evening and she had a lot to do between now and then. The sooner she got started, the better. Focusing on that, she headed for the kitchen to polish Myrtle's antique silver serving pieces.

Long into the night, Phoebe cleaned like a woman possessed. After she polished the silver, she hand-washed Myrtle's prettiest set of china and carefully returned it to the French étagère in the dining room that her grandmother had owned as long as Phoebe could remember. Half expecting Taylor to come downstairs for an evening snack, she set out a plate of cheese and fresh fruit, as well as homemade brownies, on the sideboard, but he didn't so much as stick his nose out of his room. Not sure if he was avoiding her or so caught up in his writing that he didn't want to leave it, Phoebe left him alone.

That didn't mean, however, that she didn't think about him.

Every time she let her mind wander, every time she dropped her guard, she found herself listening for his step in the hall upstairs, wondering if he was thinking about her, remembering what it was like to lie in his arms under the stars. Then she would reach for another plate, another glass, another piece of silver. And when she ran out of place settings to clean and polish, she started on the kitchen itself. By the time she went to bed at two o'clock in the morning, the glass doors of the kitchen cabinets were gleaming and her grandmother's antique O'Keefe and Merrit stove was sparkling.

Exhausted, she fell asleep the second her head hit the pillow. But even in sleep, she couldn't escape thoughts of Taylor. He walked into her dreams as though he owned them, and with nothing more than a smile, he charmed her into letting him stay. When the alarm went off at six the next morning, she was still dreaming of him.

Groaning quietly, she dragged herself out of bed and told herself that this had to stop. She had to get the man out of her head! It should have been easy—he obviously regretted making love with her. If she had a lick of pride, she'd pray that he'd forgotten his promise to help her clean the house and he'd spend the whole damn day in his room working. Better yet, maybe he'd decide to do some research and visit the other ranchers Joe had introduced him to. Then she'd have the house to herself and could forget, at least for a while, that she'd ever met him, let alone started to have feelings for him.

Clinging to that wishful thought, she dressed, then headed downstairs, wondering if Taylor would stick around for breakfast if he was going to spend the day doing research. Surely, he would get an early start....

"Good morning."

Lost in her thoughts, she stopped short at the sight of him sitting at the kitchen table eating a bowl of cereal. Before she could say a word, he said, "I hope you don't mind me grabbing some cereal—I thought I'd save you the trouble of cooking breakfast. So where do you want to start cleaning the house? If you'll give me a list of what you want done, I'll get started."

Chapter 8

For the rest of the week he helped her get the old house ready for the guests who would be arriving on Friday. Phoebe couldn't believe it. When he'd said he'd help her, she'd never expected him to throw himself into the job with complete abandon. In fact, considering the way he'd holed up in his room after the camping trip with the McBrides, she hadn't held out much hope that he would help her at all. She couldn't have been more wrong.

He not only mowed the lawn for her and trimmed the walkways, he painted the picket fence, front and back, repaired a leaky faucet in one of the bathrooms upstairs, and rehung some of the shutters that had needed fixing for as long as Phoebe could remember. And all without a word of complaint.

"You're doing too much!" Phoebe protested Friday morning when she stepped outside and discovered him scraping all of Myrtle's vintage lawn furniture with a wire brush in preparation for repainting it. "You're a guest, too. I never expected you to do all this. You should be writing."

"I promised to help you," he replied. "And I can work tonight, after your guests arrive. I'm at a standstill right now, anyway. I'm hoping that all this exercise will recharge my brain cells."

Put that way, Phoebe could hardly complain, but she still felt guilty. As she went back to her own chores inside the house, vacuuming upstairs and down, then dusting the antique furniture and whatnots that made Myrtle's house so perfect for a bed and breakfast, her thoughts kept drifting to Taylor. Every time she passed a window, she found herself looking for him, watching him, dreaming. He was a man she could get used to seeing around the house. Who would have thought that he'd be so handy?

Don't go there, a voice in her head warned. *Don't get any more ideas about him. He's not interested, remember?*

That wasn't something she was likely to forget. Even though he'd gone out of his way to help her, she didn't fool herself into thinking it was for any other reason than that he'd given her his word. He was still keeping his distance. Oh, he was no longer avoiding her like the plague and hiding out in his room, thank God, but there was a reserve in his eyes every time they met hers. He still regretted making love with her, and she'd be a fool to forget that.

Assuring herself she was no one's fool, she threw herself into washing all the windows, upstairs and down, until they were gleaming. The house was huge, and by the time she finished with the last window, a stained glass beauty in the front hall upstairs, she was hot and sweaty and in need of a break. Realizing that Taylor must be, too, she grabbed her cleaning supplies and hurried downstairs to the kitchen.

In a matter of minutes, she'd made a pitcher of fresh-squeezed lemonade, arranged some sugar cookies on a dessert plate, and had that and two glasses of ice loaded on a serving tray. Carefully lifting it, she stepped out onto the back porch and went looking for Taylor.

The last time she'd seen him, he'd been on the west side of the house, still working on the lawn furniture. But there were few trees in that part of the yard, and when she followed the veranda around to that side of the house, she wasn't surprised to find it deserted. It was two o'clock in the afternoon, and the sun was scorching.

"Taylor?" she called, glancing around. "Where are you?"

"Over here. I'm taking a break."

Following his voice around to the east side of the house, she said, "Good. So am I. It's too hot to be working so hard. When I was cleaning the windows in the attic, I thought I was going to have heat stroke. I hope you're thirsty. I made a gallon of lemonade. I'm so hot right now, I feel like I could drink the whole gallon by myself—"

Coming around the side of the house, she stopped short at the sight of him lying in the hammock. In the time that he'd been staying there, she'd seen him tense, intense, uptight...but never relaxed. Her eyes traveling over the long, lean length of him as he lay stretched out in the hammock under the shade, she couldn't help but think that he should take it easy more often. Even dressed in dirty jeans and a T-shirt that was damp with sweat, his dark hair mussed, he was one good-looking devil. Her heart kicked just at the sight of him. Who would have thought that physical labor would agree with him so well?

"Hey, that looks great!" he said, spying the cookies and lemonade. "Here…let me help you with that."

He jumped up to take the tray from her, and for a split second, they were touching close. Their eyes met, breaths caught, and for a moment, Phoebe thought she saw something flash in his eyes, a spark of heat, that set her heart thumping crazily in her breast. But then he turned away to set the tray on a nearby patio table, and she was sure she must have imagined it.

Irritated with herself—how many times did he have to throw a No Trespassing sign between them before she got the message?—she said stiffly, "I hope you like lemonade. There's some tea in the fridge if you don't."

"Are you kidding? I can have tea any day. This looks great!" Taking the glass she handed him, he swallowed its contents in five seconds flat.

Amazed, Phoebe had to laugh. "Well, that was impressive. Did you even taste it?"

For the first time in days, a smile pulled at the corners of his mouth. "Yeah. Did I mention I was dying of thirst?"

"I would never have guessed," she said dryly, her own mouth twitching with a grin. "Would you like some more?"

For an answer, he grinned and held out his glass.

Just that easily, the mood changed, and the tension that had been standing between them like a brick wall was gone. Sinking back down into the hammock while she claimed an old-fashioned lawn chair, they laughed and talked as they finished off the lemonade and cookies and didn't even realize how much time had passed until they both reached for another cookie and discovered they were all gone. Break time was over.

She knew she was in trouble when she wanted to run inside and dump the entire contents of the cookie jar onto the serving tray. But who could blame her? It had been days since he'd relaxed enough with her even to smile, let alone talk and laugh. She didn't want it to end. Unfortunately, she really did have to get back to work. She still had some last-minute chores to do before her guests arrived.

Knowing that, she still had to force herself to rise to her feet and start collecting the dishes. "I hate to break this up," she told him huskily, "but six o'clock will be here before I'm ready for it, and I've still got a ton of things to do."

The logical, analytical part of Taylor's brain told him that she was right. She had work to do and he would be wise to let her do it. But his brain didn't always function properly whenever she was within touching distance. Especially when she looked so pretty. How she managed that after she'd been working so hard for the last five days, he didn't know. But there was a sparkle in her eyes and smile on her lips, and even though she wore her worst clothes and she had a streak of dirt across her cheek, he couldn't take his eyes off her.

Take a clue from the lady and go back to work, a voice in his head growled. *Now!*

He should have. He'd been successfully keeping his distance all week, and he'd finally worked out his priorities. He'd do well to remember them.

So why was he still lying there in the damn hammock, teasing himself with the sight of her? he wondered, frowning. The answer came all too easily. Because he'd missed her.

That alone should have been enough to send him running for the hills. But when he moved, it wasn't to
run…it was to reach for her.

"Taylor! What are you doing?"

"Something I've been thinking about doing from the
moment I first lay down in this hammock," he growled,
and pulled her down into his arms. Before she could do
anything but gasp, his mouth covered hers.

Every time he held her, kissed her, was better than
the last. Sometime in the future, he knew he was going
to have to deal with that, but not yet. Not when her
body rested softly against him and her legs tangled with
his. Not when he could feel the beat of her heart against
his chest. Not when her mouth opened sweetly under
his and she told him with nothing but her kiss that the
last five days had been just as lonely for her as they
had been for him.

"Come upstairs with me," he rasped, pressing a kiss
to the shell of her ear, then trailing kisses down her
throat, making her moan. "I want to make love to you."

Her senses swimming and her heart pounding,
Phoebe clung to him and tried to remember why she
couldn't do this. There was a reason—a good one—but
she couldn't think when he kissed her, couldn't remember anything but his name. Taylor. She wanted to chant
it, groan it, call it over and over again until the very
rhythm of it echoed in her heart, and it was all because
of him, his kiss, the sure, tender knowledge of his touch.
His hands roamed over her, trailing down her back to
her waist and hips, then back again, stroking her, caressing her, slowly driving her out of her mind with
need.

Aching for more, she felt the hammock shift under
them and only vaguely recalled that they were outside,

in full view of the neighbors and anyone who cared to drive past Myrtle's corner lot, which was right in the middle of town. Somewhere in the back of her mind, the thought registered that they had to stop, but then he kissed her again and the world just seemed to slip away until there was only Taylor and the heat of his kiss on a lazy summer day.

Lost in the magic of his arms, she didn't see Mighty Mouse, the next-door-neighbor's huge black-and-white cat, suddenly dart into the street with no warning, but luckily, the driver of the UPS truck proceeding down the street at a fast clip did. He slammed on the brakes and hit the horn, just missing the cat by inches. Jerked back to her surroundings, Phoebe stiffened. Dear God, what was she doing? she wondered in horror. Nadine Hawkins, the worst gossip in town, lived right next door to Myrtle, and it was common knowledge that she spent half her day looking out the window for something— preferably *someone*—to talk about. Catching Phoebe and Taylor making out in Myrtle's hammock would make her year. Phoebe could hear her now, telling the preacher and the gossip columnist at the town newspaper all about it. Knowing her luck, she'd already called them both.

Mortified at the thought, she pulled free of his arms and scrambled to her feet. "I have to get back to work," she told him. "The guests will be here soon." Her eyes not quite meeting his, she whirled and hurried into the house, hot color turning her cheeks crimson.

You're acting like a sixteen-year-old who got caught necking in the back seat, she told herself sternly, and for the life of her, she didn't know why. So what if Nadine saw them kissing? It wasn't as if she had anything to be ashamed of. It was just a kiss, for heaven's sake! Nothing more.

But as much as she tried to convince herself that there was nothing out of the ordinary about what they'd shared, she knew there was nothing ordinary about Taylor's kiss and the feelings he stirred in her so effortlessly. Every time he touched her, every time he kissed her, every time their eyes met, heat lightning seemed to sizzle between them and she wanted him more and more. And sometime in the not-too-distant future, she was going to have to decide what she was going to do about that.

But not yet, she told herself quickly. She didn't have time to make a decision about Taylor now. She put fresh sheets on all the beds and made sure all the rooms had candles and potpourri and other little touches she knew her guests would appreciate. The pièce de résistance, however, was the apple pie she put in the oven. Her grandmother had taught her a long time ago that there was nothing that made people feel more welcome and at home than the scent of fresh-baked apple pie.

Satisfied that she had everything under control, she hurried upstairs to take a bath. Her guests were scheduled to arrive in less than an hour, but as she settled into the old-fashioned tub and slid down into the steaming hot water so that it could close around her shoulders, she couldn't make herself rush. Not when it seemed as if she'd been moving in Fast Forward for the last two days. Sighing in contentment, she closed her eyes and lay her head back against the rim of the tub.

She couldn't have said when Taylor slipped into her thoughts. He was just there, seducing her with memories of his kiss, his lovemaking, the hot, tender moments in the hammock. Her heart started to pound, her blood to heat, and all she wanted to do was lie there and daydream about him until the water turned cold.

That's when she realized she was in trouble. She had guests who would be there any minute, she reminded herself. She had to stop this!

She tried, but she was fighting a losing battle. When she drained the tub and reached for a towel, she could feel his hands on her. When she stepped in front of the medicine cabinet mirror to comb her hair, all she saw was the dark, turbulent need in her eyes. Frustrated, her heart aching for something she was sure she couldn't have, she forgot all about her wet hair and jerked open the bathroom door, her only thought to escape the emotions that swirled inside her like a storm gathering strength. Instead, she ran full tilt into Taylor, who was, apparently, on his way to his own room across the hall.

"Oh!" Her heart slamming against her ribs, she felt his fingers close around her upper arms and draw her imperceptibly closer. "I need to check on the pie," she said huskily, the need to melt against him almost more than she could bear. "The guests will be here soon, and I want everything to be just right. My whole future could be riding on this weekend."

"I know," he replied softly, drawing her closer still. "I hope you don't mind, but Joe told me all about it."

Surprised, she said, "He did?"

A wry grin tugged at his mouth. "I think he wanted to make sure that I didn't do anything that would ruin this weekend for you." At her look of chagrin, he chuckled. "Relax, Phoebe. I wasn't offended. You're like family to the McBrides—they're just looking out for your interests. I assured Joe that he didn't have to worry. You're very good at what you do, and I'll do everything I can to make sure your guests leave on Sunday singing your praises. Not that that will take much work,'' he added.

With nothing more than words, he touched her heart and set tears welling in her eyes. Embarrassed, she dropped her gaze and tried to shrug off the moment with a self-deprecating laugh. ''You won't be saying that if I burn the pie. I need to check on it.''

He should have let her go, but he couldn't, not when her eyes still glistened with the remnants of tears and she was kissing close. Did she know how soft her skin was under his hands? Or how intoxicating she smelled, fresh from her bath? He'd been thinking of nothing but her since he'd pulled her down into the hammock with him, and that only made him want her more. With a soft groan, he growled, ''In a minute,'' and leaned down to cover her mouth with his.

Sweet. Did she knew how the taste of her went to his head? he wondered, groaning as she kissed him back with a quiet hunger that was nearly his undoing. Given the chance, he would have swept her up in his arms and carried her off to his bed, where he would have spent the rest of the day and night making love to her.

But that wasn't an option, and she knew that as well as he did. ''I have to go,'' she said huskily, pulling out of his arms. ''The guests will be here soon—''

Downstairs, the doorbell rang, startling them both. Horrified, Phoebe looked down at the robe she'd pulled on after her bath. ''Oh, my God! They're here and I'm not even dressed! And the pie! It's going to burn—''

She would have turned and rushed down the stairs, but Taylor caught her by the arm, stopping her in her tracks. ''I'll take care of the pie and the guests. You get dressed. Go,'' he said, gently pushing her toward her room. ''Everything's going to be fine.''

She wanted to argue—it was her responsibility to take care of her guests—but she knew he was right. If she rushed downstairs like a madwoman and greeted the new arrivals in nothing but a robe while the pie burned in the oven, Myrtle would probably never again have another paying guest.

"I'll be down as quickly as I can," she assured him, hurrying toward her room. "Give me five minutes."

It was more like ten minutes than five before she made her way downstairs, but she quickly discovered that Taylor had everything well in hand. The pie was cooling on a wire rack in the kitchen, and Taylor was visiting with an older couple in the front parlor. Surprised, Phoebe stopped short at the sight of them. She was expecting two couples...the Coopers and the Winstons, both of whom were newlyweds. She had forgotten that Myrtle had told her that the Coopers were octogenarians.

Spying her in the doorway, Taylor turned to her with a smile, his brown eyes twinkling. "Here's Phoebe now. Phoebe, this is Lawrence Cooper and his bride, Doris. They just got married this morning in Albuquerque."

Doris Cooper grinned. "I know, dear. Isn't it outrageous, two old-timers like us getting married? But it was better that than living in sin. Our children would have had a stroke!"

Liking her immediately, Phoebe had to laugh. "I think it's wonderful. How long have you two known each other?"

"Since I was an MP in the Second World War," Lawrence said with a boyish flash of dimples. "She was a WAC who stole my heart, then got shipped to England. I hadn't seen her in fifty years, then suddenly she tracked me down on the Internet two months ago, after her husband died. We've been together ever since.''

"Our kids wanted to send us on a cruise," Doris confided, "but we didn't care about all that. We just wanted to go somewhere quiet where we could just relax and enjoy each other." Glancing around at the parlor, which Myrtle had decorated so beautifully with exquisite antiques, she smiled. "This is perfect. It reminds me of my grandmother's house."

"It *is* my grandmother's house," Phoebe told her. "She's on a cross-country trip right now, but she'll be pleased that you like it. Can I show you to your room? I gave you the suite overlooking the garden. It gets the morning sun."

"Oh, that would be lovely," Doris said. "I love waking up with the sun. How early is breakfast served, dear? Can we have coffee in our room?"

"Of course," Phoebe said easily as she led the way to the stairs. "I'm usually up by five-thirty. All of our pastries and bread are made from scratch each morning, so I have to get an early start. The first rolls are usually ready by seven, but I start the coffee the minute I come downstairs. I can send some up to your room if you'd like. Just call me on the house phone when you wake up."

Following with the luggage as Phoebe and the Coopers made their way upstairs, Taylor couldn't help but marvel at the way Phoebe treated the older couple. She was as comfortable with them as if she'd known them their entire lives, rather than a matter of moments, so consequently they were completely at ease. Lawrence shared a joke with her, Doris asked if she could trade recipes with her, and by the time they reached their room, Phoebe knew the names and ages of all their grandchildren.

Amazed, Taylor had to smile when she invited the older couple to join her and Taylor for dinner and they eagerly accepted. How had she known that they would want company for dinner? They were on their honeymoon, for heaven's sake! But they did seem to enjoy meeting and talking to people, and they must have recognized a kindred spirit in Phoebe. How could they not? She was a natural.

The Winstons, however, were a completely different kettle of fish. Phoebe had hardly settled the Coopers in their suite when the other couple arrived. Young and obviously very much in love, Peter and Heather Winston were quiet and private, but Phoebe was still able to draw them out as she showed them to their room. "I was going to put you in the bridal suite on the second floor, but I really think you'll enjoy the third-floor suite more. You'll have the entire floor to yourself, and you'll also have a great view of the mountains. You're going to have to climb two flights of stairs, though. If that's a problem, the second-floor suite is just as nice."

The decision was theirs. The bride and groom exchanged a silent look, and suddenly, hot color was rising in their cheeks. "This third floor will be fine," Peter Winston said huskily.

Carrying up their luggage, Taylor liked to think that he was an astute man, but he had to admit that it had never crossed his mind that the young newlyweds might be worried about their privacy—after all, the old Victorian house was huge. Still, the Winstons were young—they looked as if they were barely out of high school—and this was their first night together as man and wife. Phoebe had not only sensed that they were nervous about spending their wedding night right down the hall from a house full of strangers, but she'd also tactfully found a way to make them more comfortable without stating the obvious.

"If you need anything, just let me know," she added as Taylor set their luggage just inside the door of their suite. "And champagne and dinner will be served at seven, compliments of the inn. If you'd like, you can have it on the balcony outside your room. It's no trouble to send it up to you—there's a dumbwaiter in the hall right outside your room. When you're finished, you can set your tray of dishes back in the dumbwaiter and send it back down to the kitchen."

"Oh, that sounds great!" Heather said. "I've never been in a house with a dumbwaiter."

"Then why don't I send everything up a little before seven?" Phoebe suggested with a smile. "A buzzer will sound in the hall when it reaches your floor."

Just that easily, Phoebe offered the young couple complete privacy. Watching her, seeing the smiles on her guests' faces, Taylor found himself incredibly proud of her. Just a week ago, that would have scared the hell out of him. Always a cautious man, he'd never allowed himself to get involved enough in a woman's life to feel anything other than desire and liking for her. For no other reason than that, he should have taken a step back from Phoebe and immediately put their relationship back on a less personal level. But the more he got to know her, the more she fascinated him. Considering that, the last thing he could do now was step back.

So, when she went back downstairs to begin the meal for all the newlyweds, he didn't retreat to his room as he normally would have. Instead, he lit the candles in the front parlor and dining-room, then built a fire in the dining room fireplace. It might have been the middle of June, but the nights were cool, and considering the newlyweds in the house, the evening seemed to call for the romance of a fire.

"Oh, that's nice!" Phoebe said with a pleased smile when she stepped into the dining room carrying a tray of hors d'oeuvres and found the room aglow with candlelight. "Doris is going to love it."

"She seems like an easy touch when it comes to romance. Does your grandmother have any music? It's a good night for a little Frank Sinatra."

"According to my grandmother, it's always a good night for a little Frankie," she retorted with a grin. "The music cabinet in the front parlor is filled with his albums. Take your pick."

Taylor had never considered himself a romantic—he'd never felt the need to give a woman hearts and flowers and candlelight—but he found himself enjoying the idea of setting the stage for Doris's wedding night. Poor Lawrence wasn't going to know what hit him.

Grinning at the thought, he found a Sinatra album he instinctively knew Doris would love and immediately started the phonograph. Within minutes, the familiar strains of Frank Sinatra drifted through the downstairs. Almost immediately, Doris and Lawrence appeared in the doorway of the front parlor. Her blue eyes sparkling with delight, Doris grinned at Taylor, who she caught in the act of adjusting the volume. "Don't touch that dial, young man! Us old folks don't hear as well as we used to."

"Old folks, my eye," Taylor retorted, his brown eyes glinting with humor. "You won't be old when you're ninety, Mrs. Cooper."

"That's Doris to you," she replied sweetly. "How did you know I liked Frank Sinatra?"

"All the best people do," he said simply, grinning. "And just for the record, I wasn't turning it down. I was turning it up."

"A wise man," Lawrence said with a wink. "She can turn nasty when anyone gets between her and Frank Sinatra."

"My grandmother's the same way," Phoebe said from the dining room as she stepped from the kitchen with an ice bucket and a bottle of chilled champagne. "Come to think of it, I'm pretty fond of Old Blue Eyes, myself. There's just something about the way he sings a love song. Speaking of which—"

"What?" Taylor teased. "Love songs?"

"Love," she corrected him, offering champagne to the newlyweds, then Taylor. "I think it's time for a toast." With a smile at the Coopers, she held up her glass. "To love…"

"And marriage," Taylor added, raising his glass.

"And Viagra," Lawrence said with a wicked smile.

"Lawrence!"

"What?" he asked with pretended innocence when his wife tried to frown reprovingly. "I bought stock in the company. I hope it goes up."

For a moment, no one said a word. Then Doris's eyes met those of her new husband and she giggled. "Me, too."

Phoebe couldn't remember the last time she'd laughed so much…or enjoyed an evening more. When she came downstairs the next morning at five-thirty to start the coffee cakes and pastries that Myrtle had taught her to make when she was just a child, she was still grinning over the stories Doris and Lawrence had told over dinner. If she ever got married, she hoped she was lucky enough to have the same type of relationship the Coopers shared. They were made for each other.

"Good morning."

Lost in her thoughts as she gathered the ingredients she would need for the morning baking, she jumped, her heart in her throat, and whirled to find Taylor standing in the kitchen doorway. "Oh! You startled me! I didn't think anyone else was awake. Did you want some coffee? It'll just take a minute—"

"No, I'll do it," he said, and stepped toward the pantry at the same time she did.

Phoebe couldn't have said who bumped into whom, but suddenly, Taylor's hands were on her arms, holding her just inches away from him, and her body was humming with need. Her heart pounding, she only had to look into his eyes to know that he felt it, too, that same, familiar need that haunted her dreams and made her ache for him whenever he stepped into her thoughts.

"I'll make the coffee," he said huskily. "You concentrate on your baking. I'll help with the rest of the meal. What do you need done? Is it too early to cook the bacon? Or were you going to serve sausage? What's on the menu?"

Phoebe couldn't have been more surprised if he'd stood on his hands and done a back flip right there in her grandmother's kitchen. "You know how to cook?"

"Watch it, sweetheart," he said with a grin. "That remark was more than a little bit sexist. Of course I can cook. My mother believed that a man should know how to cook and clean and take care of himself. I may not be a gourmet, but I can handle bacon and eggs, and I make a damn good hollandaise."

Surprised, she arched a brow at him. "Your mother taught you to make hollandaise?"

"Actually, I worked in a restaurant when I was in college," he admitted with a wry grin. "So what would you like me to do? Bacon and eggs? Hollandaise? Or my specialty…cinnamon toast?"

"All of the above," she replied, flashing her dimples at him, "but you need to hold off on the eggs and toast until the newlyweds buzz for their coffee. In the meantime, you could squeeze some fresh orange juice for me, if you wouldn't mind. The oranges are in the refrigerator."

"No problem," he said easily. "But first, I'll start the coffee."

He strode over to the pantry as if he'd lived there all his life, and, within minutes, he had the coffee perking in the coffeemaker and fresh juice squeezed. Without having to ask what needed to be done next, he washed strawberries and grapes for a fresh fruit platter, then cored a pineapple with the skill of a sous chef.

Busy with her pastries, Phoebe tried to concentrate on her own work, but he made that nearly impossible. There was just something so sexy about a man who knew his way around the kitchen. She'd never seen him so relaxed before. He hummed "Strangers in the Night" under his breath, and every time he came within touching distance of her, he seemed to brush up against her.

Her blood heating, she told herself the first time it was just an accident, but it happened a second time, then a third. Looking up from the pastry dough she was rolling out, she wasn't surprised to find him watching her with dark eyes that glinted with amusement. He was flirting with her, she realized, and started to smile.

Cocking her head at him, she lifted a delicately arched brow. "What are you doing?"

"Nothing," he said innocently, only to dip a finger in the bowl of flour on the kitchen island, then playfully draw a smudge down her nose. "What did you think I was doing?"

"Oh, nothing," she replied with a shrug, then slipped around him to retrieve a loaf pan from the cabinet behind him. As she returned to her work station at the kitchen island, she trailed her fingers down the back of his neck and grinned when he caught his breath. He wasn't the only one who could flirt.

She was a witch, Taylor thought, swallowing a silent groan. A beautiful, tempting, sensuous witch. Over the course of the next few hours, she took his own game and turned it back on him, teasing and flirting with him until he was so hot for her, he could hardly string two sentences together without help. And he loved it. She made him want her with just a smile. And during breakfast, when her foot played with his under the table and she smiled at him with mischief in her eyes, all he wanted to do was sweep her up in his arms and carry her upstairs to his room.

There was, however, no time for loving. Once both newlywed couples had had breakfast and the dishes were done, she had a busy day running her grandmother's antique store. Locals, as well as tourists on their way to Aspen stopped in to browse and buy, and the old-fashioned cash register rang on and off throughout the late morning and early afternoon.

Taylor knew he should have kept up his pretense of doing research and made himself scarce for the day, but he couldn't bring himself to leave Phoebe. He was enjoying her company too much. She visited with tourists as if they were old friends, greeted locals with true affection, and invited them all into the shop as though she was inviting guests into her home. She even set out a platter of homemade cookies for anyone who might be hungry!

Amused and delighted with her lack of pretension, Taylor volunteered to carry out the customer's purchases to their cars, just like a proud husband helping his wife. That's when he knew he was in trouble.

When had he got so caught up in her life that he forgot his own? he wondered with a scowl. He was in Liberty Hill for one reason and one reason only—to make the McBrides pay for what Gus had done to his mother—and lately, he had even begun to question the wisdom of that. Everything had seemed so clear when he'd first arrived in town, but now, he didn't know what to do. And that annoyed the hell out of him. He was a decisive man, or at least, he always had been in the past. He still felt that his brothers and sisters needed to know what kind of man their father had been, but he was beginning to wonder if telling them would really serve any purpose. They were going to believe what they wanted to believe, regardless of what he said, and he couldn't blame them for that. They'd known Gus all of their lives growing up—he was their father. The odds were better than good that they'd known him better than even his mother had.

Disturbed, troubled, he needed some time to think, to decide what he wanted to do, and he couldn't do that helping Phoebe with her grandmother's antique store. "I've got some errands to do," he told her gruffly after carrying out a set of Windsor chairs for a woman. "Can you get someone to carry out the heavier objects if I'm gone for a few hours?''

"Of course," she assured him. "Is everything okay? You look...upset."

"I'm fine," he assured her. "I've just got some things to take care of. I'll be back in a couple of hours."

Not giving her a chance to ask questions he wasn't prepared to answer, he made a quick exit and headed for his car. A few minutes later, he found himself taking the road from town that led to his father's ranch, and he couldn't even say why. He just knew he had to go there.

Chapter 9

The ranch was deserted; there wasn't a McBride anywhere in sight. Normally, Taylor wouldn't have felt comfortable trespassing on someone else's property without at least getting their permission first, but Joe and Zeke had made it clear on a number of occasions that he was welcome to look around as much as he liked. Without even thinking about it, he headed straight for the family cemetery.

Nestled under the trees, high on a hill overlooking the homestead, it was just as he'd remembered it…quiet, peaceful, ageless. In the valley below, the house that had been home to countless McBrides was a testament to the survival of the family, but here on the hillside, time was measured not in years, but in the graves.

Surrounded by silence, Taylor stood under the old pine tree that hovered protectively over his father's grave and waited for the old bitterness and anger to twist in his gut, just as it always did whenever he thought of Gus McBride. This time, however, he was stunned to discover that the only emotion he felt was regret. Regret that he'd never had a chance to know the man his brothers and sisters called Dad. Regret that he'd never shared a holiday with him or a birthday. Regret that Gus McBride had died without ever knowing that his eldest son existed—because everything would have been different if he had.

Pain squeezed his heart at the thought of what might have been. Before he'd come to Liberty Hill, he'd have sworn that nothing could ever change his opinion of Gus McBride. As far as he was concerned, he was a deadbeat father and the biggest loser in the world. He had to be—otherwise, he would have come for him and his mother and taken them out of the nightmare of poverty they'd lived in for all of Taylor's childhood.

His brothers and sisters, however, had shown him that Gus had been nothing like the monster he'd thought he was. He'd been loving and giving and had always been there for his wife and children. After hearing the stories of what a good man he'd been, Taylor was forced to come to only one conclusion. The only reason Gus hadn't been there for him was because he hadn't known of his existence. How could he hate him for that when his mother was the one who'd chosen not to tell him she was pregnant?

With that realization, a load lifted from his shoulders, and he was stunned by the emotions that swamped him like a tidal wave. How long had he hated his father for what he'd done to his mother? It seemed like forever, but the truth was, his mother had never shared his feelings for Gus. In fact, she'd loved him until the day she died…because she'd known he was a man worth loving.

Why had it taken him so long to see that? To realize that he didn't have to hate him, either?

Years. He'd wasted years, made himself bitter and churned with anger. He'd thought revenge would heal the gaping wound in his heart, but he realized now that revenge was a double-edged sword. He was tired of the hate, the anger, the resentment. He wanted a relationship with his family, with the brothers and sisters he hadn't had the opportunity to know as a child. And to do that, he had to tell them who he was. It was the right thing to do. The question was…how was he going to break the news to them after lying to them for weeks?

He would find a way, he promised himself as he returned to his car and headed back to town. He wasn't going to lose the only family he had left now that he'd realized how much they meant to him.

The heady scent of flowers floated on the warm summer breeze, along with the quiet hum of honey bees as they busily worked their way through the garden that was just steps away from the dining room's French doors. For as long as Phoebe could remember, Myrtle had talked about thinning out the overgrown plants and bringing some order to the flowers that had taken over the yard years ago, but her granddaughter was thankful that she never had. Roses and rhododendrons, daisies and black-eyed Susans, plus dozens of other blooms that Phoebe didn't know the names of, created a profusion of colors that looked like a Monet painting.

Happily cutting flowers for the dining room and front parlor, their heady scent teasing her senses, Phoebe was unaware that she had company until she heard a step on the crushed gravel path behind her. Startled, she turned to find Taylor heading straight for her, and images of the last time they'd been alone together in the backyard swirled in her head. Almost immediately, her heartbeat jumped into a crazy rhythm, and all she wanted to do was walk into his arms. A quick look at the house next door, however, kept her right where she was. Nadine was working in her own garden and watching everything that was going on in the neighborhood. She must have had super-human hearing, because the second Taylor walked through the side gate, she looked up and made no effort to hide the fact that she was watching both him and Phoebe like a hawk.

Taylor noticed—he shot the older woman a quick look—but if he was concerned by her nosiness, he gave no sign of it. Giving Phoebe a smile that warmed her heart, he said, ''Hi, sweetheart. Can I help you with that?'' And with no more warning than that, he strode up to her, leaned over and kissed her on the side of the neck.

She melted—there was no other way to describe it— and completely forgot about Nadine. ''Hi, yourself,'' she said huskily and stepped into his arms for a hug. ''I was just cutting some fresh flowers for the house,'' she said with a smile as she drew back. ''What have you been up to?''

''Not much,'' he said easily. ''I just went for a drive.''

Her eyes searching his, Phoebe immediately sensed that something was different about him, but she couldn't quite put her finger on what it was. He looked just as he always did, only…more relaxed. And that was a rarity for Taylor. From the moment he'd first knocked at her grandmother's front door, his intensity had been impossible to ignore.

Cocking her head, she frowned. ''That must have

been some drive. You look like you don't have a care in the world. What's going on?''

He shrugged, his smile turning wicked as he drew her back into his arms. "Nothing. Can't a man spend some time with a beautiful woman in a garden without raising a fuss?''

"Of course, but—"

"But Mrs. Hawkins is watching," he said with a grin. "She's not going to stop me from kissing you, you know. I've been thinking about it for hours.''

"Taylor…"

"Say it again," he murmured, kissing the side of her neck again. "I love it when your voice gets all husky when you say my name.''

She shouldn't have. She would only encourage him and she needed to keep her head about her. And Nadine *was* watching! But when he whispered her name and trailed a string of kisses across her cheek to her mouth, she could no more resist him than she could stop her heart from thundering at his touch. With a sigh that was his name, she slipped her arms around his neck and kissed him back with a hunger that matched his own.

That's when it hit her. Nadine might be watching…or the entire population of Liberty Hill…it didn't matter. She was never going to be able to summon any defenses against him, even though she knew he was going to break her heart.

In the past, that realization alone would have been enough to send her running into the house to think about the hurt she was opening herself up to. But she didn't want to think about the future, didn't want even to contemplate the day he drove out of her life and returned to California. He was going to leave her with a broken heart, regardless of when he left, and worrying about that wasn't going to change anything. In the meantime, they had today. Nothing else mattered.

Pulling back, she smiled up at him with her heart in her eyes. "As much as I'm sure Nadine is enjoying the show, I think we should take this upstairs—"

"My sentiments exactly," he said and grabbed her hand to pull her with him toward the house.

Tugging against his hold, she laughed, "Wait! I didn't mean now. I have to finish cutting flowers and meet with Heather and Doris in the kitchen at four. We're making strawberry jam. Then I have to start dinner."

Too late, he remembered her guests and wanted to kick himself. She was right, dammit! As much as he didn't want to think of anything but her and how he wanted to spend the rest of the afternoon making love to her, she had a responsibility to her guests that could not be ignored. Their own plans would have to wait.

But only until tonight, he promised himself. As soon as her guests had retired to their own rooms, Phoebe was his. For the rest of the night.

Grinning ruefully, he said, "See what you do to me! I lost my head, and it's all your fault."

"Thank you," she replied with twinkling eyes. "I do what I can."

And she was damn good at it, the little flirt. Fighting the need to sweep her up into his arms and carry her off to bed, he growled, "Shall we make a date for later?"

"Ten o'clock sounds good to me. How about you?"

"Ten it is. My room or yours?"

"Mine," she said promptly. "I'll wear something special." With nothing more than a few simple words, she conjured up an image that heated his blood, then gathered up her flowers and hurried inside. Already aching for her, the feel of her lips still warm against his cheek, Taylor stared after her like a man who hadn't seen a woman in a decade. How, he wondered, groaning, was he going to make it until ten o'clock without going quietly out of his mind?

Four hours later, he was still wondering the same thing. The strawberry jam had been made hours ago, dinner was cooked and eaten and the hands of the clock on the mantel in the front parlor seemed frozen in time. He'd been watching them on and off for the past thirty minutes and he'd have sworn they hadn't moved at all.

"Are you all right, Taylor?" Doris asked as she finished telling the story about how Lawrence had asked her to marry him with a cookie bouquet. "You keep looking at the clock."

Caught in the act, Taylor swallowed a silent curse and forced a smile. "Sorry. I'm waiting for ten o'clock. I'm supposed to take some medication."

"Oh, I know how that is," she said, sympathizing. "If you don't take things exactly on time, it can screw up your whole system. I told Lawrence that's why he's dizzy all the time—he never pays attention to the clock. Didn't I tell you that, honey? You need to listen to Taylor. What are you taking, Taylor? Or would you rather not say? I'll talk about anything, but some people like to keep their medical conditions private...."

Fighting a smile, Taylor doubted there was much of anything that Doris kept private, but all he said was, "I really would rather not talk about it. I wouldn't want to raise any eyebrows."

From the corner of his eye, he saw Phoebe bite back a quick smile and wasn't surprised that she'd guessed *she* was the private medical condition he didn't want to talk about. If her eyes had met his, he was sure Doris would have guessed that his clock-watching had nothing to do with medication and everything to do with a date with the lady of the house, but Phoebe luckily kept her gaze focused on the older woman.

Making a quick exit while he could, he rose abruptly to his feet. "I'm sorry to cut the evening short, but it is nearly ten. So if you'll excuse me, I'll say good night. I'll see you all in the morning."

"That's all right, dear," Doris assured him as she, too, rose. "It's time we turned in, too. We've got a long drive ahead of us tomorrow. We need to get a good night's sleep. Thank you for a wonderful evening, Phoebe. Dinner was fantastic."

"My pleasure," Phoebe said with a smile. "I'm glad you enjoyed it."

Good-nights were exchanged, then while Phoebe was locking up, the older couple followed Taylor up the stairs and made their way to their room at the end of the hall. Slipping into his own room, Taylor glanced at his watch and wondered how long it would take Phoebe to slip into the special outfit she'd teasingly promised to wear. He'd give her ten minutes, and she'd be lucky to get that. He'd already waited hours for her. He couldn't wait much longer.

His imagination running wild at the thought of what she planned to wear, he didn't notice the disturbance that had erupted down the hall from his room until Doris cried, "Help! Somebody help us! Lawrence fell!"

Taylor didn't wait to hear more. Jerking open his door, he ran out into the hall and reached the Coopers' room just as Phoebe hurried up the back stairs from the kitchen. "What happened?" she asked as she and Taylor followed Doris into the suite, where they found Lawrence flat on his back just inside the open bathroom door. "Oh, my God! Lawrence, are you okay? Where did all this water come from? Did the tub overflow?"

"A pipe broke under the sink," he said, only to groan as he struggled to sit up. "It was already all over the floor when we stepped into our room. I was trying to find the shut-off valve when I slipped."

Frowning, Taylor stepped over to the sink and took a quick look. "The break's below the shut-off valve," he said grimly. "The water will have to be cut off outside. Where's the cutoff?"

"Out by the street, next to the front gate," Phoebe said as she hurriedly moved to Lawrence's side when he tried to stand up. "Maybe you shouldn't get up just yet. You took quite a fall."

"She's right," Taylor said with a frown. "You should see a doctor. Let me turn the water off and I'll drive you to the hospital. Just to make sure you didn't crack a bone or something."

"Aw, heck," the older man grumbled, "the only thing I cracked was my pride. A man doesn't like to make a fool of himself on his honeymoon."

"But you could have seriously hurt yourself," Phoebe argued, "and I feel responsible. Let me at least call Janey McBride and have her check you out. She's a nurse and will know if you need X rays."

"I don't need a nurse to check me out," he said stubbornly. "I just jarred my bones. Ask Doris. She'll tell you I'm a tough old goat."

Her smile worried, Doris nodded. "He's like that watch that keeps on ticking when you hit it with a hammer. But he's not as young as he used to be," she added, shooting her new husband a frown. "And he's all wet. I've got to find him something to wear."

She turned toward their suitcases, which they'd left on the floor, only to notice that they were sitting in a puddle of water. "Oh, no! Our clothes! We had everything packed except our night-clothes and what we were going to wear tomorrow when we leave."

"Don't worry," Phoebe assured her as she slipped her arm around her to give her a hug. "I'll throw everything into the dryer for you and find a way to dry your luggage. In the meantime, we've got to move you to another room, and you can help Lawrence change into his pajamas."

"But I thought all the suites were taken," Doris said, surprised.

"They are, but you can have my room," she replied easily. "I can move into my grandmother's room. Just give me a few minutes to collect my things. Taylor, there's a flashlight in the utility closet under the stairs. While you're turning off the water, I'll help them make the move to my room."

"No problem," he replied. "Then I'll let the Winstons know about the pipe breaking and call a plumber for you."

Relieved that he was there to help her, Phoebe hurried down the hall and breezed through her room, snatching up things she would need for the night and putting away items that would be in the Coopers' way. It took all of two minutes to change the sheets and hang fresh towels in the bathroom across the hall, then she rushed to her grandmother's room and dropped her things right inside the door. By the time she made it back to the older couple's suite, Doris had found a dry towel and draped it over her husband's shoulders. He was standing on his own, but he was pale and obviously still shaken.

"Lawrence, are you sure you're all right?" she asked worriedly. "I just feel so badly about this."

"You didn't have anything to do with that pipe breaking," he pointed out reasonably, "so don't beat yourself up over it. I'll admit I'm a little stiff, but who's not at my age? I'm fine, dear. Quit your worrying. Doris'll rub a little Ben-Gay on my back and I'll be good as new in the morning."

Phoebe doubted that he'd get over the fall quite that easily, but she couldn't very well force him to see a doctor if he didn't want to. "I hope so," she said, "but if you start feeling worse, I want you to let me know immediately."

"If he doesn't, I will," Doris promised as Phoebe escorted them to her room. "Thank you so much, sweetie, for all your help. When I saw Lawrence fall, I was scared to death."

Phoebe could well understand that—she'd felt the same way. Impulsively hugging them both, she said, "I don't want either one of you to worry about anything. I'll take care of your clothes and see that everything's dry. And the water'll be turned back on as soon as possible."

Her mind already jumping to everything she had to do, she quickly wished them goodnight and hurried down the hall to the utility closet next to their suite. Taylor had turned off the water, but the broken pipe was only the beginning of the problem. Grabbing her grandmother's shop vacuum, which had been bought for just such an emergency, she went to work extracting the water from the bathroom and bedroom floors.

By the time the plumber had fixed the pipe, Phoebe

had vacuumed up all the water and Taylor had rolled up the sodden rag rug and carried it outside to dry, it was going on midnight. And Phoebe still had to wash and dry two suitcases of the Coopers' clothes. If she was lucky, she might be finished by two or three in the morning.

"Can I help?"

In the process of putting the first load of clothes in the washer, Phoebe looked up to find Taylor standing in the laundry-room doorway. Smiling tiredly, she said, "Not really. But thanks for all your help. If you hadn't been here, I don't know what I would have done."

"You'd have done fine, but I'm glad I could help. You look beat. Are you sure you can't do those things in the morning? It's been a long night, and you have to be up early to start breakfast."

"Don't tempt me," she began, only to remember the plans they'd made for the evening. Her eyes widening, she said, "Oh, Taylor, I'm so sorry! I completely forgot about our plans."

"It's okay," he assured her, his grin rueful. "You had other things on your mind. There'll be another time."

She hoped so, but time was slipping through their fingers. Soon, her grandmother would return and she would have to go home and decide what she was going to do with the rest of her life. How could she even contemplate a future without Taylor? Pain squeezed her heart at the thought.

"I wanted to be with you," she said huskily, honestly, tears squeezing from her eyes. "I had this special nightgown—"

Eliminating the space between them with a single step, he stopped her simply by gently pressing his hand to her mouth. "Stop," he rasped. "Don't ruin the surprise. We'll get another chance." And leaning down, he shushed her with a kiss.

In the days and weeks she'd known him, she'd lost track of the number of times he'd kissed her, but none of his kisses had ever been anything like the one he gave her at that moment. Hot and sweet and oh, so tender, it called out to her heart in a way no other kiss ever had and said things she was afraid to put into words. Tears pooling in her eyes as he lifted his head and slowly released her, all she wanted to do was melt into his arms. She knew if she did, however, she'd never finish cleaning the Coopers' clothes. Considering how close Lawrence had come to seriously hurting himself, that was the least she could do for him and Doris in compensation.

"I'll see you in the morning," he said huskily. "Call me if you need me."

She needed him more than he could possibly imagine, more than she was prepared to admit, but all she could manage to say was a quiet, "Good night."

Later, she couldn't have said how long it took her to finish drying the Coopers' clothes. As the hours lengthened and the quiet of the night settled over the house, all she could think of was Taylor, upstairs in bed without her. She'd never been so lonely in her life.

Taylor knew the exact moment Phoebe came upstairs—it was going on three o'clock in the morning and there was no question that she was exhausted. Her steps were slow and heavy as she quietly made her way down the hall to her grandmother's room.

Considering the circumstances, no one would have blamed her if she'd slept late the next morning, but she didn't shirk her duties so easily. Not long after dawn, the scent of fresh-baked bread drifted through the house, quietly waking him and the other guests one by one.

And though Taylor half expected to find her bleary-eyed and tired, he should have known better. Dressed in a soft white blouse and a feminine yellow skirt with a little frill at the hem, she looked rested and relaxed and incredibly beautiful. She greeted the Coopers and Winstons with an easy smile and pastries that would have done a gourmet chef proud. Just looking at her, no one would have guessed that she'd only had a few hours sleep.

She was amazing, Taylor thought, and was glad he wasn't the only one who appreciated her. Biting into a raspberry Danish, Doris closed her eyes and sighed dreamily. "Oh, that's so good! I don't know how you do it, Phoebe, dear. I could never have made this kind of breakfast after only three hours' sleep. You have to be exhausted!"

Grinning, Phoebe shrugged. "I'll admit my brain's not operating on all cylinders, but I'm okay. I can catch up on my sleep later. I wanted to make sure that all of you had a good breakfast before you left."

"This is better than good," Lawrence assured her, popping another Danish into his mouth. "It's fantastic! I bet I gained five pounds this weekend."

"I'm glad you enjoyed it," she replied with twinkling eyes.

"Oh, we more than enjoyed it," Lawrence said. "We're going to tell all our friends about this place. We've had a wonderful time."

"We have, too," Heather Winston said shyly as she and her husband exchanged a loving smile. "My parents are celebrating their twenty-fifth anniversary in

September. I'm going to tell them to come here. They'll love it.''

''We'd love to have them,'' Phoebe said, pleased. ''I probably won't be here then—I've got to go back to my real job, unfortunately—but my grandmother will. I'm sure your parents will love her. She'll make them feel right at home.''

''The question is…how good a cook is she?'' Lawrence asked with a teasing grin. ''If she can't make Danish like you can, there's no point in coming.''

''She taught me everything I know about cooking and baking,'' Phoebe assure him. ''That's one of the reasons she asked me to take over for her while she was on vacation. I'm the only one she knows who can cook like she does.''

''You're also her granddaughter and she trusts you with everything she owns,'' Doris said. ''Not to mention the fact that she must love you dearly.''

Unable to argue with that logic, Phoebe flashed her dimples at her. ''I'm her favorite granddaughter.''

''And her only one, I'll bet,'' Taylor added teasingly.

''That has nothing to do with anything,'' she tossed back, grinning. ''I'd be her favorite if she had a dozen granddaughters. We're very much alike.''

''Then I'm sure she's a wonderful person,'' Doris said with a smile. ''She certainly has a fantastic house. I wish we could stay longer, but Lawrence has a dentist's appointment tomorrow, so we've got to get back.''

''We do, too,'' Peter Winston said. ''We've both got to go back to work tomorrow, and we don't want to get home late. It's a six-hour drive, so we'd better get going.''

That's just what Taylor had been waiting to hear.

Rising quickly to his feet, he said, "I'll help you carry your luggage out."

Fifteen minutes later, the newlyweds said their good-byes, traded hugs as if they were all family and drove away. Feeling as though she was walking on air, Phoebe couldn't stop smiling. In spite of the near disaster last night with the broken pipe, the weekend had turned out to be amazingly successful. And the Coopers and Winstons were going to tell all their friends and family what a wonderful time they'd had. There was no better advertising than word of mouth!

Thrilled, Phoebe couldn't wait to tell her grandmother. They were a hit! But the second Taylor followed her back inside the house and shut the front door, she threw herself into his arms. "Thank you, thank you, thank you!"

Laughing, he pulled her close. "For what?"

"All your help, of course!"

"But you were the one who did all the work," he pointed out. "And last night, you were incredible. All I did was call the plumber—"

"And turn the water off and move the furniture and help me get the rug up," she finished for him. "I'm sure I would have panicked if you hadn't kept your head the way you had. I could just see the Coopers telling all their friends that the place had leaky old pipes and they'd be taking their lives in their hands if they went anywhere near it."

"Are you kidding? That was never going to happen. They were crazy about you. And nobody blamed you for the pipe breaking. It could have happened to anyone."

"Maybe," she acknowledged. "But you still were a

big help all weekend. Except for the pipe breaking, everything was perfect...because every time I turned around, you were there to help me. Thank you." Giving into impulse, she rose up on tiptoe and kissed him sweetly on the lips.

How long had he been waiting for just such a moment? Taylor had long since lost track. He just knew he had to have her...now! Burying his hands in her hair, he slanted his mouth over hers and kissed her as though he was starving for the taste of her. Then, before she could do anything but gasp, he swept her up in his arms and started up the stairs.

"Taylor! What are you doing?"

"Carrying you up to bed," he said promptly. "We're both a little late for the date we made last night, but better late than never."

"But it's not even ten o'clock in the morning!" she protested.

"So? What has that got to do with anything?"

When he put it that way and gave her that dark, hungry look that always made her go weak at the knees, there was no way she could resist him. "Not a damn thing," she replied, then laughed and threw her arms around his neck. "I like the way you think, Mr. Bishop."

"So do I," he retorted with a grin as he reached the second floor and turned down the hall to her room. "Now, Ms. Chandler, I believe you mentioned last night that you were going to wear something special for our date. How long will it take you to get ready?"

She didn't even have to think about it. "Two minutes."

Setting her on her feet just outside her grandmother's

room, where her things still were, he grinned. "The clock's ticking."

He would have given her more time if she'd asked for it, and if they'd been able to keep their date last night as planned, she certainly would have taken more than two minutes to get ready, but it seemed as if it had been ages since they'd had any time alone together, and even longer than that since he'd made love to her. Suddenly, all she wanted was to be with him, but she had promised to wear something special. "I'll meet you in your room," she promised huskily, and shut the door in his face.

Alone in his room, Taylor didn't need to set the mood for himself—he'd dreamed of her, reached for her in the night more times than he could remember—but making love with her wasn't just about him. No woman had ever captivated him the way she had, and he needed to show her that. So he hurried down the hall to the closet where he knew supplies for the inn were stored, then rushed back to his room.

Five minutes later, when she knocked at his door, he was ready for her. When he opened the door, he felt his heart stop in his chest. He'd seen her in dozens of different situations: lying on a sleeping bag under the stars in the mountains, baking in the kitchen, her cheeks dusted with flour, and then there was that night she had stepped into the hall still damp from her bath and dressed for bed. She'd stolen his breath every time. That didn't begin to describe what she did to him today.

Dressed in a cream-colored antique satin gown, her blond hair falling in a golden wave past her shoulders, she looked as if she'd just stepped out of a dream from the past. Every beautiful inch of her was covered. The full sleeves of her gown were gathered at her slender wrists, spilling lace onto her hands, and the long skirt just brushed her bare toes. The bodice was made of lace, but here, too, every sweet inch of her was covered, all the way to her throat.

She looked incredibly beautiful, incredibly feminine, incredibly sexy. Taylor took one look at her and forgot his own name. "My God, you're gorgeous!"

A shy smile curled the corners of her mouth. "Thank you. I thought you might appreciate it."

"Sweetheart, that's an understatement," he said hoarsely, and reached for her.

She melted into his arms and only then noticed the changes he had made to the room. "Oh, Taylor! It's beautiful!"

He grinned ruefully. "I sort of raided your supply closet. I hope you don't mind."

"Mind?" she said incredulously. "No one's ever done anything like this for me before." Glancing past him again, tears pooled in her eyes at the sight of the dozens of candles that cast a soft romantic glow over the room in spite of the fact that the late-morning sun streamed through the windows. "It's beautiful," she said again, this time in a husky whisper.

"Don't cry," he murmured, leaning down to kiss away the tears that spilled over her lashes and trailed down her cheek. "I just wanted to make you smile."

That *did* make her smile, and that was his undoing. Groaning, he swept her up in his arms and carried her to his bed, where he gently laid her down on the turned-back covers. "Do you know how long I've wanted to do this?" he asked as he came down beside her and once again took her into his arms. "Ever since—"

"—we made love under the stars in the mountains," she finished for him. "I have, too."

She made the simple admission softly, huskily, honestly and had no idea how she destroyed him. The ache inside him tightening, he leaned closer and eliminated the distance between them with a kiss. There was no more need for words.

Outside, a dog barked down the street, and on the two-lane highway that cut through town, the sudden screech of brakes drew the attention of other drivers. Phoebe never noticed. Every thought, every nerve ending, every fiber of her being was focused on Taylor and a soft whisper of a kiss that teased and seduced and went on and on and on.

Her thoughts blurring and her breath catching on a moan as his hands slid slowly over her, rubbing the satin and lace of her gown against her bare skin, she moved against him, aching for more. "Taylor..."

"Easy," he murmured huskily, pressing a lingering kiss to the side of her neck. "There's no one here but you and me. We have all day."

Heaven. With a few simple words, he'd offered her heaven. Ever since the moment they'd first made love, it seemed as though they'd been looking over their shoulders. On the camping trip into the mountains, the McBrides had almost always been nearby, then when they'd returned home, it was the neighbors and even the guests they'd had to worry about surprising them. But the guests were all gone, the house was quiet, and she hadn't realized just how much she'd needed to be alone with him until now.

Settling against him, she tangled her legs with his and drew him close for a slow, lingering kiss that was sweet and hot and oh, so intimate. "How's that?" she breathed when she finally drew back far enough to give him a sultry smile. "Slow enough for you?"

"Perfect," he assured her thickly. "Do it again."

He didn't have to ask her a second time. Delighted by the taste of him, the feel of his lean, hard body against hers, his hands caressing her with gentle, sure strokes that were guaranteed to drive her crazy, she couldn't seem to stop kissing him. Pushing him onto his back, she rolled over onto him and trailed kisses across his freshly shaved cheek to his ear, making him shiver in pleasure.

Caught up in the pleasure of having her way with him, she would have sworn she was the one seducing him, but suddenly he was the one kissing her, teasing her with nibbling little kisses, cupping her breasts in his hands, playing with her, making her moan. And she loved it.

She loved him.

The thought slipped past her defenses, stunning her, but before she could even begin to come to terms with it, he reached for the hem of her gown and slowly drew it up her body and over her head. With a will of their own, her hands went to the buttons of his shirt and unbuttoned them with agonizing slowness.

She loved him. The thought whispered through her head again like the soft summer breeze that whispered through the open window, and the need to tell him, to share the joy and wonder that filled her, was almost more than she could bear. But she couldn't say a word. Not yet. Not when he hadn't even hinted at his own feelings. Marshall told her he loved her after she'd confessed her own deepening feelings for him, then ruined everything by asking her to loan him money. Taylor had shown no interest in her money, thank God, but she couldn't risk having her heart thrown back in her face a second time...not until he'd at least hinted that he felt the same way.

So she kept her love to herself, but it wasn't easy. Every time he touched her, every time he kissed her, every time he made her moan, all she could think of was that she loved him. And when he rolled her under him and tenderly eased into her, those three magical little words became a chant in her head. I love you. I love you. I love you. But all she said was his name, over and over and over again. "Taylor...Taylor... Taylor...."

Something was wrong. Taylor couldn't put a name to it, but he wasn't a dense man. And something had changed between him and Phoebe ever since they'd made love that morning. Oh, her response had been everything that he could have wanted, and she'd held nothing back then, or later, after lunch, when they'd made love again. But something wasn't quite right, and it was driving him crazy.

Changing a lightbulb for her in the entry hall, he stood on a ten-foot ladder and scowled at the sound of her humming in the kitchen as she cooked dinner for the two of them. She sounded happy enough, but he didn't fool himself into thinking her current mood had anything to do with him. She loved to cook and generally hummed to herself whenever she was in the kitchen. She'd stop soon enough if he joined her.

"So ask her what's wrong," he grumbled out loud to himself. "You're never going to know if you don't ask."

Caught up in his conversation with himself, he didn't notice that there was a visitor at the front door until there was a perfunctory knock. An older woman pulled open the screen door and stepped inside. ''Oh, hello,'' she began, catching sight of him on the ladder. ''I—''

Whatever she was going to say next was lost as she suddenly froze, her eyes widening as they locked with his in the shadowy afternoon light of the hall. Every ounce of blood drained from her face. ''Gus!'' she whispered in horror, and passed out cold.

Chapter 10

Bending over to check the chicken she was baking in the oven, Phoebe straightened abruptly at the sound of something falling in the front entry. Images flashed through her head of Taylor, up on the ladder, reaching for the burned-out bulb in the old-fashioned hanging brass fixture and losing his balance. With no effort whatsoever, she could see him falling ten feet to the floor below. Alarmed, her heart stopped in her breast.

"Taylor?"

Her only answer was silence, and that scared the hell out of her. Slamming the oven door, she ran toward the front of the house. "Taylor? What was that noise? Are you all right?"

Sick with fear when he still didn't answer, she burst into the entry hall, only to find Taylor down on his knees on the floor, bending over a woman who lay unconscious on the floor just inside the front door. "Oh, my God!'' she cried, horrified as she rushed forward to help. ''What happened?''

''I don't know. She walked in, took one look at me and passed out.''

Dropping to her knees beside him, Phoebe reached for the unconscious woman's hand to feel for a pulse, only to gasp as she finally got a good look at her. ''It's Sara McBride! I mean...Michaels. Joe and Zeke's mother,'' she explained, when he looked up sharply. ''I thought she was still on her honeymoon.''

Worried, she leaned over Sara and patted her gently on the cheek. ''Sara? Are you okay? C'mon, wake up. Don't make me call an ambulance. Think of what that would do to Zeke and Joe and the girls. And Dr. Michaels—he'd be worried sick about you. You don't want that.''

For a moment, Phoebe thought Sara wasn't going to respond and she'd be forced to call Dr. Michaels and all four of the McBride children, but something she said must have finally gotten through to the older woman. Moaning, Sara frowned and pressed a hand to her head. When her eyes slowly fluttered open, they were dark with confusion.

''Thank God!'' Phoebe breathed in relief. ''Are you all right? Did you hit your head?''

Still dazed, the older woman frowned up at her in confusion. ''Phoebe...what happened?''

Smiling reassuringly down at her, Phoebe took her hand and squeezed it comfortingly. ''I was going to ask you the same thing. I heard a thump and ran in here to find you passed out cold on the floor. Are you hurt? Can you sit up? Maybe I should call Dr. Michaels or the kids. You're awfully pale.''

''No,'' Sara said weakly, closing her eyes.

"Please…don't. There's no need to worry them. I'm fine—just a little light-headed. I shouldn't have skipped lunch. Just give me a minute and I'll be fine."

"Maybe some hot tea would help," Taylor suggested gruffly. "My mother used to say there was nothing like hot tea to get a person back on their feet."

At his first words, Sara's eyes flew open and, for the first time, she noticed the man kneeling at Phoebe's side. Her heart stopped dead at the sight of him. "Oh, my God!"

"It's okay," Phoebe assured her when she struggled to sit up. "You don't have to be embarrassed. This is Taylor Bishop. He was putting a lightbulb in the chandelier when you passed out."

The roar of her blood loud in her ears, Sara hardly heard her. Gus. Dear God, he looked like Gus! The way he tilted his head and the cut of his angled jaw. And his eyes—they were a hard, steely brown, not Gus's laughing, kindly blue—but the shape of them was the same. She could almost see him looking out at her through this man's eyes.

"Who are you?" she cried hoarsely, shrinking back from him. "What are you doing here? What do you want?"

"He's a guest here," Phoebe answered for him. "Didn't Gran tell you she was turning the place into a bed and breakfast? Taylor's been staying here all month, doing research on a book. He's a writer. Are you all right?" Frowning at her, she started to rise to her feet. "I think I'd better call an ambulance, after all."

"No!" Her eyes searching Taylor's face, she tried to convince herself that her imagination was just playing tricks with her mind, but there was no question that he favored Gus. ''Are you from around here?'' she asked him, frowning. ''Do you have family in the area?''

''Not any that claim me,'' he retorted dryly. ''Why?''

''You just look so familiar,'' she admitted. ''That's why I fainted. When I saw you up on the ladder, I thought…''

When she hesitated, Phoebe said, ''What, Sara? What did you think? Whatever it was, it must have been pretty upsetting. You fainted!''

For a moment, Phoebe didn't think the older woman would be able to answer her. Tears misted her eyes, and she looked as if she was going to burst into tears any moment. Concerned, Phoebe slipped an arm around her. ''Whatever it is, it can't be that bad, Sara. Just say it.''

''I thought he was Gus!'' she blurted out. ''The light wasn't good, and he looked just like him.''

Surprised, Phoebe glanced over at Taylor. She didn't see the resemblance, but she didn't expect to. Gus McBride had died when she was just a child, and she'd only seen a few pictures of him.

''Gus was—''

''I know who Gus was,'' Taylor said gruffly when she started to explain. ''I'm sure seeing me was a shock.''

Over the past few weeks, he'd tried to plan how he was going to tell the McBrides who he was, but he hadn't been able to come up with anything. Never in a million years had he thought Sara McBride would give him the perfect opening to end the lies and reveal his true identity.

''He was Sara's husband and the father of her children,'' he added coolly, never taking his gaze from the woman who was, technically, his stepmother. ''He was also my father.''

For a long moment, the words hung in the air, echoing like a scream. From the corner of his eye, Taylor saw Phoebe stiffen and could just imagine what she was thinking. Don't! he thought fiercely. Don't judge me until you know the full story. But he couldn't explain anything to her yet, not until he'd dealt with Sara McBride Michaels.

Even though he didn't know his father's wife, he'd had plenty of time over the course of the last few weeks to imagine what her reaction would be when she learned of his existence, and she didn't disappoint him. Pale as a ghost, she ignored the helping hands he and Phoebe held out to her and pushed quickly to her feet, her blue eyes snapping with fury. "I don't know what your problem is, sir, but you're not my late husband's son. He only had two sons—*my* sons." Dismissing him, she turned to Phoebe. "Who is this man, Phoebe? What's he doing here? Why is he saying such outrageous things?"

"I'd like to know the answer to that myself," Phoebe replied tightly. "All I know is what he told me—that his name is Taylor Bishop and he's a writer working on a book about the history of the local ranchers. He never mentioned anything to me about Gus or about being his son."

"Because I knew you probably wouldn't introduce me to the McBrides if I did," he said, defending himself. "My name really is Taylor Bishop, just as I told you it was, but I'm not a writer. I'm a lawyer from San Diego. I just found out who my father was in April, after my mother died. She left me a letter." Taking it out of his wallet, where he had carried it since, he held it out to Sara.

For a long moment, he didn't think she was going to

take it, let alone read it. Her blue eyes dark with mistrust, she stared at the letter as if it was a snake that was going to strike her. Then, just when Taylor was sure she was going to tell him to go to hell, she snatched the letter from his hand and unfolded it with fingers that were far from steady.

Watching her as she began to read, Taylor knew every word she read. He'd memorized the letter's contents months ago.

To my dear son,
    You'll never know how much I love you. You've been the greatest joy of my life, a blessing I thanked God for every day. I know how difficult it was for you, growing up without your father, and I'm sorry for that. But your father wasn't the unfeeling monster you think he was, dear. He was a good man who had no idea you even existed. His name is Gus McBride, and when we met, he lived in Liberty Hill, Colorado....

It was obvious when Sara reached the words naming Gus as his father. She stiffened like a poker and the little bit of angry color that tinged her cheeks drained away. Stricken, she shoved the letter back into his hands and choked, "I have to go!" Whirling, she ran for the door. A split second later, she was gone.

With her leave-taking, silence fell like a cold and heavy shroud. His face carved in grim lines, Taylor couldn't have said how long he stood there, staring after her. For weeks, all he'd thought about was the satisfaction he would feel when he revealed to Sara McBride Michaels just what kind of man she'd loved and had children with. It was something she needed to know, and he was just the person to tell her, he'd reasoned. The truth had to be told—he'd convinced himself it was the only just thing to do.

But as Sara drove off as though the hounds of hell were after her, all he could see was the pain in her eyes when he'd told her the truth. He'd hurt an old woman. The last thing he felt was satisfaction.

Beside him, Phoebe stood as still and cold as a statue, and for a moment, he didn't think she was going to say a word to him. But then her eyes met his head-on, and she only had one question for him. "Is it true?"

Cornered, he knew she wasn't going to be able to handle the truth any better than Sara had. Considering that, he should have talked his way out of trouble. It would have been the smart thing to do, and relatively painless—after all, he was a lawyer and had ample experience at slanting the truth in whatever direction he wanted. But he was tired of the lies, tired of hiding who he was. He'd known when he'd decided to come to Liberty Hill that he was going to make his share of enemies when the truth came out. He hadn't thought he'd care. He'd been wrong. Unfortunately, there wasn't a damn thing he could do about it now. The deed was done—it was too late to turn back the clock. Like it or not, he'd have to live with the consequences of his lies.

His mouth hardening into a flat line, he nodded curtly. "Yes. Gus McBride was my father."

"And you knew that when you came here?"

"Yes."

"So you lied…to me and everyone else in town. There was never any book, no research to be done. You never gave a rat's ass about the history of the local ranchers. It was all just a lie to get close to the Mc-Brides."

She had him nailed. Again, he nodded curtly. "Yes."

"You used me."

She didn't yell and scream at him the way most women would have—that he could have handled. Instead, she looked at him with eyes full of reproach. With nothing more than that, she made him feel guilty as hell. "Phoebe, sweetheart, if you'd just let me explain—"

He took a step toward her, but that was as far as he got. Abruptly stepping back, she gave him a look that warned him not even to think about touching her. "There's nothing to explain," she said coldly. "You kept your identity a secret because you came here to cause trouble. Congratulations. You succeeded. You just devastated an old woman who never did anything to hurt you. Are you proud of yourself?"

Stung, he growled, "Of course not!"

"Why not? You couldn't hurt your father, so you hurt his widow. Isn't that what you wanted?"

"I did what had to be done," he said stiffly. "I'll admit I was angry when I came here. I had every right to be. While Gus McBride was living the life of a cattle baron and giving the four children who carry his name everything they wanted, he had another son who was being raised by a single mother in the projects in San Diego. My mother worked two jobs just to put a roof over our heads and food on the table when I was growing up, so don't tell me who's hurt here, Phoebe. You don't have a clue!"

Arching a brow at him, she gave him a look that made him feel like a worm. "Want to take a bet on that?"

Cursing his choice of words, he sighed in frustration. His communication skills weren't usually so poor, dammit! "I wasn't trying to hurt anyone," he said quietly.

"I just wanted to set the record straight. After all these years, I felt it was time. These people robbed me of a relationship with my father. I had the right to confront them."

"If all you were interested in was a confrontation, you would have been up-front about who you were from the beginning," she retorted. "This was about revenge, Taylor, pure and simple. Why don't you just admit it and be done with it?"

Guilty that she was right, he snapped, "Okay, so I'm human! My whole reason for coming here *was* to make Gus pay for everything he put my mother through. But that changed after I got to know Zeke and Joe and the girls. I like them and I want them to know who I am—their brother. That's why I told Sara the truth. Not to hurt her, but because I want a relationship with my brothers and sisters. And she made the connection between me and Gus the second she laid eyes on me. The truth would have come out eventually. It just seemed better to do it now and get it over with."

Her eyes searching his, Phoebe wanted to believe him, but she didn't know if she'd ever be able to take his word for anything again. Hurt, suddenly furious with him, she said, "You lied to me, you used me and now you want me to believe you? How can I? While you were kissing me and making love to me, you were planning to hurt my friends. Do you have any idea how that makes me feel? I *trusted* you. And what did you do with that trust? You stomped it into the ground."

To his credit, he didn't offer her empty excuses. "I'm not proud of what I did," he said huskily. "All I can say is I'm sorry. You're the last person I would ever want to hurt."

"Then why did you?"

He didn't have an answer for that, but to Phoebe, the answer was obvious. He'd never cared for her—she'd just been a means to an end. He'd needed to meet the McBrides, to find out all he could about his father's family while he plotted his revenge, and she'd made that possible. While she'd been foolishly falling in love with him, he'd just been using her.

And it hurt—more than she'd ever thought possible. Sick at heart, she felt tears sting her eyes and desperately tried to blink them away, but she was fighting a losing battle. Her vision blurred, and before she could stop it, a single tear spilled over her lashes. Horrified, she tried to gain control. She wouldn't cry in front of him! she told herself furiously. She wouldn't let him see just how devastated she was by his betrayal, wouldn't let him guess how much she cared.

"I have nothing more to say to you," she choked, pushing past him. "Just stay away from me."

Hurrying outside, she rushed over to her grandmother's antique store next door, and had barely unlocked the front door and stepped inside before the tears started to flow. As a child, she'd always loved the store. Packed with old furniture and items from the past that had been strange and fascinating to a six-year-old, she'd found ways to entertain herself for hours, playing games of make-believe and what-if. While her grandmother tended to her customers, Phoebe had imagined herself in another time, another land, another life.

But she was no longer six, and as she escaped into the quiet shadows of the closed shop, she found little solace in the games of make-believe she'd played as a child. All she could think of was Taylor...and how much he'd hurt her. How could she have been so stupid? she wondered, furious with herself. She'd actually begun to hope that he was falling in love with her, just as she was with him. Fat chance. The only thing Taylor Bishop loved was his need for revenge.

So she wanted to be left alone, did she? Taylor fumed as he put the ladder away and retreated to his room. That was fine with him. She was quick to defend the McBrides because they were her friends. Well, he was her lover, dammit! The least she could have done was consider his position. Did she think it was easy, growing up not knowing who his father was? And what about his mother? She could have at least sympathized with her and the hardships she'd endured.

But, no! he raged. She'd only been concerned with the McBrides and their pain. Well, here was a news flash for her. He *was* a McBride! And his half brothers and sisters had a right to know that. Granted, he'd hurt her and Sara McBride, and he deeply regretted that. The truth was finally out, though, and he wasn't sorry about that.

Even though you hurt an old woman? a voice chided in his head. *And Phoebe? Are you really that cold?*

He readily admitted that there'd been a time in the not-too-distant past when he'd had a reputation for having ice water in his veins. He'd been ruthless when he was in court, sometimes even with his own clients, and he hadn't apologized for that. The only thing that had mattered was winning. He hadn't cared about anyone...except his mother.

But that was before he'd come to Liberty Hill, before he'd let down his guard with his brothers and sisters, before Phoebe had showed him a side of himself he hadn't known was there. He'd let himself care, dammit, and he was afraid he was going to live to regret that.

Because he may have just blown any chance he'd ever have of having a relationship with any of them. He'd hurt Sara, and in all likelihood, her children would never forgive him for that. He couldn't say he blamed them. His father had hurt his mother, and he couldn't forget it, let alone forgive it.

As for Phoebe, he didn't think he'd ever forget the look in her eyes when she'd realized who he was and just how much he'd used her. If looks could kill, he'd have dropped in his tracks right then and there. He wouldn't have been surprised if she never spoke to him again. He'd given her every reason to hate his guts.

"What is it? Are you all right?"

"Mother, what's wrong? You sounded frantic on the phone."

"You're as white as a ghost. Are you sick?"

"Dan, do you know what the problem is? How long has she been this way?"

"Ever since she got back from Myrtle's," Dan told Zeke, frowning worriedly at his wife. "I tried to get her to talk about it, but she insisted that I call a family meeting. She was only going to talk about what was bothering her once—when the entire family was all together."

Shooting his mother a sharp look, Joe growled, "Mother? What's going on? What happened at Myrtle's?"

In spite of her paleness and the agitation she wasn't quite able to hide, Sara had been in relative control of her emotions up until then. But when all four of her children looked at her with such love and caring, tears welled into her eyes. "I—I don't know how to tell you all this...."

"Whatever it is, it's okay, Mom," Merry said, stepping forward to hug her. "Just tell us. We're here for you."

"I know, dear," Sara sniffed, giving her daughter a watery smile. "I—I have always been so proud of all of you. I'd never do anything to hurt you."

"Geez, Mom, we know that," Zeke said gruffly. "You wouldn't hurt a fly. So what happened at Myrtle's? What were you doing there, anyway? She's not back from her trip yet, is she? Phoebe said she'd be gone at least another week." Suddenly frowning, he growled, "Did Phoebe say something to you that upset you? That doesn't seem her style at all—"

"Let her talk, Zeke," Janey cut in quietly. "She'll tell us when she's ready."

"Thank you, dear," Sara said thickly, reaching for Janey's hand to give it a squeeze. "This is just so hard! I don't know where to begin."

"Who upset you, sweetheart?" Dan asked huskily. "Did someone say something to you? Or do something? I've never seen you so agitated before."

"It was that man at Myrtle's," she choked, fighting and losing the battle to hold back tears. "He was changing a lightbulb in the entry—"

"What man?" Joe interrupted, scowling. "Are you talking about Taylor Bishop?"

"Taylor did this to you?" Zeke demanded, shocked. "I thought he was a nice guy. He certainly seemed likable enough when he went camping with us. What did he say to you?"

Sara hardly heard his last question. Stunned, she gasped, "You've met him? When? How? What did he say to you?"

"We've all met him," Janey said, frowning in confusion at the panic she heard in her mother's voice. "Phoebe introduced us. He's writing a book on the ranchers in the area."

"What do you mean... *What did he say to us?*" Merry asked, perplexed. "What do you think he said? What's going on, Mom? And don't say it's nothing. I've never seen you so upset before."

Wanting to protect them, knowing she couldn't, Sara would have rather cut off her arm than hurt her children, but she couldn't protect them from Taylor Bishop's claims. He would have his say, and the only way she could counteract the damage he was determined to cause was to tell Zeke and Joe and the girls first.

But it hurt, dammit! Gus should have been there to deal with Taylor Bishop. *He* should have been the one who had to tell his children the truth and give them the explanation they deserved. After all, he was the one who created this mess! Instead, it was left to her.

Just thinking about it clogged her throat with tears, but she could no longer put off the inevitable. "I'm upset with good reason," she choked. "He claims he's your father's illegitimate son."

For a long moment, the only reaction to her announcement was stunned silence. Then Joe growled, "That's a damn lie!"

"The son of a bitch!"

"Dad would never have cheated on you!"

"He was crazy about you!"

Touched by their faith in their father, Sara couldn't hold back the tears that filled her eyes. "I knew you wouldn't believe it," she sniffed. "There has to be another explanation."

"Of course there is," Dan agreed, slipping his arm around Sara's shoulders. "I knew Gus all of his life. I never saw him look at another woman after he met you, sweetheart. Obviously, this Taylor character's mistaken or you misunderstood him."

If she hadn't loved him before, Sara would have loved him then for standing up for Gus. They had been good friends, and Dan had known Gus all his life. Unfortunately, all the faith in the world couldn't change what she'd seen with her own two eyes.

"Oh, I understood him, all right," she sniffed, wiping the tears from her cheeks. "He didn't need to say a word. I saw the resemblance between him and Gus the second I laid eyes on him."

For a second, her words didn't register. When they did, Zeke rasped, "What are you saying, Mom? You can't really believe that Dad would...that he..."

"Betrayed me and got another woman pregnant?" she finished for him when he couldn't find the words. "I don't want to believe it, but what else can I think? He looks so much like your father, it's frightening. I took one look at him and fainted."

"Oh, Mom, no!" Merry said, moving to her mother's side to hug her. "That must have been awful for you."

"It didn't get awful until he told me he was Gus's son."

"That doesn't mean he is," Joe retorted. "Maybe he's one of Todd Smith's bastards. People used to say he and Dad looked more like brothers than second cousins. And Todd certainly played the field when he was younger. Every time you saw him, he had a different woman on his arm. He's still a flirt, and he's got to be pushing seventy!"

Sara would have given anything to believe that, but she shook her head sadly. "Taylor Bishop's mother wrote him a letter before she died. I read part of it. It clearly states that his father was Gus McBride of Liberty Hill, Colorado.''

"But Dad loved you!" Janey argued, tears glistening in her eyes. "He wouldn't have cheated on you. He wasn't that kind of man."

"He certainly wasn't," Joe said flatly. "Personally, I think this is all nothing but a scam Taylor concocted to try to get his hands on this ranch. Well, he can think again. It's not going to happen."

His mouth set in a flat line, he stormed over to the phone and punched in Myrtle's number. When Phoebe answered, he growled, "Phoebe, this is Joe. I need to talk to Taylor. Is he there?"

"I'll put you through to his room," she replied. "Is Sara all right?"

"She's fine," he retorted. "She'll be a lot better when this garbage with Taylor is dealt with."

"I'll put you right through," she said, and patched him through to Taylor's room.

Taylor answered on the second ring. "Hello?"

"I want to know what the hell you think you're doing, lying to my mother about who your father is."

Taylor wasn't surprised that Joe had called—he'd known one of the McBrides would call the minute Sara told her children what had happened. "It's not a lie," he said coolly. "Gus *was* my father."

"The hell he was! He loved my mother from the moment he met her when he was fourteen. He would never have cheated on her."

"I didn't say he did," Taylor retorted. "You can't cheat on someone you're not involved with."

"What the devil are you talking about? I just told you that my father was in love with my mother ever since he was fourteen. From the time they met, they were never *not* involved!''

"Oh, yes, they were," Taylor growled. "If you don't believe me, ask your mother about the summer of 1962."

"Why?" he asked, suddenly suspicious. "What happened then?"

"They broke up and Gus went to the Cheyenne rodeo. That's where he met *my* mother."

"That's a lie!"

"Is it? Ask your mother."

Even to his own ears, his voice was smug and confident, and there wasn't a doubt in his mind that Joe heard it, too. His half brother hesitated, and when he finally spoke, his words were cold and hard and held a warning that only a man who felt threatened by the truth would need to make. "If you're after the ranch, you can forget it. You're never going to get your hands on it."

Whatever Taylor had been expecting, it wasn't that. Stunned, he said, "This has nothing to do with the ranch, Joe. That's not why I came here."

"Yeah, right," Joe sneered. "You come here pretending to be somebody you're not, and I'm supposed to believe you're not after what you can get? Do you really think I'm that stupid?"

"I never said you were stupid. I just want—"

"What?" he growled when he hesitated. "To be friends? For us to welcome you into the family like a long-lost brother? You're not our brother. You're a liar and we want nothing to do with you. If you come anywhere near the ranch or any member of this family again, you're going to find yourself in more trouble than you ever imagined. Leave us alone!"

Slamming the phone down, Joe turned to find his

mother and the rest of the family watching him with expressions of varying degrees of fear and anger. Merry asked the question they were all silently asking. "He still claims to be Dad's son, doesn't he? Even though you told him he would have never cheated on Mom."

Frustrated, he nodded. "He claims Mom and Dad broke up in the summer of '62, and Dad went to a rodeo in Cheyenne. According to him, that's when his mother met Dad."

Up until then, Sara had almost convinced herself that this was all some terrible mistake. But with Joe's words, the years rolled back, and in the blink of an eye, she was back in that awful summer of '62, when, without warning, her world had turned upside down and she'd almost lost Gus for good. "Oh, my God!"

Lost in her own private hell, she didn't realize she'd spoken aloud until Dan stepped to her side and took her hand. "What's wrong, sweetheart? You've gone pale as a ghost again."

"Gus and I did break up that summer," she said, stricken. "It was so many years ago, I'd forgotten about it. We didn't speak to each other for three weeks."

"But you still loved each other," Janey argued. "He wouldn't have cheated on you just because you weren't talking for a couple of weeks."

She made it all sound so simple—and it should have been. The only problem was…nothing was ever simple when it came to love. Tears welling in her eyes, she choked, "You don't understand, Janey, dear. We thought our breakup was for good. We hadn't spoken in nearly a month. It was horrible. I was so lonely, I cried myself to sleep every night. Mother was so worried about me, she sent me to Denver to visit my cousin, Harriet. I kept hoping Gus would call, but he never did.

Harriet finally convinced me that I had to go on with my life. When the brothers of some of her friends asked me out, I went.''

"Why?" Zeke asked, frowning in confusion. "You were in love with Dad. Why would you go out with someone else?"

"Because I didn't know how else to get over him," she replied. "I'd never been so miserable in my life. I hated dating other men—even though they were all very nice. I just wanted Gus. After two weeks, I couldn't stand it any longer, and I went home. That's when I discovered that while I was gone, Gus had been on a trip of his own."

"Let me guess," Joe said flatly. "He went to Cheyenne."

She would have given anything to deny it. They'd have believed her if she'd lied, but she couldn't bring herself to do it. They were entitled to the truth, regardless of how much it hurt. "He'd been thinking about trying bronc riding on the rodeo circuit, but he didn't want to leave me. After we broke up, there was no longer any reason not to go. The first rodeo was Frontier Days...in Cheyenne."

"Oh, my God," Merry whispered, tears filling her eyes. "It's true, isn't it? Taylor really is Dad's son, isn't he? He's our brother."

Her heart aching, Sara nodded. "Yes, dear, I believe he is."

Chapter 11

For the first time since his mother had died, Taylor was glad she was dead. She would have been thoroughly ashamed of him, and with good reason. In his quest for revenge, he had, no doubt, destroyed the only illusion Sara McBride had left about the man she had loved all of her adult life...his faithfulness.

Just thinking about it sickened him. Pacing the confines of his room, he wandered over to the window and stared blindly out, the hurt in Sara's eyes forever etched in his memory. Wincing, he silently cursed himself. What the hell had he been thinking? He might be a bastard at times—especially when he was in the courtroom—but he didn't make a habit of hurting old ladies. Or young ones, either, he added grimly. But within a matter of seconds, he'd not only devastated Sara McBride, he'd done the same to Phoebe.

God, he was a jerk! How could he have ever thought that he would actually enjoy telling Sara that Gus had played around on her? What kind of unfeeling monster was he? He might as well have stabbed her in the heart with a knife. And then there was Phoebe…

She had to hate him, he decided. He'd given her no choice. Just as she'd guessed, he'd used her to get to her friends. From the moment he'd first appeared on her grandmother's doorstep, he'd done nothing but lie to her. He'd thought he was being so smart, that she wouldn't find out, and if she did, he wouldn't care. Talk about arrogance.

He cared, all right. He loved her—and it scared the hell out of him. The lack of a father in his life had taught him at an early age not to let himself care about anyone but his mother. He'd built a wall around his heart and no one had come even close to scaling it until he'd met Phoebe. And like a fool, he'd made her hate him because all he'd thought about was revenge—and his own anger. And now he was paying the price for that.

Idiot! he silently raged. Selfish, self-centered, vindictive idiot. The minute he'd found out his father was dead, he should have immediately turned around and gone back to San Diego. So what if his car was wrecked? He could have hired a taxi—or taken the bus, for that matter—to Colorado Springs, then flown home. Once his car was repaired, he wouldn't even have had to come back for it. He could have just had it shipped home.

But, no! He'd stayed…and fallen in love with a woman who could now no longer stand the sight of him. Then, to make matters worse, he'd actually started to like his brothers and sisters. And they'd seemed to like him…until they'd found out he was their brother.

God, what a mess! He couldn't have screwed things

up more if he'd tried. For a moment, he considered packing his bags and heading back to San Diego first thing in the morning. After all the hurt he'd caused, it was the least he could do. But, dammit, he cared too much to just give up and walk away. He couldn't even think about leaving Phoebe. And what about Janey and Merry and his brothers? They were his family now. How could he forget that when he'd wanted siblings his entire life?

They might not want anything to do with him, but that was too damn bad, he thought grimly. He couldn't turn his back on them any more than he could on Phoebe. He just had to find a way to fix this. The problem was…he didn't have a clue where to begin.

He went to Ed's Diner for dinner.

Seated at her grandmother's kitchen table, her appetite nonexistent as she apathetically pushed around the cereal she'd poured for herself, Phoebe told herself she didn't care where he was. After the way he'd lied to her, he could go lose himself in the woods, and she wouldn't so much as blink. In fact, she hoped he did. Then she'd never have to see him again.

That's right, that irritating little voice in her head mocked. *You don't give a flip about the man at all. That's why you spent the last hour crying your eyes out—and why you haven't eaten two bites of that bowl of mush that used to be cereal. You always lose your appetite over people you couldn't care less about.*

Disgusted that she couldn't lie to herself, Phoebe abruptly rose to her feet and crossed to the sink to dump her cereal. Okay, she thought bitterly, she admitted it. She still loved him, and that infuriated her. How could she have any feelings but contempt for a man who deliberately set out to destroy a family he didn't even know? He didn't care about her. How could he? Time and again, he'd done nothing but lie to her—even after they'd made love! While she'd been falling in love with him, the only thing he'd been thinking about was the McBrides and getting revenge.

Images flashed before her eyes…his first morning at her grandmother's, when she'd introduced him to Merry…the night she'd gone with him to dinner at Joe's and he'd met the entire family. And then there was the camping trip…the loving they'd shared, the access he'd gained to the ranch, his face as he'd stood at his father's grave. She should have known then that something was wrong, but she'd never thought to suspect he might not be who he said he was. Why would she? He'd seemed so honest.

So much for trusting her gut, she thought with a sniff. She couldn't even believe the desire she would have sworn he felt for her. There couldn't have been any real emotion behind it, no caring for her as a person. She'd been a means to an end, nothing more. If she hadn't known the McBrides, he probably never would have given her a second glance.

And it was that, more than anything, that hurt. She'd made it so damn easy for him to use her. Had he suspected she was falling in love with him? She'd never said the words, but he had to know that she wasn't the kind of woman who gave herself to just anyone. Just thinking of the way she'd melted in his arms made her cringe. Even now, was he laughing at how naive and trusting she'd been?

Tears welled in her eyes at the thought, but before she could give in to them, she heard the front door open and knew Taylor was back from his solitary dinner at

Ed's. Horrified, she quickly brushed the tears from her eyes. She would not let him find her moping around the kitchen with wet eyes, crying over him. Her heart might be breaking, but if she had anything to say about it, he'd never know it!

Her chin set at a determined angle, she hurriedly stepped over to the pantry and pulled out everything she needed to make a chocolate cake. Her heart pounding, she couldn't think of a single recipe, but she didn't let that stop her. Grabbing a bowl, she began sifting flour, then adding salt, sugar and cocoa to the bowl without measuring anything.

She knew the exact moment he stepped into the open doorway. Suddenly, her mouth was dry and her palms damp and she dropped the wooden spoon she was using to stir the concoction on the floor. Swearing softly, she picked it up and carried it to the sink. With every step she took, she felt Taylor's eyes on her.

"Are you all right?"

His gruff question reached out and stroked her like a caress, making her want to cry all over again. Don't! she wanted to yell at him. Don't pretend you care when we both know you don't. But she couldn't say that—not without crying. Instead, she kept her eyes on the awful mixture she was stirring in the bowl and said stiffly, "I'm fine."

"I thought maybe we could talk."

So now he wanted to talk to her, she thought, amazed. After weeks of using her and lying to her and not telling her the truth about himself, he now wanted to spill his guts? She didn't think so. "I don't have time tonight. I have to get this cake in the oven."

"Maybe later, then?"

"I doubt it. I'm busy."

She knew she was being rude, but she couldn't help it. She didn't want to talk to him, didn't want to hear his story. He'd lied to her and everyone else in town, and as far as she was concerned, there was no excuse for that. She was sorry that he'd grown up without a father, sorry that he'd never known Gus McBride, but that didn't justify what he'd done. Two wrongs didn't make a right.

She couldn't have said how long he stood there, obviously hoping she would change her mind. It seemed like forever. She finished mixing the cake, then greased and floured a sheet pan, and still he stood there, watching her. Ignoring him, she slipped the pan into the oven. She didn't realize he was gone until she turned around and found the doorway empty.

The tears came in a flood then, and there was nothing she could do to stop them. Collapsing in a chair at the kitchen table, she buried her face in her folded arms and cried and cried. Why did she have to love him so much? she wondered tearfully. She could never trust him again, not after what he'd done. She didn't even know who he was. Oh, sure, he'd told her that his name really was Taylor Bishop and he was a lawyer from San Diego, but so what? He'd told her a lot of things, and only God knew how much, if any, of it was true. All she could say for sure about him was that she knew next to nothing about the man himself. Had the tenderness of his touch been real or feigned? Had he ever been interested in her or had that just been another part of the lie he'd perpetuated from the moment he hit the city limits of Liberty Hill? She liked to think she could tell when a man was just pretending, but he'd fooled her from the moment he met her.

She didn't have much faith in her own judgment anymore, and it was all his fault. He'd done this to her, to *them,* and she hated him for that. He'd destroyed something wonderful, something she'd never felt for anyone else, and it was gone forever.

That was what she cried for—the love she'd lost and would never have again. And it hurt. Just hours ago, she'd thought there would never come a time when she didn't want to be with him, but now, she just wanted him gone. Maybe then she could start to forget.

She hadn't planned to ask him to leave, but now she realized that she couldn't continue to let him stay there. It just hurt too badly. Every time their eyes met, every time she heard his step in the hall, she was reminded of everything she had lost. She couldn't stand the pain any longer.

In the morning, she would ask him to leave, she promised herself. The decision made, she should have felt better. But when she finally went upstairs an hour later, she couldn't close her eyes without seeing Taylor reaching for her. Long after the house had grown quiet, silent tears trailed down her cheeks. She'd never been so miserable in her life.

The next morning dawned gray and rainy. Exhausted, her eyes scratchy from too little sleep and too many tears, Phoebe would have liked nothing better than to pull the covers over her head and spend the day in bed. But she hadn't forgotten her resolve to ask Taylor to leave. Putting it off would only make it harder in the long run.

Resigned, she rolled out of bed and winced at her image in the mirror. There was no way she could face Taylor looking the way she did. She was pale and drawn, her eyes still swollen and red from crying. He'd take one look at her and know she'd spent the night crying over him.

"So clean yourself up," she muttered to her image in the mirror. "Put on some makeup, for heaven's sake!"

In the end, she not only put on makeup, she pulled on her favorite summer dress and washed her hair, brushing it dry until it fell in a soft cascade of golden waves past her shoulder. A final look in the mirror assured her that she looked presentable. Satisfied, she headed downstairs to start breakfast. She still didn't know how she was going to tell Taylor to leave, but she didn't have to come up with the words right now. He wouldn't be down for at least another hour.

Her thoughts on what she would make for breakfast, she stepped into the kitchen, only to stop at the sight of Taylor ladling fresh ground coffee into the coffeemaker. "You're up early," she said stiffly. "Here, I'll do that."

"I've got it under control," he replied as he added water. "I was just making a cup of coffee before I go."

Phoebe's heart stopped dead in her chest. "Go? Where are you going? To Ed's for breakfast? You don't have to do that. You're still a guest here. Breakfast is included with the price of your room."

"I'm leaving," he said quietly. "I think it's for the best."

He couldn't have stunned her more if he'd slapped her. He couldn't leave! she thought, completely forgetting that she'd planned to ask him to do just that. He couldn't just walk away...not after what they'd shared. Didn't he realize that she loved him? They needed to talk. She had to tell him—

But even as she opened her mouth to do just that,

images from yesterday swam before her eyes and she stiffened like a poker. What in the world was wrong with her? Where was her pride? This was the same man who had lied to her and taken advantage of her, and she was going to tell him she *loved* him? She didn't think so!

Her arms folded stiffly at her waist, she said, "I'll figure up your bill. Excuse me."

Later, she never knew how she made it to her grandmother's study without falling apart. Her heart aching, she wanted to throw herself down on the old-fashioned chaise that had been in Myrtle's office for as long as she could remember, but she didn't dare. If she let herself cry now, she didn't think she would ever be able to stop. So she sat down at the desk instead and turned on the computer.

It only took a matter of seconds to print out his charges. Staring down at the single piece of paper, Phoebe felt tears threaten all over again. He'd been there for weeks and this was the only record she had to show that he'd been there at all. How could this be? Where was the charge for breaking her heart? How did she put a price on that? What about the lies he'd told her and everyone else in town? Surely there had to be a price to pay for that. What number did she put on the pain he'd caused?

She didn't have an answer for that…because the pain kept getting worse. After paying his bill, he would walk out the door and not look back. And in the process, he'd rip her heart out by the roots.

No! she wanted to cry. Don't go!

But she couldn't stop him from leaving or stop herself from hurting. She'd set herself up for pain the second she let herself love him. There was no turning back the clock now. All she could do was learn to manage the pain, starting now.

It wasn't easy. Where she got the strength to face him she didn't know, but when she returned to the kitchen, her eyes were, thankfully, dry. "Here you go," she said quietly, and handed him the itemized bill.

Hardly sparing it a glance, he paid with a credit card, and within a matter of moments, the transaction was complete. When he hesitated after she handed him his copy of the receipt, she thought he might have changed his mind. His eyes met hers, her heart jumped, and she found herself holding her breath, waiting for him to say something...*anything*...that would make it possible for her to forgive him.

But he only growled, "I guess I'd better get going. Take care of yourself."

His face carved in somber lines, he grabbed his suitcase, which she hadn't noticed sitting by the refrigerator, and strode out without once looking back. Her worst fears realized, Phoebe couldn't have said how long she stood there, staring after him with her heart in her eyes. It seemed like an eternity. She tried to convince herself that any second now, he would change his mind and come back. He didn't.

When she started to cry, she couldn't have said. Suddenly, tears were running down her face. She didn't even try to stop them—there was no longer any reason to. Taylor was gone.

Standing on Myrtle's wide front porch, Janey McBride knocked sharply on the front door and told herself there was no reason to be nervous. She'd just come there to talk to her brother. Surely Taylor wouldn't re-

fuse to speak to her. She was his sister. They had a lot
of catching up to do.

The problem was...she didn't have a clue where to
begin. What did you say to a brother you'd never known
existed until yesterday? *Hi, you look like Dad?* She
didn't think that would be a very good idea. According
to Joe, Taylor was full of anger, and she couldn't say
she blamed him. He'd never had a relationship with
their father, never played catch with him or been tucked
into bed by him when he was a little boy. Even though
he now knew who his father was, he still didn't know
the color of his eyes, the shape of his face, the sound
of his voice...and he never would. No wonder he was
angry. She would be, too.

Lifting her hand to knock again, she frowned. Where
was Phoebe? She usually didn't take so long to answer.
Granted, it was early yet, and the mornings were the
busiest part of the day at a bed and breakfast. Maybe
she should have called first....

Lost in her thoughts, she didn't see Phoebe through
the frosted half glass of the front door until she heard
the dead bolt turn. Relieved, she smiled. "There you
are—"

Whatever she was going to say next vanished at the
sight of Phoebe's red-rimmed eyes as she pulled the
door open just a crack. "Phoebe?" she gasped. "My
God, what's wrong? Are you all right? What happened?"

"Nothing."

"Don't be ridiculous," Janey scolded, pushing her
way inside. "You've been crying your eyes out. Why?
It's not Myrtle, is it?" she asked in alarm. "Nothing's
happened to her, has it?"

Wiping her eyes with a tissue she pulled from her

pocket, Phoebe shook her head and sniffed, "She's fine, as far as I know. I'm just sad."

Janey didn't have to ask about what—suddenly, she knew. Glancing past her, she looked up the stairs. "Where's Taylor? I know it's early, but I need to talk to him."

It was a simple request, but suddenly Phoebe's eyes were swimming. Her heart aching for her, Janey slipped an arm around her shoulders. "What is it, Phoeb? Did you and Taylor have a fight? Is that why you've been crying?"

Miserably, Phoebe nodded. "I'm sorry I'm being such a baby, but the last twenty-four hours have been very emotional. I still can't believe he lied to me the way he did. I told him what I thought of him last night and was going to ask him to leave this morning, but he didn't give me the chance. Before I could say anything, he told me he thought it would be better if he left."

Surprised, Janey said, "He's gone back to San Diego?"

"I don't know," she said huskily. "He just paid his bill and left. He didn't say where he was going." When Janey looked stricken, she frowned in confusion. "Why do you want to talk to him? He lied to you, too. I didn't think you would want anything to do with him."

Throughout the night, Janey had asked herself the same thing, and time and again, the answer had always been the same. "We share the same blood," she said simply. "That makes him family."

"But how do you know he's telling the truth?" she argued. "We only have his word that his mother wrote that letter that names Gus his father. What if this is all just a scam to get his hands on the ranch? It happens, you know. Scam artists impersonate people all the time.''

"But he hasn't asked for anything," Janey pointed out. "He just wanted us to know who he was."

"That's all he appears to want now. He's a lawyer, Janey. If he decides he wants part of the ranch, trust me, he'll find a way to get it."

"But that's just it," Janey said with a frown, "I don't think he wants the ranch. He wants family."

"Then why didn't he say who he was from the beginning? If you want people to accept you and give you a chance, you don't start the relationship by lying."

"You and I wouldn't," Janey replied, "but we grew up knowing who our fathers were. Taylor didn't. Don't get me wrong," she added quickly. "I'm not excusing what he did. He should have been up-front and honest. But he had no reason to trust us with who he was. For all he knew, we would have slammed the door in his face. He was just doing what he thought he had to do to find out who his family was, and I can't condemn him for that. If our circumstances had been reversed, I might have done the same thing."

Put that way, Phoebe found herself wishing she hadn't been so quick to judge him. He'd wanted to talk, to explain himself, and she hadn't let him. And now it was too late. He was gone, and even though she had his home phone number from his registration card, she couldn't call him. Not after he'd walked away so easily. If he'd cared about her at all, he wouldn't have left without insisting that she at least listen to him.

Glancing in his rearview mirror, Taylor watched Liberty Hill grow smaller and smaller and knew he'd done the right thing by leaving. Bruised feelings needed time to heal, and they could heal a lot faster if he wasn't underfoot to remind everyone of his lies.

Knowing what was right and doing it, however, were two different things. Leaving Phoebe had turned out to be the hardest thing he'd ever done. He'd wanted to grab her and hold her close and make her listen to him, but she hadn't been in the mood to hear anything he'd had to say. So he'd left and he'd been fighting the need to turn around and go back to her ever since.

But she thought the worst of him, and that tore him apart. Granted, he hadn't handled the situation well, but dammit, he wasn't the monster she thought he was. He wasn't vindictive—he'd never deliberately hurt anyone in his life. From the moment he'd found out who his father was, every move he'd made had been about Gus. He'd told Sara the truth about him for one reason and one reason only—because he couldn't let Gus continue to enjoy a sterling posthumous reputation when he considered him to be nothing but a deadbeat dad. He was just sorry that in the process of learning the truth, Sara and his brothers and sisters were hurt.

But if they hated his guts for that and wanted nothing to do with him in the future, he'd find a way to accept it. Phoebe, however, was another matter. How long had he been looking for her without even knowing it? Now that he'd finally found her, he wouldn't, couldn't, lose her.

He'd never considered himself an impatient man, but at that moment, it took all his self-control not to turn around and race back to her. He wouldn't do either one of them any good if he pushed her now, he told himself grimly. She needed space, and he was giving it to her. He wasn't, however, going very far…just to Colorado Springs. There, he'd find a room and wait. Once Phoebe had had a chance to calm down and cool off, he would ask for her forgiveness. He hoped she didn't make him wait long.

Finding a room wasn't difficult. Waiting was. In the silence of his empty hotel room, his thoughts drifted again and again to Phoebe. Did she miss him yet? Was the house quiet without him? Was she wondering where he was?

Before he could stop to think, he picked up the phone to call her, only to slam it back down again. No, dammit! He wasn't calling her! Pressuring her now, when she was still so upset, would be nothing but a mistake. Her hurt was too fresh, her anger too strong. She'd say something she didn't mean and put him on the defensive, and he'd end up losing her.

He wasn't letting that happen, he promised himself grimly. He had work to do. If he had to tie himself to his computer, then so be it. He wasn't calling her!

Setting up his laptop at the small table in the corner, he opened up the file on an upcoming case and proceeded to spend the rest of the day working. Phoebe, however, didn't make it easy for him. She slipped into his thoughts whenever he dropped his guard, and time and time again, he found himself staring out the window, remembering the feel of her in his arms. Frustrated, he dragged his attention back to his work and once again concentrated on the brief he was writing…until she drifted into his thoughts again. The day was one of the longest of his life. He worked through lunch and dinner, and didn't make nearly as much progress as he'd have liked. By the time he turned off his computer later that evening, a headache throbbed at his temple like a jackhammer. He turned on the TV for noise, only to grimace at the romantic comedy with Meg Ryan playing on one of the cable stations. Frowning, he switched to the local news.

A pretty blue-eyed news anchor looked into the camera and said somberly, "The federal government announced today that it plans to enlarge the Liberty Hill National Wildlife Refuge by purchasing thousands of acres of surrounding ranchland from private ranchers in the area. The refuge currently comprises fifty thousand acres and will double in size by the end of the year. Now, on to sports..."

A fresh-faced sportscaster who looked as if he couldn't have been a day over eighteen rattled off the latest national league baseball scores, but Taylor hardly heard him. Instead, the previous story echoed again and again in his head. *The federal government announced today that it plans to enlarge the Liberty Hill National Wildlife Refuge...*

What the hell was that about? he wondered with a scowl. The story itself sounded innocent enough, but Taylor had fought the government before, and he knew how they operated. If the current administration, which favored big business over conservation, was after land, it wasn't because the government wanted to protect the environment and animals in the area. They were after something else, and they'd stop at nothing to get it.

And the McBride ranch was right in their way.

Whatever's going on, it's none of your business, his common sense growled. *Stay out of it.*

He should have. It would have been the smart thing to do. His name was mud with the McBrides, and Joe had made it clear that the ranch was theirs. They wouldn't appreciate him giving an opinion when it wasn't asked for.

He knew that, accepted it, and reached for the phone anyway. The second Joe came on the line, he said, "This is Taylor. I need to talk to you—"

"Tough," he growled. "I'm not interested in anything you have to say. Goodbye."

"Wait, dammit! I saw the news. What have you got on the ranch that the government wants? And don't tell me nothing," he snapped. "I'm not an idiot. Washington wouldn't be going to this much expense for nothing."

Hesitating, Joe almost told Taylor he was imagining things and hung up on him. After all the trouble he'd caused, it was no more than he deserved. But they were in a hell of a mess with the government, and he shouldn't have been surprised that Taylor had been able to read between the lines of the government's announcement. He'd been impressed with his shrewdness from the first moment he'd met him—and until he'd claimed to be his father's illegitimate son, he'd trusted him. Part of him still wanted to. And he was a lawyer. Maybe he could help.

"We had a geologist come out to the ranch a couple of months ago," he said stiffly. "He found oil."

Taylor swore softly. "I knew it! Where is it?"

"Near the western boundary of the ranch."

"Close to the wilderness area," Taylor said. "Why am I not surprised? When you wouldn't sell out, one of the brainiacs in Washington decided it was time to enlarge the public lands in the area, didn't he? Dammit to hell!"

"My sentiments exactly," Joe said dryly. "We've been told that if we don't sell, the feds will harass us until we do. I've heard stories—"

"They're not just stories," he warned him. "The

government doesn't always play fair, Joe. If you don't want to lose the ranch, I suggest you get a good attorney. Before this is over with, you're going to need one."

"Are you volunteering for the job?"

Taylor hadn't called him for that reason, but now that Joe had brought the subject up, he was glad that he had. "As a matter of fact, I am. In spite of what you may think of me, I'm an excellent attorney. I've taken on the government before and won, and I can do it again."

"And you'd do that for us? I thought you hated us."

"I don't hate you," he said honestly, "though I can see why you might think that. I never had any animosity toward any of you. I certainly don't want you to lose the ranch...or sell it. It may not be part of my heritage, but it was yours and Zeke's and the girls'—not the government's. If I can keep them from taking it from you, I will."

He'd never been more sincere about anything in his life, but he wasn't surprised when Joe didn't immediately accept his offer. "This isn't a decision I can make on my own. The family will have to vote on it. I'll have to get back to you."

"I've got a new number," he said quickly, and rattled off the hotel's number before Joe could ask why he'd left Liberty Hill and Phoebe. "Call me after you talk to the family." Not giving Joe a chance to ask any questions he didn't want to answer, Taylor quickly hung up.

Chapter 12

"Two family meetings in three days," Zeke said as he joined the rest of the family at the homestead. "What's Taylor done now? File a lawsuit against us, claiming his share of the ranch?"

"Not quite," Joe said dryly as he accepted the glass of home-made lemonade his mother had just poured for him. "He saw the story on the news last night about the wildlife refuge. He's not an idiot. It didn't take him long to put two and two together—he called me almost immediately and asked what the feds were after."

"You didn't tell him, did you?" Merry asked worriedly. "What if he decides to go after his share of the ranch? Then we'll be fighting him *and* the government."

"Oh, I don't think he would do that," Janey said with a frown. "He just doesn't seem the type."

"I agree," Sara said as she took a seat at the pine table that had been crafted by the first McBride when he came to Colorado back in the 1800s. "He might be full of anger, but he didn't seem greedy at all. And if the only thing he was after was his share of the ranch, he'd have filed a lawsuit the minute he got in town," she reasoned. "It wouldn't have cost him a thing, other than the filing fee. He's a lawyer. So why did he call, Joe? What did he want?"

"He said we're going to need a good lawyer if we're going to beat the government. He offered his services."

"What?"

"You've got to be kidding!"

"This is a joke, right? C'mon, Joe. What did he really want?"

"I told you," Joe said, his brown eyes twinkling with rueful amusement. "He offered his services, and I told him I'd get back to him. I had to run it past the family first." Sobering, he added, "He was right about one thing—we do need an attorney. We should have hired one as soon as Thomas retired."

"We didn't need one then," Janey pointed out. "And who were we going to get? Someone in Colorado Springs that we didn't even know?"

"Thomas spoiled us," Merry agreed. "He represented the family for thirty years. We knew we could trust him. That's not going to be so easy with someone new."

"I don't know about the rest of you," Zeke said, "but I don't want to put the future of the ranch in the hands of someone we don't know from Adam."

"So what are you saying?" Joe asked with a frown. "You want to hire Taylor?"

"I don't know," Zeke admitted honestly. "I don't know if we can trust him."

"He resented Dad all his life," Merry pointed out.

"If he still wants revenge, he couldn't pick a better way to get it than to tank the case and give the government whatever it wants."

"I don't think he would do that," Janey said quietly.

"I don't, either," Joe said. "He may have resented Dad all these years, but we didn't do anything to him. Why would he take it out on us?"

No one had an answer for that. Seated at the head of the table, Sara said, "I think Joe and Janey are right. From what you've all said about him, you liked him until I came home and he hit me with the truth. I think you should give him a chance."

"But he lied to us about who he was," Merry argued. "How can we trust him after that?"

"He made a mistake," Sara replied. "That doesn't mean he's a bad person any more than your father was. People make mistakes. Any one of you might have done the same thing if you'd been in his shoes. He's still your brother."

Touched that she could be so forgiving of their father's mistake, Joe took her hand and squeezed it warmly. "You're something else, Mom. I thought you'd hate him."

Tears glistening in her eyes, Sara gave him a watery smile and lovingly patted the hand that held hers. "How could I do that? He's your father's son just as much as you and Zeke are, dear. I only had to look at him to know that. I can't hate him for telling me the truth. It was a shock, but that wasn't his fault. Your father should have told me that he saw another woman when he was in Cheyenne all those years ago. At least then, I might have halfway expected something like this to happen one day."

Joe couldn't argue with that. Glancing at his brother

and sisters, he lifted a brow at them. "Well? What do you think?"

Merry hesitated. "I don't know," she finally said with a shrug. "Mom's never steered us wrong yet. If she thinks we should give Taylor a chance, I guess I don't have a problem with that. What about you, Zeke?"

"Mom's instincts have always been right on the money," he replied. "I won't object to meeting with him and seeing what he suggests. If he says the right things, I won't object to hiring him."

"What about you, Janey?" Joe asked. "Is that all right with you?"

"It's the right thing to do," she said simply. "I'm fine with it."

Satisfied, Joe nodded. "Good. I'll set up a meeting."

When the phone rang an hour after he'd talked to Joe, Taylor braced for the worst. He'd had time to think about it, and he knew in his gut that they weren't going to accept his offer. Why should they? He'd hurt Sara and lied to the entire family, and that didn't exactly inspire trust. If he'd had any sense, he'd have just kept his mouth shut and his nose out of their business and let them handle their own problems. The ranch was, after all, theirs, and none of his concern.

Still, it really bothered him that they might lose part of it to the government. He might not carry the McBride name or have any claim to the ranch, but the McBrides had been living on that land for well over a hundred years, and the government had no right to it. If they'd just let him help, he knew he could convince the feds to back off.

Reaching for the phone, he said, "Hello, Joe. What'd the family say?"

"How'd you know it was me?"

"You're the only one who has this number. Well? What's the verdict? Yes or no?"

"We'd like to meet with you and discuss the situation," he said simply.

That was more of a chance than he'd hoped for. Humbled, he said, "That sounds fair to me. When do you want to meet?"

"How about tonight?" Joe suggested. "We're all here at Mom's. Where are you?"

"In Colorado Springs. I'll be there as soon as I can." He started to hang up, only to say, "Hey, Joe? Thanks. I know you probably had to talk some of the others into this. I appreciate it."

"No problem," Joe said gruffly. "It was the right thing to do."

He hung up before Taylor could say anything else, leaving him shaking his head. He'd never met anyone quite like the McBrides. They never ceased to amaze him with their generosity of spirit.

Still, he didn't know quite what to expect when he arrived at the homestead a little over an hour later. Approaching the front door, he couldn't forget the look on Sara's face when he'd told her who he was. He'd been brutally honest with her and she had every right to hate his guts.

But when he rang the doorbell and she answered the door, she greeted him with an easy, understanding smile. "Hello, Taylor. You made good time. Please, come in. Everyone's in the dining room. We just had dessert. Can I get you something?"

"Oh, no," he said quickly. "Thank you." Taken

aback by her graciousness, he realized that he'd never had anything to fear from her. If his father had been alive, she would, no doubt, have accepted him as easily as she did now. That was just the kind of lady she was. And that blew him away.

His eyes meeting hers head-on, he said huskily, "I'd like to apologize for hurting you."

"That's not necessary, Taylor—"

"Oh, yes, it is," he said, interrupting her. "You never did anything to me. I had no right to take out my resentment on you."

"You were hurting," she said quietly. "I can certainly sympathize with that. You were looking for someone to blame. But I'm not your enemy...and your father wouldn't have been, either. If he'd known of your existence, he would have been as involved in your life as he was in our children's."

"I want to believe that."

"You can believe it. I knew him better than anyone. He would never knowingly have turned his back on you."

She was so sincere that Taylor had no choice but to believe her. "Thank you for saying that. He obviously wasn't the man I thought he was all these years."

"No, he wasn't," she replied. "I wish you could have known him. He really was a wonderful husband and father."

Holding out his hand, he said, "No hard feelings?"

For an answer, she placed her hand in his. "No hard feelings. Now that we've made peace, please come in. The family's going to think I won't let you in the door."

"I'm sure they know you better than that," he replied and stepped inside.

She led him to the dining room, where his brothers

and sisters and Sara's husband, Dan, were waiting. Greeting them all, Taylor said huskily, "Before we go any further, I need to apologize to all of you. I should have been honest with you about who I was from the beginning, but all I could think of was making somebody pay for the fact that I grew up without a father. I thought if you knew who I was, you'd never let me inside the door."

"We might not have if we'd known you were going to lay the truth on Mom the way you did," Zeke growled. "What the hell were you thinking?"

"He's apologized," Sara said, shooting her youngest son a reproving frown. "I suggest we all forgive and forget and focus on the only problem we've got right now—losing part of the ranch to the government."

"Mom's right," Joe said quietly. "So what do you think, Taylor? Can we win this fight?"

"If we're lucky—and we play our cards right." Taking a seat at the table next to Zeke, he said, "While I was waiting for Joe's call, I did a little research. We've got several things working in our favor. First of all, the wilderness area was originally set up by a donation of land by the first McBride who settled these mountains."

Surprised, Merry said, "How'd you know that?"

"I read the original agreement that established the wilderness area," Taylor said with a smile. "The point is we've got to find a way to use that to our advantage. How do you think the public is going to feel about the fact that the government was *given* thousands of acres of McBride land over a hundred years ago, and now they're threatening to *take* more?

"And then there's the executive orders signed by the last administration," he added. "The president is violating those orders with his current policies, and it's an election year. We need to get the word out there, hit the talk shows, place some ads in newspapers and magazines, and put some pressure on the administration to back off.''

''And if that doesn't work?'' Janey asked.

''Then we fight them in a very public court fight,'' he replied. ''We'll throw everything we can dig up at them and have cameras rolling the entire time. Trust me, it won't be pretty.''

Considering that, Joe sat back in his chair and gave the rest of the family an arch look. ''Well? What do you think? Do we hire Taylor or take our chances with someone in Colorado Springs?''

''Taylor,'' Janey said promptly. ''If it comes to a fight, I want him on our side.''

Seated across from her, Merry openly studied Taylor, obviously trying to make up her mind. ''I want to trust you,'' she told him. ''If you just hadn't lied to us, this would be a lot easier.''

''I know, and I'm sorry about that,'' he said sincerely. ''I wish I could go back and start over, but unfortunately, I can't. All I can say is that you have my word—for what it's worth—that I won't ever lie to any of you again. I've never done anything like this before, and trust me, I never will again. I hated what I'd done the second I saw the look on Sara's face when I told her who I was.''

''We all make mistakes,'' Sara said quietly. ''As long as we learn from them, that's what matters. And personally,'' she added shooting a glance at her children, ''I agree with Janey. When it comes to a fight with the government, I think we need Taylor in our corner. What about you, Merry?''

Merry, to her credit, was able to admit she'd had a

change of heart. "I feel that he can get down and dirty if he has to. That's a compliment," she told Taylor with a smile. "And I do think you've learned from your mistakes with us...which is the only reason I'm willing to trust you."

"I'll second that," Zeke added. "Don't take this wrong, Taylor, but you're going to have to prove yourself. I'm not trying to be ugly, but after the way you lied to all of us, that's all I feel I can do at the moment."

"A chance is all I ask," Taylor said, understanding perfectly. "You won't regret it. Now that we've got that settled, let's get started. I need to know everything you can tell me about where and when the oil was discovered...."

Phoebe stood at the open door of her grandmother's refrigerator and wrinkled her nose in distaste. Nothing looked good. She was tired of her own cooking, and she'd been hanging around the house too much. Maybe getting out would help spark her appetite. She'd go to Ed's for breakfast. When she was a little girl, he'd always made her something special whenever she'd visited Myrtle. If she remembered correctly, his chocolate chip pancakes were fantastic. Maybe she'd order that.

But as she changed into a frilly yellow blouse, white slacks and sandals, she knew she wasn't really going to Ed's for his pancakes or anything else on the menu. She was going for one reason and one reason only. She was tired of listening for Taylor's footsteps in the front hall.

It was time to get on with her life, she told herself sternly, forcing back the tears that inevitably welled in her eyes at the mere thought of Taylor. It had been four days since he'd left. He obviously wasn't coming back. The sooner she accepted that, the better.

But knowing that and doing it were two different things. She wanted to hate him, but that was impossible. Regardless of how he'd lied to her, she still loved him. She dreamed of him, she ached for him with every breath she took. She couldn't step into any room in the house without thinking of him, and it was driving her crazy.

When the next round of guests came on the weekend, she hoped she'd be too busy to think about him, but in the meantime, she needed a distraction. Ed's was it. Checking the mirror one last time to make sure her makeup covered the dark circles under her eyes, she grabbed her purse and stepped outside. It was only two short blocks to the diner, and the morning was beautiful. She walked.

Not surprisingly, Ed's was packed. All the local ranchers liked to meet there in the morning for coffee, gossip and one of Ed's great breakfasts. Smiling at the sight of all the pickup trucks parked out front, Phoebe stepped inside to a hail of greetings.

"Hey, Phoebe! Just the girl we wanted to see."

"Why didn't you tell us Taylor Bishop was Joe McBride's half brother? And don't tell us you didn't know. He was staying with you. He must have mentioned it."

"I thought he was a writer, but now everybody's saying he's a lawyer. Is that really true?"

"Of course it's true! Didn't you hear? He's going to help Sara and the kids fight the government. They wouldn't trust him to do that if he wasn't some hotshot fancy lawyer from San Diego. What I want to know is who his mama is. Has anybody heard?"

Stunned by all the questions and comments that hit her as she made her way to the lone seat at the far end of the counter, Phoebe sank down onto the red vinyl bar stool in a daze. Taylor was still in town? But how could he be? He'd left four days ago, and there was no other place in town to stay.

Unless he'd gone to the McBrides'.

He couldn't have, she thought, shaken. The McBrides were furious with him. They wouldn't have taken him in. What was going on? This all had to be a mistake.

"Well?" Preston Star, a friend of her grandmother's and one of the more colorful local ranchers, demanded with an arch look. "Have you got your grandmother's blood in you or not, young lady? Taylor Bishop was at Myrtle's for weeks. By now, you ought to know everything there is to know about that old boy, right down to his shoe size. So what gives?"

"I was going to ask the same thing," she replied. "Where did all of you hear this? Taylor checked out days ago. I thought he'd gone back to San Diego."

"That's not what Joe said."

"Joe?" she said, shocked. "*Joe* told you Taylor was his half brother?"

"He sure did," Augie Montgomery said from across the room before Preston could say a word. "I heard him myself this morning in the feed store. He said Taylor was one hell of a lawyer, and with his help, they were going to send the feds packing."

Dozens of questions whirling in her head, Phoebe couldn't believe what she was hearing. Augie had to be mistaken. She'd witnessed Sara's reaction to Taylor's announcement that he was Gus's son. She'd been devastated. And when Joe had called later that evening and asked to speak to Taylor, Phoebe hadn't imagined the anger she'd heard in his voice. He'd been outraged that Taylor had upset his mother, and she couldn't say she'd blamed him. Taylor had been incredibly insensitive when he'd told Sara who he was.

So how had he made peace with the McBrides so quickly? she wondered, frowning in confusion. And then there was the matter of trust. Even if Taylor had found a way to convince the McBrides to forgive him for tricking them into letting him into their lives, earning their trust back wasn't something he was going to be able to do easily. Trust, especially trust that had been carelessly destroyed, wasn't automatically restored with an apology. If anyone knew that, she did. Taylor may have apologized to her, but she wasn't sure if she could ever trust him again. So how could Zeke and Joe and the girls?

What was going on? Had she somehow misunderstood the entire situation? She didn't see how she could have, but what other explanation was there? The McBrides were putting the ranch itself in Taylor's hands, and for the life of her, she didn't know why. Confused, sick at heart at the idea that she might have totally misjudged Taylor, she completely lost her appetite.

"I've got to go," she choked, and turned to hurry toward the door.

"Hey!" Ed called after her. "Where're you going? This is the first time you've been in since Myrtle left. I was going to make some chocolate chip pancakes for you!"

"I just remembered I left something on the stove," she fibbed, and rushed outside.

Later, she never remembered the two block walk home—it passed in a blur. Pain squeezing her heart, all she could think of was Taylor. She had to talk to him, had to find out what was going on, but she didn't have

a clue where he was. She'd have to call the Mc-
Brides....

Lost in her thoughts, she didn't see the Mercedes
parked at the curb in front of her grandmother's house
until she was almost there. Then she looked up and felt
her heart lurch in her breast. Immediately, her gaze
jumped to the front porch, and she wasn't surprised to
see Taylor standing there, obviously waiting for her. He
had, no doubt, watched her rush down the street all the
way from Ed's.

She wanted to run to him, to throw herself into his
arms and never let him go. But her heart was still
bruised from the way he'd misled her, and she couldn't
just act as if nothing had happened. Halfway up the
front walk, she stopped in her tracks. The thunder of
her heartbeat loud in her ears, she couldn't bring herself
to go one step further. The next move was his.

Aching to hold her, Taylor knew that any chance he
had of finding happiness with her was riding on what
happened in the next few minutes. God, he'd missed
her! Did she know how much he'd wanted to call her?
To come to her? Every minute that he was away from
her seemed like an eternity. But he wouldn't risk losing
her, so he'd kept his distance.

Had she forgiven him yet? He panicked just at the
thought of spending the rest of his life without her.
There had to be a way to make her understand why
he'd done what he had...and what she meant to him.
All he asked was that she just listen to him.

"Are you busy?" he asked huskily. "I was hoping
maybe we could talk."

For a moment, he thought she was going to say no.
She hesitated, then nodded. "I have a few minutes."
Stepping up to the porch, she took a seat in the old-

fashioned wicker porch swing. "I just heard you were representing the McBrides in their fight against the government. I was shocked."

"To be perfectly honest, so was I," he replied. "I thought they would send me packing. They gave me a chance, instead. I hope you will, too."

"I want to," she admitted honestly, "but I'm afraid to trust you. You already hurt me once. I can't let you do it again."

She didn't pull any punches, and he appreciated that. As long as they were able to communicate, he had a chance of winning her back. "I can understand why you don't trust me," he said quietly. "I lied to you, and even though I felt justified at the time, nothing justified hurting you. I would like to explain everything to you, and if you don't want anything to do with me after that, I promise I won't bother you anymore. Okay?"

"That sounds fair enough," she replied.

He thought it would be easy, telling her about what it was like, growing up without a father, but suddenly, emotion was clogging his throat. "For as long as I can remember, I always wondered who my father was," he said roughly. "All my mother would ever say on the subject was that he was a wonderful man. I could never understand how she could say that. If he was so wonderful, why wasn't he with us? Why wasn't he at least sending a child support check so my mother didn't have to work two or three jobs just to support us?"

Just thinking about how hard his mother had worked set anger burning in his gut. "You know something? She never made more than eight dollars an hour in her life. She never had a new car—until I bought her one once I graduated from law school—and it took her years of scrimping and saving to have a home of her own.

Don't get me wrong," he told her. "I'm not telling you this to make myself look good, or to make you feel sorry for us. I just want you to understand what it was like for my mother. Imagine yourself with a baby, and no one to help you raise that baby. No boyfriend or husband, no parents. My grandparents disowned her when they discovered she was pregnant."

"Oh, Taylor, I'm sorry," she murmured. "That must have been awful for her."

"She never complained," he said huskily. "But I knew how hard life was for her, and I hated my father for that. The problem was...I didn't have a name or face to put with whoever the man was who fathered me. My mother would never tell me who my father was. I think she was afraid I would go looking for him," he confided. "She was right."

"But she left you a letter when she died," she said.

He nodded. "That's right. That's when I decided to come to Liberty Hill to find Gus. I had no idea he was dead until I got here."

Phoebe's heart hurt for him. "I'm sorry things worked out the way they did for you," she said quietly. "Gus really was a remarkable man. Everybody liked him."

"All I wanted was revenge," he said simply. "Then, through you, I met the McBrides, and I found myself liking them. That, of course, was the last thing I wanted. They were supposed to be these horrible people who'd stolen my father from me, but I still couldn't make myself hate them. They were just too likable. The more I got to know them, the more I realized that it wasn't revenge that I wanted. I wanted a family. And you."

Those two little words slipped right past her guard

and caught her unawares. Her heart suddenly pounding in her breast, she stiffened, afraid to hope. "Taylor—"

"I hadn't counted on falling in love with you," he said huskily, "but I couldn't stop myself. Before I met you, all I cared about was work…and making my father pay for not being there for me and my mother. I never took any time for myself or did anything fun. You showed me another side of life."

A rueful smile curled the corners of his mouth. "I thought I knew what I wanted. I was a partner in the city's biggest law firm, lived in the right part of town, and dated women who were rich and beautiful and could help my career. Then I met you and it all seemed so empty and shallow. You helped me see that happiness had nothing to do with money or success and everything to do with love and family and liking who you are as a person.

"I didn't like the man who came to Liberty Hill for revenge," he admitted huskily. "Or the man who lied to you and used you to get close to the McBrides. That's not who I am or who I want to be. I have family now, something I never thought I'd have, and someone to love."

Stepping over to the swing, he took her hands and drew her to her feet. "I love you so much I can't find the words to express it. I never thought I would say this to a woman, but I want the kind of life with you that Sara had with my father. They had a home and children and a love that grew stronger with every passing year, and that's what I want with you."

Tears threatening to choke her, Phoebe couldn't doubt his sincerity. She only had to see the love shining in his eyes to know that he meant every word. "I love you, too," she said huskily, "but—"

"Whatever it is, we can work it out," he assured her. "Just tell me what it is."

"I'm not sure love is enough," she blurted out as tears spilled over her lashes and trailed down her cheeks. "You know as well as I do that we're as different as night and day. You're a class-A personality who is obviously very ambitious, and I just want to have my own bed and breakfast so that I can do what I do best…help people relax and enjoy life."

"But you can do that, sweetheart."

"No, I can't. The two don't mix. I don't have a clue how to be the wife of a big-city lawyer, let alone a senator or governor or—knowing how ambitious you are—the president. I'm a tree-hugger, Taylor. Look at me. I dress like a hippie. I'm a throwback to a different century, one that your law partners would never understand. How can a relationship between us possibly work? We'll only end up hurting each other, and that's the last thing I want to do to someone I love."

Any last lingering doubts Taylor had ended with her words. Delighted, he snatched her into his arms for an exuberant kiss. "Dear God, I love you!" he laughed when he finally let her up for air. "We're going to have a great life together!"

Confused, Phoebe frowned. "What are you talking about? I just told you—"

"I know, sweetheart. I heard every word. You love me and would never deliberately do anything to hurt me. I feel the same way about you. If we go through our life together remembering that, then there isn't a doubt in my mind that we can make it."

"But I can't be the kind of wife you need me to be!"

"Yes you can," he insisted, kissing her again. "My plans for the future have changed. I don't need to get

ahead to prove myself any more. I know who I am—
the son of Gus McBride and Alice Bishop, and they
were both great people. I have brothers and sisters, a
stepmother, a family history. I know who I am and have
everything I want…as long as you agree to marry me.''

''But—''

''I know,'' he interrupted her with a grin. ''You don't
know how to be the wife of a big-city lawyer. You don't
have to worry about that. I'm resigning from the firm
and hanging out my shingle in Liberty Hill. I'll be a
small-town lawyer, and you can help your grandmother
run the bed and breakfast, and we'll live happily ever
after as Mr. and Mrs. So what do you say? Will you
marry me?''

He made it sound so simple…and that, more than
anything, convinced Phoebe they had a chance. He
knew what he wanted to do with the rest of his life—
and so did she. She wanted to spend it with him. Somehow they would make it work.

Tears once again filling her eyes, she stepped back
into his arms. ''Yes. Yes. Yes!''

Epilogue

"It was a beautiful wedding," Phoebe sighed, lying in her husband's arms as she watched the snow fall outside the cabin they'd rented in Vail for their honeymoon.

"You were beautiful," he said huskily, kissing the side of her neck. "Did I mention that?"

"At least a dozen times, but a bride never gets tired of hearing it," she replied solemnly, her blue eyes twinkling.

"I'll remember that," he said just as solemnly, and kissed her again.

"It was worth the wait."

Taylor liked to think he was an agreeable husband, but he couldn't go that far. "I wanted to marry you the same night I proposed. You were the one who wanted to wait."

"Only because we both had some business to take care of. And it was for the best. I found a buyer for

Dad's business. When the sale closes next week, I can invest in my grandmother's bed and breakfast and my partnership with her can become permanent.''

"I'll draw up the papers whenever you say, sweetheart,'' he replied. "Now that I've convinced the government they don't want the McBride ranch, after all, I've got some time on my hands.''

"Oh, speaking of the McBrides, I forgot that Sara and Joe gave me a couple of things they wanted me to give you. I put them in my suitcase. I'll be right back.''

Giving him a quick kiss, she jumped up and hurried into the walk-in closet to retrieve the items from her suitcase. When she returned to the bedroom, it was to find Taylor pulling a sealed envelope from the top drawer of the dresser. "What's that?'' she asked in surprise when he held it out to her.

"I have no idea. Your grandmother asked me to give it to you.''

"It looks like our families are up to something,'' she said with a grin as she exchanged the items she held for the envelope from her grandmother. "You go first.''

Settling on the bed with her, Taylor reached for the box that was wrapped in white. "It's from Sara,'' he said, reading the small card lodged under the edge of the bow. "She's been really great. Ever since we made peace, she's treated me just like one of the family.''

"I always liked Sara,'' she replied. "She doesn't hold grudges.'' Watching him tear off the paper, she started to smile, only to frown when he lifted the lid off the box and reached out hesitantly to whatever was inside. "Taylor? What is it?''

"It's pictures of my father,'' he said huskily, stunned. "Look! There's some when he was a boy, and when he graduated from high school. And later, fishing with all the kids." Flipping through them, he shook his head in amazement. "I can't believe she gave these to me. How did she know I needed pictures?"

Tears glistening in her eyes, Phoebe smiled. "She's a wonderful woman."

"You can say that again." Picking up the envelope from Joe, he grinned ruefully. "I'm almost afraid to open this. What do you think it is?"

"I have no idea. Open it and find out."

She didn't have to tell him twice. Lifting the edge of the sealed flap, he carefully tore it open and pulled out several folded pieces of paper. Surprised, Phoebe said, "That looks like a legal document."

"It is," he said, unfolding it. "My God, it's a deed to part of the ranch!"

"You're kidding!"

A slip of paper fell out with the deed, and he picked it up with a hand that wasn't quite steady. "Dad would want you to have this and so do we," he read. "Not for saving the ranch, but because you're our brother. Love, Joe, Janey, Zeke and Merry."

"Oh, Taylor, that's wonderful!" she said, hugging him. "What a fantastic thing for them to do for you."

"I'm shocked," he said huskily. "I had no idea they were going to do something like this. Did you?"

"No one said a word to me. After all this, what do you think is in the envelope from my grandmother?"

"There's only one way to find out," he replied, grinning. "Open it and find out."

Her heart pounding, Phoebe opened her envelope as carefully as Taylor had his. Unfolding the contents, which looking incredibly similar to what Taylor had just opened, she gasped. "Oh, my goodness!"

"What is it, sweetheart? It's looks like a deed."

Tears flooding her eyes, she couldn't speak. Without a word, she handed it to him, along with a short note from her grandmother. Smiling tenderly at her, Taylor slipped his arm around her shoulder and began to read.

Dear Phoebe,
   I know we had a deal, sweetheart, but the more I thought about it, the more I realized that I didn't want you to invest in the bed and breakfast. The money you get from your father's business is your inheritance—I can't ask you to give that up to invest in my business. So I'm giving you the bed and breakfast as a wedding present.

"Oh, no! Taylor, I can't let her do this!"
Grinning, Taylor continued to read.

   I can hear you now, saying you can't let me do this. Of course you can! I loved traveling so much last summer that I decided I didn't want to be tied down any more. I'm thrilled that I was able to give the B and B to someone who loves it as much as you do. So enjoy, sweetheart. And be happy.

Stunned, Phoebe wiped at the tears in her eyes. "I can't believe she did this. I never expected anything so generous."

"She loves you," Taylor said huskily, tightening his arm around her to pull her close for a kiss. "So do I. So are you?"

Her blood heating from his kiss, she blinked, trying to keep up with the conversation. "Am I what?"

"Happy," he replied. "It's what your grandmother wanted for you."

Overcome with joy, she laughed, ''Oh, I'm way beyond that. I've never been happier in my life.''

''Me, either,'' he said with a grin, and pulled her back into his arms.

* * * * *

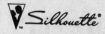

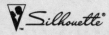
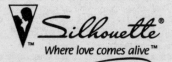

COMING NEXT MONTH

#1237 SOME MEN'S DREAMS—Kathleen Korbel

Single father Dr. Jack O'Neill could work miracles in the E.R., but he needed help healing his own family, stat. His young daughter was in danger, and only Dr. Genevieve Kendall knew what to do. By revealing a secret from her own past, Gen might be able to save the child's life, but would any amount of love be enough to save the father's frozen heart?

#1238 TRUTH OR LIES—Kylie Brant

The Tremaine Tradition

To catch a criminal, detective Cade Tremaine turned to Dr. Shae O'Riley, the beautiful surgeon who had caught the eye of a suspected drug runner—and the officer on his trail. But neither Cade nor Shae expected the spiraling path of danger and corruption they faced. And they didn't anticipate finding love—love they were terrifyingly close to losing forever....

#1239 FREEFALL—RaeAnne Thayne

When a tragic accident left Sophie Beaumont to care for her sister's children, she was reunited with Thomas Canfield, the children's paternal uncle and her former lover. Soon old passions reached new heights. Sophie feared falling for Tom again, but he was the only man who made her feel safe. Especially once she learned that her sister's death was no accident, but murder....

#1240 RISKING IT ALL—Beverly Bird

How to defend a guilty man? That was the question attorney Grace Simkanian faced with Aidan McKenna, an allegedly crooked cop who claimed he'd been framed. Though mistrustful of men, Grace couldn't deny the crackling chemistry they shared. But could she let go of past prejudices in time to save his career—and her hardened heart?

#1241 HEARTBREAK HERO—Frances Housden

Kiss-and-tell, a sweet-sounding name for a deadly drug. It was up to DEA agent Kell Jellic to track down the woman carrying the formula. But when he unwittingly fell for Ngaire McKay, his prime suspect, he found himself torn between duty and desire. With the world watching, Kell had to prove that she was actually innocent before they both wound up dead.

#1242 NO PLACE TO HIDE—Madalyn Reese

A stalker was hunting Emma Toliver, and the only man who could protect her was Anthony Bracco, the ex-corporate raider who had once tried to steal her company—and her heart. Though she thought Anthony was out of her system, one look into his enigmatic eyes sparked a heat too intense to ignore. Suddenly Emma wondered who the *real* threat was....